PIPER'S CHILDREN

FBI agents race to solve a surreal mystery

IAIN HENN

THE
BOOK
FOLKS

Published by The Book Folks

London, 2023

© Iain Henn

ISBN 978-1-80462-085-4

www.thebookfolks.com

THE PIPER'S CHILDREN *is the first standalone book in a new series by Iain Henn about a special FBI unit set up to investigate seemingly unsolvable mysteries. Look out for the other titles, coming soon!*

Details about Iain's other novels, the mystery DEAD SET ON MURDER *and the romantic thriller* THE GREATEST BETRAYAL, *can be found at the back of this book.*

"The bard known far and wide
The travell'd rat-catcher beside
A man most needful to this town."

Johann Wolfgang von Goethe

"When, lo, As they reached the mountain-side,
A wondrous portal opened wide,
As if a cavern was suddenly hollowed;
And the Piper advanced and the children followed,
And when all were in to the very last,
The door in the mountain-side shut fast."

Robert Browning

Prologue

Before

He remembered the long walk up the hill, his legs feeling as though they were weighed down, the air heavy, the sun hot and beating down and the dust in the air stinging his eyes.

He'd been told not to look back, they all had, but as he reached the top of the steep rise he threw a glance over his shoulder, staring down at the village.

The people were coming out of their cottages, milling about in the open, the crowd growing. Confusion. And then there was pointing and shouting.

He would never forget the wails that erupted from the women's mouths.

He strained his eyes, wanting to see his mother and his father but the distance was too great, the adults just stick figures from this long view.

He looked ahead of him again. The other children were stumbling as they climbed. His mind clouded over, ending the brief moment of clarity.

Up ahead he saw the back of the tall, lean figure, his long coat trailing out behind him.

The boy wanted to return to the cottages, to his parents, but he had a terrible sense that was something he could never do.

PART ONE

Chapter One

Crying out, the boy startled awake. Opening his eyes, he was instantly gripped by panic thinking he must be blind as he could see nothing. Shivers raised the hairs at the nape of his neck and he imagined nightmare creatures crawling unseen toward him. Mounds of earth rising like living things, slithering across the ground, licking at his flesh. Where was he?

His back ached from lying on the hard, cold ground and he forced himself to sit up. Relief surged as his eyes began adjusting to the darkness and he became aware of a pinprick of light in the distance. He could just make out the rocky cavern walls and with a sharp intake of breath, he remembered the long journey, remembered entering the cave.

How long had he been asleep?

He called out for the others. "*Wo seid ihr?*" But there was no reply. Nothing. No sound at all, just the eerie stillness of this dark cavern.

He rose to his feet, his whole body trembling, and shuffled toward the light. As he approached, the light grew and he saw that it was the opening to the cave. Terrified at being alone he called out again, praying the others were just beyond the entrance.

Or had they moved on, leaving him behind?

His heart beating rapidly, he started to run, desperate to find his friends. He reached the opening and ran out into an area of long grass and clumps of tangled shrubs surrounded by wooded hills.

He looked back. The cave from which he'd come was partly obscured by overhanging branches. At that moment he heard a torrent of whispers coming from what must have been the tree spirits, and he froze.

A strong breeze whipped his hair, and he remembered his mother telling him the forest whispers were caused by the wind as it rustled the tens of thousands of quivering leaves. But his friends didn't believe his mother had told him the truth. They believed there were sinister creatures that lurked in the shadows of the woods.

He ran forward, shouting out for his friends, a sinking feeling in the pit of his stomach, his eyes squinting under the glare of the sun. He ran over fallen logs and branches, through ferns and lichen and elderberry shrubs, a forest of conifers, pines, and cedars towering high above. Overhead, the multi-layered canopy was a verdant canvas of filtered sunlight.

Why had they all been out here in the wilderness? Why had they made that long, exhausting trek that had led them to the cave?

The light faded unexpectedly; the sunlight painted away by a large, ominous, wide-reaching shadow. A sudden change. Columns of rain clouds driven by the wind scrolled across the sky.

The boy stopped, panting for air, leaning against the broad trunk of a tree. Rain suddenly began beating down on him. And then he remembered. Fragmented images resurfacing, coming together. Something his mind had been blocking. He gasped at the memory, icy shivers radiating up his spine.

Der Rattenfänger.

Chapter Two

A person wakes up more than twenty-five thousand times during an average lifespan. Most of those wakings are unremarkable and for the most part, have no details worth remembering. But this was one waking I knew I would often think back on. The call that started it all. The morning when the changes began.

My eyes came into focus slowly as I reacted to the shrill ring. When I registered that it was my phone's ringtone, I jolted fully awake.

I was an early riser but even for an FBI agent like me a 5 a.m. call was not normal. Not when it was from a supervisory special agent. And not when that SSA was the ex-lover I'd heard very little from for the past two years.

Even so, I surprised myself at becoming so quickly clear-headed and alert.

"Ilona, it's Will. Sorry about the ridiculous hour."

It was hardly the opening line I would have expected from him after all this time. "That's one word for it," I said.

"I have an unusual case. I could use your expertise but I need you here as early as possible."

Straight down to business. Fine with me. "Where?"

"FBI resident agency in Poulsbo. There'll be a car outside your apartment in fifteen minutes and there's a chopper on standby. And don't worry about your boss, he's been advised."

I frowned. *Really?* "What's the situation?"

"Better if you're briefed on arrival."

"Okay, I guess." No one likes short notice, but this wasn't the first time I dressed and packed in under fifteen. Adrenaline kicked in. I brewed coffee while I brushed on a touch of make-up in eight minutes flat. I tied my shoulder-length chestnut hair into a ponytail and pulled on a leather jacket over a blouse and black suit pants. I took a few mouthfuls of the coffee and then headed out.

Will McCord wanting my expertise? After all this time?

Early streaks of dawn light filtered through the cloud over the small aerodrome on the outskirts of Seattle as my ride entered the grounds.

I boarded the helicopter, a four-blade, single-engine Bell 407. I watched the dawn breathe life into the heavens as the pilot flew northwest. The early rays of sun glinted off the glass and steel of the skyscrapers, high-rises that were dwarfed in turn by the world-famous Space Needle that dominated the cityscape.

I had seen the sun rise many times but never like this, as I swept across the rooftops, peering out from the window of the helicopter. Far below there was a sliver of movement on 14th Avenue – the first vehicles, the early birds – but nothing like the tide of traffic that would erupt in a short space of time.

I loved Seattle, had adopted it as my own since moving here from DC. My gaze wandered from the waters of Puget Sound and the thickets of trees in the green spaces that dotted the urban sprawl to Lake Washington in the distance. Beyond that, just a hint of the peaks that were The Cascades. The sun's soft blue and orange glow swirled with the shifting mists of those mountains. It reminded me of the rising tendrils of a flame.

Were there still any embers of the flame I'd once felt for Will? I hadn't thought about him for a long time now… So, what did I feel?

Curiosity, that was for sure.

All of the FBI's field offices and resident agencies had access to the aviation program. The choppers were used for surveillance, transport of equipment, and crisis situations. Why did they need one for me? For this?

It was only an hour and a half, if that, from Seattle to Poulsbo along the I-5 and the WA-16 W and WA-3 N. I remembered doing that drive a couple of years ago. The chopper would take around thirty minutes.

Typical Will McCord, I thought. Ambitious and impatient. Pushy. A special agent when we'd been together and now an SSA. Will should've been able to accept the same intense needs in me when we'd been together but I wasn't certain he ever truly did.

The pilot was one of those easy, laconic characters, chirpy at an hour when most people wouldn't be able to string two coherent sentences together. He had a booming voice that was almost audible over the whirr of the blades.

I had no idea what he was talking about. I was straining to listen but not taking anything in – the sound of Will McCord's voice had drawn me back to memories from two years earlier.

I wasn't certain what his last words to me had been but the ones I remembered were: 'I didn't plan for any of this, Ilona, but I think maybe we both need to move on.'

I'd been furious. I'd gone through a rapid escalation to anger, then depression and self-doubt. And just as quickly I'd pulled myself together and got on with my life and my career. My close friend Clara said I'd gone through the usual phases of breakup grief except that, as with everything else in life, I did it on fast-forward. Clara knew me too well.

Worst of all was the realization that Will wasn't a total jerk and certainly not the near-superhero he'd been in my eyes. He was just a normal man who, living and working in another city, had become interested in another woman. He was right; we'd grown apart and maybe we both just needed to move on.

I really didn't need to be revisiting any of those memories now.

I wondered again, looking out on the light flooding the horizon, what was so unusual that I'd received a 5 a.m. call and special transport?

Chapter Three

Will met me in the front lobby and walked with me through the main suite of offices to the interview room. It was as though I'd last seen him just the day before. Square-jawed, sharp-eyed, and stoic. A seasoned professional who was passionate about the Bureau. His on-the-job manner had always been a little different from his after-hours persona, even with me, even during the time we'd been an item, and that certainly hadn't changed. Apart from "Thanks for coming," there was no 'long time, no see,' or 'how have you been?' As always with Will, he was straight to the point. *Almost* as if we had never been something more than just colleagues. Almost. "Don't know if you're already familiar with the Olympic National Forest here. Lots of rugged trails through old-growth conifers."

"Of course, I'm familiar with it."

"This agency received a call from the local sheriff. Park rangers found a kid lost in the forest yesterday, dressed like something out of the Middle Ages and speaking German. The local chief contacted head office for assistance, requesting linguists and child handlers."

"And they asked you to look into it further?"

"Yes."

Something about that didn't sit right with me. "All of this for one lost kid? Why is the Bureau even involved in something like this?"

He glanced at me as we walked. "Taking this on and resolving it has a dual purpose, Ilona. Part of a trial run."

"A trial run for what?"

"A special project."

I rolled my eyes. I wasn't in the mood for vagueness. Certainly not from Will McCord. After all, *he'd* called me. "Stop being so damn mysterious, Will. If you want me to work with you on this then tell me what it's all about. *Now*. Not later."

A half-smile crossed his lips. "Same old fire…" He cleared his throat. "It's only because I was keen for you to meet with the boy first. He's just ahead. But if you insist, just briefly…" His eyes locked with mine. "Over the past year, I've been part of a panel that's been discussing, amongst other things, a new, specialized unit. It's an idea that's been on the back burner for a while…" Breaking eye contact momentarily as we walked, he chose his words carefully. "This boy's appearance has brought the project back to the attention of the big boys."

"What kind of special unit?"

"We can go into that later. It's about targeting cases most likely to be unsolvable."

"Okay. But who says this is unsolvable?"

He continued with his explanation, sidelining my question. "The Bureau has been looking at creating a team specific to those kinds of cases. Agents with a track record that fits the profile."

"And you think I'm one of those?"

"Your closure rate on cold cases, alone, speaks for itself. The big boys have had their eyes on you for a while."

"That's called stalking."

He grinned. "I see some things haven't changed. You've still got that in-your-face attitude."

"So there are some things you still remember."

He waved away my comment, his expression serious again. "The concept is to identify, early on, those cases likely to fit the long-term, difficult to solve, risk-of-becoming-high-profile cases. We'd assign the special unit to act before any of that develops."

"Are there more cases like that coming to light?"

He stopped in the corridor and turned to face me – his expression thoughtful – and I was reminded of how those blue eyes complemented his dark brown hair. "I don't know that there's more but they are getting more public exposure." He made a sweeping gesture with his right arm. "These days, with the explosion of social media, containing the fallout gets more and more difficult every day. The powers that be believe it's undermining public confidence in law enforcement and I'd have to agree." His words were measured. "Let's face it, there's an ever-increasing wave of paranoia out there these days about *everything*. So, we want to move faster on certain cases and control the narrative."

"And you think this is that kind of case?"

"Has all the hallmarks. It's highly unusual and it's already made it into the media. Local county news website. Their print newspaper's in stores tomorrow with the story." He resumed walking, and I fell back into step beside him. "The scaremongers and the fake news brigade will love a lost kid mystery like this. State radio jocks are already on air talking about it this morning. It's *that* fast."

"How?" I asked. I was beginning to see how this could be an ideal test case for a new unit. "Local authorities wouldn't go running to the media, they know to keep matters under wraps."

"Ellie Goodman, one of the rangers that found the boy, shares a house with her younger sister. She mentioned it that evening, didn't think anything about telling a family member, and after all, it's an odd story."

I raised an eyebrow, impatient. "And?"

"Turns out the sister's a junior reporter on the local paper and she filed a story that night for the website. She called her editor, and it just made it into the print version. Great local news content with a weird angle."

"Okay, so it's a prime example of unwanted early media attention."

Will took in a ragged breath, expressing his frustration. "A lost kid turning up in the middle of nowhere, speaking German, who doesn't seem to know who he really is. If it's sensationalized by the media then the community will start to panic, parents wanting to know if there's a danger to their kids, demanding answers before our inquiries are barely underway. The sooner we have those answers, the better."

"So, what do you think is going on with this boy?"

"Perhaps you can tell me. The kid woke early. He's already been given some breakfast."

Even as I listened to him and as we reached the end of the corridor, my thoughts were pulled back to the first time I'd met Will McCord. Four years earlier. The day I arrived in Seattle, being welcomed by Will as I entered the field office there.

I'd grown up back in DC in a great big house in Mount Pleasant. My father, an assistant director of the FBI, while not revealing any details of Bureau cases, had nonetheless regaled me with stories of the men and women he worked with – federal agents committed to their work, to the pursuit of justice and the protection of their country and its people, passionate about the core values of the FBI. I was in awe of their determination, their intelligence, their heroism, and I wanted to be just like them.

After I graduated from Quantico, I was posted to the Seattle Field Office. I'd been bursting at the seams to get started. I was fascinated by the process, I craved excitement, and most of all, for both deeply personal and professional reasons, I was obsessed with getting results. I recalled thinking, as I was ushered into those Seattle offices by Will on that occasion, that he seemed young for the position of a special agent with senior responsibilities on a major team. And he was. Just six years older than me.

He was as focused, determined, and passionate as those men and women whom my father had told me so much about. It was the very reason we hit it off so easily both on the job and after hours at social gatherings with the other team members, the very reason he'd risen the ranks at a faster rate than many others.

I shut off the flood tide of memories as we entered a viewing area next to the interview room.

The room had been made child-friendly with a large, colorful painting of a smiley face in a carnival atmosphere. There were casual chairs around the room in place of the usual interview table.

The boy sat in one of those chairs. A middle-aged woman — elegant, bespectacled, with a graying ash-blonde bob — sat facing him. A laptop and a compact recorder device were on a small table alongside her.

"Marcia Kendall," Will said, "analyst and translator, Linguist Division. Multiple European and South American languages. I brought Marcia along with me yesterday afternoon."

"What has she learned?"

"It's slow-going. He's not saying much and when he does the words are odd, his accent unusual."

"Does Marcia have any thoughts on this?" I asked.

"She believes that he's speaking Middle High German, a variant spoken for two hundred years during the Middle Ages, around 1050 to 1350. Which is weird enough on its own. What we do know is the boy's name is Dietmar. He was found alone in a deserted area of the National Forest with no one else within a radius of over fifty miles. No visible signs of how he got there. Marcia's managed to learn that he's ten years old, he was with other children, they were in a cave, and of course, he wants to go home."

We entered the room and Will introduced me to Marcia, who in turn, speaking German, introduced me to the boy. His wary eyes watched me from a lightly freckled face.

"Hello, Dietmar." I held out my hand but the boy didn't respond. He looked away.

"It takes some time to win his trust," Marcia said.

"Will tells me, even with your knowledge of this language, the boy's hard to understand."

She nodded. "It's not easy to draw much out of him. And he's easily agitated."

I glanced at the laptop on the table. The screen was positioned so the boy couldn't see it.

"The odd thing," said Marcia, "is that Dietmar looks on the most ordinary, everyday objects with absolute awe and in some cases fear. So we're taking everything nice and slow." Following my gaze to the laptop, Marcia added, "I've got a program that helps me decipher the meanings of rare or ancient German words."

"Much luck?"

"His phraseology is certainly what we'd expect from the medieval era."

I looked at the boy's tunic, stockings, and the quaint, scuffed wooden clogs on his feet. There were burn marks all over the clothing but none on the boy.

"He's been saying he wants to go home, which of course is understandable," Will said. And then, to Marcia, "Any luck with that name?"

"Yes. I'm pretty certain he's been saying Hameln."

"Hameln?" I said.

"A village near the banks of the Weser River in northern Germany," Marcia told us. She tilted the laptop screen so Will and I could see the internet search results. "We know it in the Western world as Hamelin with the *i* added in."

"Hamelin?" Will's brow furrowed.

"Not as in the Pied Piper?" I said. I knew that this was one of Germany's most famous and enduring legends. In the thirteenth century, the townsfolk of Hamelin engaged a mysterious stranger to rid the town of a plague of rats. The Pied Piper, as he became known, played a tune that entranced the creatures and he led them into the river where they drowned. When the townsfolk refused to pay the Piper the agreed amount, he retaliated by playing music that lured all of the children away, never to be seen again. The story had been handed down from one generation to another, popularized further in the nineteenth century as one of the fairy tales collected by the Brothers Grimm.

"The very same." Marcia pointed to one of the German language sites on the list. "Or *Der Rattenfänger* as the German people would say it."

The boy's ears pricked up at the mention of *Der Rattenfänger*. The Ratcatcher. Quite unexpectedly and unprovoked he began to speak rapidly, directing his attention to Marcia.

I watched the boy closely. "What's he saying?"

"Something about a long journey." Marcia took a moment, listening intently. The boy seemed to be repeating himself, becoming more and more agitated as he did. "He and the others were following a man who played a pipe."

It wasn't what I was expecting to hear. "He believes he was following a pipe player?"

Will's concern was raised. "Marcia, I think we need to give him some space."

"Leave me alone with him again," Marcia said. "I'll distract him, try to calm him down."

Will and I exchanged a glance, and nodding to Marcia, we quietly left the room.

"Bizarre," Will said to me. "And it's not just that he seems certain about what he's saying. He really is speaking an ancient German dialect. You've seen the way he's dressed. And he was out there alone in the wilds for no apparent reason."

Chapter Four

"Okay, Will, so why am I *really* here?" I asked.

"I want your expertise."

"I'm already–"

"Assigned," he cut across me, "I know, and you've built quite a rep with your unit. As I said, that's why the PTBs have had their eyes on you. We need your input."

"Your idea?"

Will nodded. "Yes."

"And how does Nadine feel about that?"

"Nadine and I separated."

I allowed a moment to pass, taking it in. "You might not think so, after all that happened between us, but I really am sorry to hear that."

"Thanks."

"How long?"

"Three months."

I allowed another beat. "Only three months…"

"Yes. And it's not–"

"And all of a sudden after all this time you want me here working with you."

"This is purely professional, Ilona."

My voice rose. "It's been two years, very little communication, and now–"

"It's because of *this* case and our plan for a special team."

I eyed him suspiciously. "It had damn well better be."

He gave me a look of disappointment. "You should know me better than that."

"You think I know you?" I said sharply.

"Ilona–"

At the same time I was having this conversation with Will, I was also having another dialogue. Just as intense. In my mind. With myself.

It wasn't the first time and I knew it wouldn't be the last, that I'd been engaged simultaneously in two conversations. Try as I might to shut down the 'other' discussion, it would often simply get louder and louder in my head and this was one of those times.

What the hell are you doing, bringing all of this up now? my inner self asked.

I'm letting it out. Expressing feelings I couldn't express to Will at the time.

Why couldn't you?

Because he'd already moved on. My lover, best friend, colleague, whatever, the son of a bitch pretty much just cut everything stone dead. Okay, so things had been strained for a while, long-distance relationship and all, but it was still… sudden.

Wasn't there a part of you that was relieved?

No… maybe. Perhaps I just needed some time, perhaps that's all either of us really needed.

And isn't that what you were given?

I ignored the response, pushing my 'other' voice away, shutting down the exchange. I needed to focus. "It's not like I'm the only agent in the Bureau with a track record," I said to Will.

"You've got a great manner with children who are crime victims. Not to mention those cold cases." He held my gaze, his look genuine. "You're exactly right for this unit. And, for God's sake, what case could be colder than several hundred years?"

I shook my head in disbelief. "You're buying into *that*?"

"Of course not. But, Ilona, this kid is talking about a world that's centuries old, speaking the lingo of the time. You've got the right kind of smarts for this. And you've worked with translators many times."

"So I'd be on loan?"

"Your department head knows it's semi-permanent for the time being."

I shot him a questioning look. "Semi-permanent?"

"Head office is looking at you to be a permanent member of the unit. If, of course, you're interested."

"On your recommendation?"

"The recommendation is from several sources."

I bit down on my bottom lip, a recurrent impulse when I was focusing, blocking everything else out. "Tell me more about the reason for this special unit. The Bureau's already well versed in unusual cases."

He took a moment to consider my question. "Yes, but we specialize in cross-border crime, child kidnap, terrorism, white-collar and cyber–" he began mansplaining.

"I know that, Will."

He raised an eyebrow but didn't pause, pressing on and getting to the point. "But not for cases that don't fit, cases that may need different kinds of experts that we would rarely call on. Not for highly unusual scenarios that attract all the wrong kinds of media attention, cases we want to keep away from the spotlight while we work on them."

"Unclassifiable."

"And likely to stay unsolved," he said, "unless we take a different approach."

I shifted my weight, allowing the tension between my shoulder blades to ease. "And who determines which cases are likely to be unsolvable?"

"We can go into that later."

"You keep saying that." The edge was back in my voice. I was reminded of how standoffish and annoying Will could be.

"The Bureau has a new program that cross-references and analyses data to determine that."

I made a face, raising both eyebrows. "You're kidding. A computer is telling us what can and can't be solved?"

"There's more to it than that."

I drew a deep breath and gave Will a hard, inquisitive stare.

"You look like you've got another question," he said.

I knew him well enough to see he was making a point of being open and patient, wanting to soften the exchange. I wasn't making it easy.

I held his gaze for a moment before giving voice to my thoughts. "Tell me more about this 'trial' business."

Will spread his arms. "Exactly what I said. The bosses want to trial a team on a case flagged as potentially unsolvable."

"A system that predicts which investigations will become tomorrow's cold cases," I expanded on the point.

"That's a good way to put it."

"Why would this 'system' highlight a case like this?"

"Initially, I wondered that myself," Will conceded, "and if I'm wondering that, then so are the directors. I think this is about more than just trialing a new team. The directors also want to test the *system* itself, its choices, and this is perfect for that, given as you said it's just one lost boy. Let's not forget also that local law enforcement called for help due to the odd nature of the case, so it fits the bill in more ways than one."

A wisp of my hair fell across my face and I brushed it back. I turned toward the two-way glass.

The boy was examining the plastic orange-juice bottle and the sticky printed label as though he'd never seen anything like it before.

"And you've formulated no early view on what's going on here?"

"At this point, no." His gaze went to the boy and then back to me. "Can I count on you?"

I looked through the glass at the boy. I recognized the fear behind his eyes.

I know how you feel, Dietmar. The sense of bewilderment. The loss of control.

Inside your head you're screaming: Where am I? What's happening?

Now I knew part of the reason Will had brought me in. If anyone understood childhood trauma, then it was me and Will was well aware of that. At age fourteen I'd been kidnapped and held hostage, emerging from the ordeal a different girl from the one I'd been before and it was something I'd partly opened up about, to Will, when we'd been a couple.

"We need to help this boy," I said. "You've already scanned the recent national missing persons lists I'm guessing?"

"Yes. No one that matches."

I snapped into organizational mode and it felt good. My comfort zone. "We'll need a list of all boys reported missing in the last ten years. If based on their age at the time of their disappearance they would be around ten now, then we cross-reference with photos and DNA if available."

"All boys, not just German-speaking?"

"All. Can't rule out that a missing or kidnapped kid wasn't schooled in the German language in the years since."

Will nodded. His eyes wandered to the boy through the window and then back to me. "We should cast this net internationally."

"Agreed. But outside the US, let's restrict it to the European countries at this early stage. And I need our researchers to send me everything they can on the Hamelin legend."

"Done."

I couldn't deny there was a part of me that felt good working a case with Will again. The old team. Like slipping into an old glove. I hadn't been expecting that. It was as though the angst of our separation had been momentarily erased and I wondered if he felt the same. "We need to get the boy out of those clothes so we can run tests, see if we can find out where they're from."

"And why there are burn marks on them," he added.

"Yes. And, Will, does this agency have a CVSA machine?"

"No. But I can have one here in a few hours. Good call."

"The Computer Voice Stress Analyzer," said Marcia. We'd noticed she'd stepped out of the interview room and now she stood in the doorway to the adjoining room where Will and I sat. "Non-invasive lie detection. You can use a hidden mic to record the boy without it stressing him out. Definitely a good call for this."

"Like any of these devices, it's not conclusive," I said, turning to her. "But it can give us a good idea of whether we think the boy's being deceptive."

"And what is its potential accuracy rate these days?" Marcia asked. "Eighty percent?"

"Better than that," Will said. "And a whole lot better than the old polygraphs."

"And we're going to need consultants." My gaze swept back to Will. "A historian, someone with special knowledge of medieval Europe. I want to know how accurate Dietmar is about life in a thirteenth-century German village. It may help point us to how and why he's telling us this. A historian who can work in unison with Marcia and, even better, help with the translation."

"Tall order," said Will.

"I specialize in them."

He allowed himself a brief grin. "I remember."

"Actually, I know just such a person," said Marcia, and even Will looked surprised.

"You do?" I looked at Marcia. My eyes were then drawn once more to the window. In the room, the boy, left alone for just a few minutes, was sipping on water and studying his surroundings. "I wasn't really expecting to get just one person with *all* those skills."

"Professor Zach Silverstein," Marcia suggested. "He not only matches your criteria but he's also close by. He's a history professor but he also has undergraduate degrees in Criminal Justice, Criminology and Forensics from Seattle University and he lectures across all those disciplines over there. More importantly, he has a special interest in European medieval studies."

"Now that's an eclectic mix," I observed.

"You could say he's something of an eclectic character."

"You know Silverstein?"

"I taught languages at the university before the Bureau recruited me," Marcia said. "Zach was a graduate student back then, studying his courses simultaneously, which is crazy but he's got an incredible memory. I remember he did his history thesis on Europe in the Middle Ages and he's produced a great deal of research that helped secure his role in teaching across multiple faculties. It must be fifteen years since I've seen him but I know he's still there and I don't think you'd find anyone else with a better knowledge of the period."

I looked to Will. "I'd say the answer to all this lies in Dietmar's story. But we need to know a lot more. Someone who understands this German medieval stuff inside out could prove useful."

"Your call," said Will. "Marcia, as one of his old alumni, could you make initial contact with him?"

"Love to," she said. "And there's something else I recall. On top of his historical expertise, Zach is – believe it or not – a self-taught expert on legends from all over the world. I seem to remember he was pretty much obsessed. He wrote a book on it that got him into a bit of bother with the university."

I shot her an inquisitive stare. "Why would it do that?"

"He's got some pretty quirky ideas." Marcia was keeping one eye on the boy in the room as she spoke. "I don't think I can explain it the way the professor does. It's always been generally accepted that some of the world's fairy tales are based on, or inspired by, real events, but greatly fantasized. Of course, most people simply believe they're allegorical tales to illustrate morals and ethics."

"Yes…" I prompted.

"The professor suggests that the tales, while exaggerated, are mostly true. That they actually happened, and that in many cases even the fantastic elements can be scientifically explained. In his book he gives examples, tying in people, places, and events and aligning them with the myths."

"Sounds like a bit of a nutter," Will said, unconvinced.

"He was called a lot worse," Marcia admitted. "One reviewer labeled him a fantasist wandering around in the wrong century."

I gave a clipped laugh. "That would definitely get the university offside."

"Yes, but he sailed through that. If anything, he's become a bit of a darling of the campus. Sometimes a little notoriety hurts you, another time it works in your favor. If a university loves anything it's a lecturer who's a minor celebrity."

"He doesn't sound like your kind of guy," Will said. I knew that my ex-partner was drawing on what he knew of me. Practical, pragmatic, down-to-earth. An agent who always believed you could unearth the evidence to solve a case via tried and tested means.

"But he may be exactly the kind of guy we need for this," I said.

Chapter Five

We all have another side to us. I knew that. Hell, we all have multiple other sides.

On the job, I was the passionate, determined, brutally honest straight-shooter. But I had a softer side. At least, I'd thought I had until Will, in the dying days of our relationship, had said, "You could lighten up, Ilona. Sometimes it feels like you treat our relationship as though it's another case you're working on."

"That's harsh."

"It's not meant to be," he'd said. "I know it can be hard to switch off but an agent has to learn to do that. *I've* had to do that."

"Will, you know the job is never far away. Nature of the beast."

"Every agent has to find that 'off' switch. Relax, kick your heels up. Even laugh."

"I laugh."

"Actually, you don't. Not lately. Not since you joined CIB and we've been spending so much time apart."

Six months earlier I had applied for and won a position with the Seattle-based Criminal Investigations Branch, within the Criminal, Cyber, Response, and Services Division. It was a step up and Will had been happy for me but working long hours apart, in different units, had taken a toll. "Never mind being on a case, I'm starting to feel like I'm on trial."

"I'm trying to reach out."

"Maybe I'm not the only one who needs to learn how to switch off."

He hadn't responded to that. Just looked at me. Frustrated. I remembered that exchange as one of the first times I'd been aware of the widening gap between us.

Three months later he'd received a promotion and was transferred to a supervisory special agent role in DC.

In hindsight, it had seemed only natural that Will, working in another city, and with a widening gap between us, might fall for someone else. Deep inside I'd known he was right. I'd needed to loosen up. We'd needed to spend more time together.

It was around that time I'd gone back to an old hobby – if *hobby* was even the right word. And as soon as I did, I realized it was a long time since I'd felt so exhilarated, so alive.

Was that the reason I'd stiffened up so much during those early Seattle days? Because I hadn't been pursuing the one thing that empowered me more than anything else ever had, not even my job? My other passion, my secret pleasure. And not something you revealed about yourself if you were an FBI professional.

Marcia came up alongside me in the kitchen alcove, breaking my reverie.

"You know, I may be a linguist and an agent and once upon a time a lecturer. But sometimes I think the real me is a mom. Just a mom."

"How many kids?" I asked.

"I raised three boys. Three young men now."

I smiled. "That sounds like a house with a hell of a lot of testosterone."

"Oh yeah." Marcia winked. "Those three boys… well, like any mom, I suppose, I've got enough stories to write a book. Probably a trilogy."

"I'll bet."

"I saw a lot of sides to my boys. Aggro, acting tough, boyish excitement. All the highs and lows. Confusion, fear, all those things."

"And what are you seeing in Dietmar?"

"Total displacement. He's confounded… in awe of all this" – Marcia gestured to the surroundings – "and he's very vague for a ten-year-old. Struggling to remember. And very scared."

"Scared by… us?"

"He's curious about us and we're earning his trust, step by step. I think there's something else… this mention of mine, using the German language, of a ratcatcher…"

"It certainly got a reaction," I said.

"I tried to ask him more about that after you and Will left the room." Marcia exuded a calmness that I liked. It was contagious. "He clammed up," she continued, "so it's going to be a matter of taking it slowly, chipping away. I can put the boy at ease and translate, but to really get inside his head–"

I completed the thought. "We need a professional. A child psychologist."

"Yes."

"Then we're on the same page."

"You would have worked with CARD before?" Marcia asked.

"A few times," I said. CARD, or Child Abduction Rapid Deployment, was the FBI's specialized unit for investigating crimes against children. "Professor Bernard Reinholdt consulted with our CIB unit on a few occasions."

"Brilliant mind," said Marcia. "Perhaps you could sweet-talk him out of retirement for this one?"

"I can try. And by the way, you've been absolutely terrific with Dietmar."

"Like I said – three boys. Just the thought of any of my boys going through anything like this…" Her voice trailed away.

I nodded my understanding. There wasn't anything I could add to that.

"When he was first brought here and you and Will arrived," I said, "how long did it take you to get the boy to open up?"

Marcia's tone brightened. "Not as long as I might've expected. But that was because the ranger who brought him in, Ellie, was in the room. He was comfortable around her."

I nodded. "Okay. And what was he saying at that point?"

The boy had been difficult to understand, so Marcia had to piece the fragments of his story together herself. "He woke in a cave, afraid, alone. Didn't know where the other children who'd been with him had gone. He ran out into the forest, calling for them, panicking."

"And the rangers heard him?"

"Yes."

We were heading back along the corridor when Will approached.

"Thanks for putting your history boffin in touch with us," he said to Marcia. He turned his gaze to me. "We're flying him over from Seattle. Should be in Meeting Room One in an hour."

* * *

For some reason I'd expected Professor Zach Silverstein to look older. Not that he looked too young. I knew from Marcia's account of the university days that he had to be late-thirtysomething. He had one of those chameleon faces, looking younger than he probably was one moment and older and wiser the next. Wiry-haired with John Lennon glasses and an expression that was half permanent grin and half WTF.

A face I'd seen before?

"You look familiar," I said.

He tilted his head toward me. "Are you psychic by any chance?"

Not the response from him I'd anticipated. "No."

"Well, then that rules that out."

"Rules what out?"

"That you once had visions of this meeting taking place."

I fixed him with a bemused stare. Appraising him. "Who thinks like that?"

"I do, I guess."

"I'll keep that in mind." I offered my hand and we shook. "Right now, on this case, being psychic might be a distinct advantage."

"Actually, every human being has some level of psychic ability within," the professor said. "As you're no doubt aware, we humans hardly ever use the whole of our brain at once. We can only guess what we'd be capable of if we did. The Scarlett Johansson movie *Lucy* speculated on that but of course, it's all conjecture. We don't really know, how could we…"

I listened, staying patient with the professor's patter. I was aware he was talking faster and faster as he went, skidding off on one tangent and then another.

"…a small number of people tap into just a little bit more of their brain, which might be what accounts for varying levels of psychic talent. I'm like you, I could use some of that – but I also fall into that great unwashed mass of those stuck back at ground level–"

"Did you just say all of that without taking a breath?"

Zach's grin widened. "I have a habit of doing that. Sorry. Tend to go off like the proverbial firecracker when I'm nervous, or on a subject dear to my heart, or both. Gotta pace the thoughts. Breathe more. Definitely got to breathe more. I'm working on it."

"Professor, we–"

"Surely you can call me Zach. The professor's that old guy who used to lecture me back in my student days and yes, I know I'm that lecturer now but I always get my students to call–"

"Zach, we asked for your help because we found a boy alone in the Olympic National Forest, miles from anywhere, speaking German. Our translator is making a good go of communicating with him, but it's difficult – the boy's use of language seems limited and… old world."

He looked confused. "Old world?"

"Yes, but what is particularly unusual is that he's wearing medieval-style garments and is telling us he's from a German village called Hameln. When our translator used the German term for ratcatcher, from the Pied Piper legend, the boy… reacted. He was fearful."

"Wow."

"That's your considered response?"

He shrugged away my comment. "You want me to verify what he says about the medieval age?"

"Yes. Depending on how accurate you say he is, it may help us identify how and where he gained that kind of knowledge."

"Such as?"

"There are medieval enthusiasts out there, right?" I said. "People who re-enact those times."

He gave this a moment's thought. "Sure. Medieval re-enactment groups, they get together for special events, usually several times a year. Fairs, games, and jousts, that sort of thing. Then back to their suburban homes and their day jobs. But that wouldn't explain the behavior of this boy, not from what you've just told me."

"What about people living in a medieval manner on a permanent basis, similar to the way the Amish maintain a colonial lifestyle?"

He stroked his chin. "No such group. If there was, I would know of them."

"It's early days," I said, "but this boy hasn't been reported missing and he believes he's from the thirteenth century. Anything you can learn from talking to him will be helpful. And I hope it will be useful to the child psychologist we're calling on."

"I'm glad you called on me. Absolutely fascinating. Like the past coming to life."

"Except the boy isn't from the past."

Zach shot me an intrigued look as we walked. "Isn't he?"

Chapter Six

I watched from behind the two-way glass as Marcia introduced Zach to the boy and then the two of them sat down. I marveled at how quickly Zach, with his banter and easy persona, managed to put Dietmar at ease.

They talked with him for fifteen minutes and I stood and watched, barely taking my eyes off the boy. Watching his every move, his every reaction, watching for any giveaway signs in his manner that he wasn't what he appeared to be.

I didn't observe even the slightest glitch in his behavior. What I saw was a nervous, bewildered, lost child, totally ill at ease as well as fascinated with everything around him.

Who are you?

I was back in my temporary office when Zach came in, stretching his arms out and then pulling up a seat. "I've always thought it's a damn shame," he said, "that there were no recording devices back in the Middle Ages. We can never really know for sure what people sounded like back then."

"I've never thought about that," I admitted.

"No reason you would. Few people ever have. Back then, as there are now, there were hundreds of spoken dialects that identified which part of a country a person was from. They existed in a kind of continuum from one region to the next, often with only slight variables."

"The further the distance the greater the difference."

"Spot on. According to texts from the seventeenth and eighteenth centuries, those dialects evolved, influenced by the emergence of written standards. Dietmar speaks in a dialect that doesn't exist nowadays, a throwback to how earlier dialects were written before those changing standards. He has an unusual way of phrasing his speech, an accent different from current-day German accents. The faster he speaks, of course, the more he becomes unintelligible to us. When we calm him down and slow his speech, we can understand him, or at the very least interpret him fairly correctly. Actually, Marcia has done an impressive job with him so far–"

"Take a breath," I said.

The professor shrugged and then grinned.

"So his language *and* his dialect are conversant with what you believe existed in a much earlier era?" I asked him.

"Yes."

"And you were able to get somewhere with him, ask him questions?"

"Yes, with Marcia's help."

"Go on," I urged.

"I tried to put him at ease," Zach said, "got him chatting, asked him where he was from and what kind of house his family lived in. He described a house made of timber logs and held together with hardened mud and a straw-thatched roof."

"That would be a fairly common understanding that people have of medieval houses."

"Perhaps. But when I asked him to describe what it was like inside, he told me about a room with a hole cut in the roof."

"What's that for?"

"Houses in medieval villages had openings in the roof through which heat and cooking smoke could escape."

"Kids wouldn't know that," I conceded.

"For Christ's sake, *adults* wouldn't know about that. You didn't."

"More the kind of little detail that historians know."

"Or a kid who actually lived there."

I waved his comment aside. "Anything else?"

"I asked him where they stored their clothing in the house."

"I'm guessing you had a particular reason for asking that?" I said.

"Yes. In medieval houses, the peasants hung their clothes from pegs in the walls."

"Not something anyone would know."

"But this kid knew." Zach leaned forward. "He described exactly that method as though it meant nothing special to him. Just the normal way of things."

"So far everything about him – language, clothing, dialect and household knowledge – seems authentic."

"Doesn't just seem that way, Ilona. Everything about him is the real deal. But he's also traumatized and he has a very limited vocabulary by our standards, which would be normal for a thirteenth-century child."

I looked at him incredulously. "You can't tell me you *believe* any of this?"

"Well, despite the obvious implausibility, I wouldn't dismiss it right now, not on what I've observed so far."

"It's impossible, Zach."

He held up his cell phone. "To a thirteenth-century villager, so is this."

"There's a plausible explanation to this and I need you to help me find it."

He nodded. "*If* there's a plausible explanation, then we will."

"Did you or Marcia ask him anything further about the Piper?"

"As you instructed," Zach said, "we're taking it slowly, one step at a time, to keep him onside, and to encourage him to open up a little bit more. Next session, we ask him about how he got here. We ask him about the Piper."

* * *

Later, after his second interview with Dietmar, Zach left Marcia with the boy and joined me in my office once again. "The lad's become more and more comfortable around Marcia."

"Mother figure," I said. I was in front of my laptop with the hand-sized CVSA device attached. It had arrived just half an hour before. Will helped me set it up and left to check on the Bureau's search for Dietmar's identity.

Zach nodded toward the machine. "You recorded our talk, analyzing his voice levels?"

"Yes. The CVSA works for any language. It's the non-verbal tones in the voice that it reads. Measures stress levels in response to the questions."

A line pulsed across the laptop screen and I gestured to a graph beneath it. "Accuracy score for each of his answers is calculated here."

Zach moved alongside me, squinting at the screen. He cocked his head toward me, appraising me. "Did you work on that five-year-old homicide cold case in Tacoma a couple of years ago?"

"Yes."

"That got written up quite a bit in press articles about the CVSA. I remember reading about it."

"The machine was crucial in solving the case," I said. "Put us back on the trail of a suspect who'd previously passed a polygraph."

"So what's the verdict here?"

"The machine gave a positive reading on all of Dietmar's responses."

"Positive?" Zach lowered his lanky frame into a chair. "So that means it didn't detect his answers as lies?"

"No."

Zach's eyes wandered to a second laptop on the desk's side annex. A paused video recording of the interview. The CCTV in the room had been configured to show a close-up of Dietmar's face. "And I believe you're a deft hand at personal observation in matters like this?"

"When a person isn't being honest," I explained, "there are subtle changes in the eyes. Lying induces a subconscious change in cognitive load."

"And that's not something that can be faked," Zach guessed.

"No."

"And Dietmar's eye movements were also consistent with telling the truth?"

"They were."

"It's all adding up then," Zach said. "Just not with a result you'd expect."

"What was he saying about this Piper that led him away from his home?"

"Marcia asked him if he knew who this Piper was? He said it was the man who came to get rid of the rats."

I shook my head. "I can't believe this." Looking past Zach, I saw that Will was back. He stood in the doorway, listening. He nodded toward me.

"I asked him why he and his friends had followed the Piper away from their homes," Zach said. "He didn't seem to know. That's when he started to get agitated again and we had to soothe him, telling him he was safe and everything would be okay." Zach rose and paced to the wall and back. Seeing the boy upset was clearly taking a toll on him as well. He took a deep breath. "He said that when the Piper played his pipe the music made them happy, they wanted to dance, and then when the Piper left they followed. Dietmar said he didn't want to, but he couldn't stop himself."

"Nothing here that any kid wouldn't know from the fairy tale," I said. "Did he say anything that isn't in the legend, anything that resonates in any other way?"

"He said the Piper led them into a cave in the hills near their village. That too fits the fairy tale. He said they were walking in the cave for a long time. When they came out the other end they were in a place of scattered woods and hills." Zach took a moment, and I could sense he was casting his mind back over the exact words that Marcia had translated from Dietmar's description. "This is where it gets a little more interesting. Dietmar described something that I would say was a natural rock formation. It was shaped like two towers and rose above him. And he said there were large, fast-moving birds with golden-brown plumage, sweeping and diving. He said they walked across that landscape for a long time and then a fire broke out in the forest. There was smoke everywhere, and flames sweeping through the trees toward them."

"Good God," I said.

"The Piper told them to run as fast as they could. They ran after the Piper through columns of smoke and ash. They reached another cave and it led them to a different place, far away from the fire. In that part of the cave, they went to sleep and when Dietmar woke, the others were gone and–"

"That's when the rangers found him wandering in the forest?"

"Yes." Zach stretched, running his fingers through his spring of curls. "Given Dietmar's limited vocabulary, I was getting this from him in fragments, but with just enough detail for me to piece it all together."

"What do you make of this other place he described?"

"If you read up on the origin of the Pied Piper legend, then you'll find most versions have the children being taken into a large cave. A nineteenth-century Scottish writer, Andrew Lang, wrote about the various theories surrounding the world's strangest historical incidents. One of these theories speculates that the Piper took the children to Transylvania."

"Transylvania?" I was unconvinced.

"There were reports that a hundred and fifty years after the Piper legend, merchants traveling through Transylvania came across a community of German-speaking people. These people didn't know how they'd come to be there. The merchants believed them to be the descendants of the lost Hamelin children, and they spread the story."

"What's that got to do with Dietmar's story?" Will moved into the office, pulling up a chair.

"There are two rock towers in the Ciucas Mountains in Transylvania. They've been carved by the elements over millennia."

"And let me guess," I said, "it's also home to the golden eagle."

"Yes. Neither the Transylvania theory nor that landscape would be known by a ten-year-old boy. But that's exactly what he described, and" – Zach motioned to the laptop screens – "according to your CVSA, the boy is telling us the God's honest truth."

"And this isn't what any of us want to hear," said Will, "but we've got feedback from Missing Persons and the photo of Dietmar that went out."

"No hits," I guessed.

"Nothing."

I vented my frustration. "If this boy wandered off and got lost, or if he was kidnapped, there has to be a report filed by his parents."

"The thing is, the boy isn't just speaking Middle High German," Zach protested. "He knows the peculiar day-to-day aspects of life in the Middle Ages, it's like second nature to him."

"And that's what we've got you here to help with."

Zach stretched again. "I'll head back in, see if I can help Marcia any further with Dietmar. We think we can get him to change into some pajamas for tonight."

"Good," I said. "We need that clothing for analysis."

As Zach left, Will motioned to me. "My office. There's something you need to see."

Chapter Seven

"Not good news," Will said as I followed him into the spare room he was using as an office. He turned his PC monitor so I could view the news website on screen.

Alarm bells rang in my head the moment my eyes settled on the headline.

Where did the Pied Piper boy come from?

The photo underneath showed Dietmar walking in the forest, heading in the direction from which the shot had been taken, the cave's partly obscured mouth in the distance behind him.

"How the hell did this happen?" I said.

"Another story from the ranger's sister. Brooke Goodman. She received the photo from an anonymous source."

"And her article has already been picked up by every news website, and Twitter news junkie out there?" I guessed.

"I'm afraid so."

"How would she know about the Piper angle?" I held up my palm before I'd even finished the sentence. "Let me guess. The same anonymous source?"

"You got it."

I read the article. It didn't say much more than Brooke Goodman's original piece, except now it included the mystifying allusion to Hamelin and the famous legend.

I zeroed in on the photo. The boy's head was tilted to the side at the moment of the shot. His face wasn't visible. "If a random hiker was out there, saw the kid, and took a photo, why didn't he approach the boy, ask if he was okay, try to help? Or if he couldn't do that then at least phone for help."

"He, or she, did. There was a call to the local emergency services," Will said. "But by then the rangers had found the boy and reported to local police, so no further action was needed."

"Why weren't *we* alerted to this?"

Will shrugged. "The information was logged but as far as Emergency was concerned the matter was closed. The information was overlooked, buried, whatever, when it came to local law enforcement calling on us."

"Sounds like you're making excuses for them." Even as I said it, I knew I was drawing from my feelings about Will, feelings that were still raw, directing them at him in the guise of my frustration with the information. Not how I wanted to be dealing with this.

"I'm telling you what we know so far." His tone turned steely.

"So someone just happens to be out there," I said, my voice sharp. "They see the boy. They shoot a good-quality pic, call emergency services, then hightail it out of there. This person then sends their photo anonymously to a reporter who'd just last night filed the story about the lost kid."

Will was on the same page. "Something doesn't add up."

"Have you spoken with this Brooke Goodman?"

"Just got off the phone to her editor and he'll make certain they don't speculate any further on this unless there's breaking news. I haven't been able to reach the reporter, so I'll get you to try getting a hold of her, as well. One of the agents here is calling a few of the other local media outlets, requesting they assist us by holding back."

"You said the emergency call that was routed to the rangers was from *he* or *she*," I said. "The emergency center worker doesn't know?"

"The person who took the call wasn't sure. Said it was muffled, couldn't say for certain."

"I'm seeing a pattern."

"Go on." Will swiveled the computer screen back into place.

I took a moment, collecting my thoughts. "Firstly, the person behind this knew there was a park patrol in the area that coincided with Dietmar being there. *Not* a coincidence. Secondly, one of those rangers just happens to have a sister who works for the local newspaper. That reporter then receives an anonymous photo the very next morning after her news article has appeared." I stabbed at the air with my right forefinger. "*Not* a coincidence."

He nodded. "Seems those events were planned."

"Someone chose that national park because they knew of those patrols, and they knew of the ranger's journalist sister."

"Agreed. And the photo?"

"We need to speak to Brooke Goodman to find out more about that." I tucked a loose strand of hair behind my ear. "And we need to check out the cave and figure out from where that photo was taken."

I watched as Will rose from behind his desk, pacing to the window and back. This was a trait I remembered well, Will's way of sifting through all the details at hand. "If the rangers take me to the area, I can stand in the spot this picture focused on. I can then extrapolate back to where the photographer must have been."

"You're hoping to find something."

"Maybe the photographic equipment is still out there," I said. "Strategically placed to get that photo and then beam it back to a control point. If that's how this was done, the equipment might still be in its hiding place."

"More likely it's been removed."

"Not if the operator didn't expect us to go out there looking for any gear left behind."

"You're hoping for fingerprints."

"It's worth a try."

"Okay."

"If I remember correctly, you were pretty good at extrapolation."

"And if I remember correctly," Will countered, "you were even better, so you won't need me. I'll follow through on having the clothing carbon-tested. Take the geek with you, let's see if he thinks the cave is some kind of Brothers Grimm time portal."

I winced at the sarcasm. "You don't want to go giving him ideas like that."

"Don't need to. He's got plenty of his own."

* * *

Back in my temporary office, I rewatched the video of Dietmar talking with Marcia and Zach. I focused even more on his eyes. I wanted to be certain I hadn't missed anything, some tiny telltale sign. I could give the video even greater focus on my own.

Nothing.

What am I missing?

I watched it again.

It was getting late. It had been a long day and I knew it was important to take a break.

I should head off to the motel that the Bureau had booked for me.

I yawned. Stretched.

I reached down into my purse and dug down until my fingers touched the edge of my personal journal.

I didn't know why I'd brought it. I knew it wasn't wise. It's not like I was going to be writing any new entries while I was here. The slim book had been safe in its private place back at my apartment in Seattle.

I pulled the notebook out. Of course, I knew why I'd brought it. If I couldn't pursue my secret pastime then the very next best thing was to sit and read over some of my old entries.

The book fell open on a random, early page and I read.

There are others like me out there.

I don't know any of them, not nowadays anyway. That would be too dangerous, the risk of exposure too great, though sometimes we interact briefly.

There are websites as well, but I'd never visit them, not from my own PC.

On rare occasions, at an internet café, I've anonymously surfed those sites and I remember in particular the words from one of the bloggers:

Keep a journal, the blogger said. Write it all down.

It's a way to relive your passion. A record just for you, of who you really are, of how it feels, of what you see, of where the emotion takes you. And when the time comes that you can no longer pursue this, then you have this priceless, timeless set of memories forever recorded in your own words.

That guy was right.

And so I keep this record, hidden away in the middle pages of a journal that otherwise appears from the cover to be a diary of do-it-yourself recipes.

Kept private, in the bottom of a drawer amongst a mix of unrelated papers and folders of no particular import.

I continued reading and I felt a lift inside. My imagination took over. I had learned how to make this work for me. It was a balm for my soul, just so long as it remained my secret, just so long as no one ever suspected.

And then I was struck by a sudden jolt of alarm as Will strode into the room.

Chapter Eight

"The researchers have compiled the material on the Hamelin legend," Will said. "They've emailed a link."

"Good. Nice and speedy." My eyes met his, and I felt a sense of relief that his gaze never fell to the slim journal in my hands.

"As I've said, the PTBs are watching this investigation closely and making us a top priority."

"I'll look over the material back at the motel." I slipped the journal back into my purse.

"I hate to admit it but on this occasion, your nerdy professor probably knows more on this than our researchers will have pulled together."

"It's been a long day and I need a break both from the professor and this place. You know me, I reach a point when I need to kick back and spend some time alone, just me and the case details."

"I remember. What are you going to do for food?"

I shrugged. "I'll figure something out."

"I'll bring takeout. Why don't I view the material with you, see if we can make some sense out of all of this."

"No, thanks. I'm fine."

"Certain?"

I fixed him with a cold stare. "I'm not a stand-in for Nadine, Will."

"That's not what I–"

"Just leave it, okay?"

"I'm bringing you some takeout, even if I just leave it at the door for you."

"Whatever." I grabbed hold of my laptop and my jacket and swept past him "Early start tomorrow," I said as I left the office.

* * *

I was still smarting as I stood in the corridor waiting for the elevator. Zach, coat slung over his shoulder, came up alongside me.

"Where have they put you up for the night?" I asked him.

"Nowhere. I've got an old friend, a college roommate from another life, who lives nearby. I'm staying with him."

The elevator arrived and we stepped in.

"I haven't read your book," I said to the professor, "but I've taken a cursory glance at the preview pages online, and I've read a few of the reviews."

"The good ones, I hope."

"There are good ones?"

He laughed. "Touché."

"I gather, from what I've read, that you're on a mission to prove there are supernatural forces in the world that can explain the fantastical elements of many folktales and legends."

"I certainly believe there's a body of information to support that."

"So that's your theory," I said, "that the natural world and the supernatural world exist side by side?"

"Yes, and that one is just as real and as scientifically plausible as the other."

The elevator doors opened and we headed through the lobby to the exit.

"But you haven't, as yet, uncovered any definitive, officially sanctioned proof." I flashed a devilish grin.

"This might be the very case where that can be achieved." Zach matched my grin with a determined, megawatt smile. He wagged his finger at me. "There's something about this boy…"

"*Or,*" I said, "learning what's real and what's not with his story, we can find out who he is and how he really came to be out there in the wilderness."

* * *

It was a short distance from the Poulsbo office to the motel and on the way, I passed an internet café, similar to the ones I frequented around Seattle when I wanted to access the net but not from one of my own devices. The earlier read of my diary had hardly been stimulating enough and I figured I could take time out, just for twenty minutes or so, to indulge myself.

I turned and went in. Using my online alias, I logged on to the site from which I could read the blogs that were the next best option to the real thing. There were several like-minded bloggers that I occasionally followed, enthusiasts like me who went by usernames such as The Loner, and StarX. I dived into one and then another and came finally on the latest from one of my favorites.

> *I'm told by others that I describe my passion with the powers of a poet but I don't believe that I do it the justice it deserves. How can I? When I'm in my element I see all the possibilities locked within, the good and the bad, the light and the dark. I am as free as any soul can be.*

These words had the power to touch me, it was as though this blogger was in sync with my spirit.

For now, for tonight, that was the best I could hope for.

* * *

It was an ordinary, fairly nondescript but reasonably comfortable motel room. I had lost count of the number of rooms like this one I'd stayed in as an FBI agent.

Before settling in, I made a call to the ranger, Ellie Goodman. I'd tried earlier without success but this time she answered almost immediately. After introducing myself and thanking her for her efforts in looking after Dietmar, I asked, "Is your sister, Brooke, at home?"

"Not at the moment," Ellie said. "I can give you her cell number."

"Already got it from the newspaper," I said. "Wasn't able to raise her."

"She runs around all over the place. Probably in a dead spot, we get a few around here. But I expect her home a little later this evening."

"I'll need to speak with her but in the meantime, when you see her, Ms. Goodman—"

"Ellie, please."

"When you see her, Ellie, if you could pass on a message that we've requested she doesn't run any more pieces on the lost boy."

"Of course. Is there a problem?"

"We're investigating his appearance out there in the forest and we'd like to keep a lid on the story until we know a little more."

"I understand. I had no idea she'd act so quickly on my discovery of the boy. You could speak with her editor."

"We've spoken with her newspaper and a few other local outlets and they will comply, but I want to make certain Brooke doesn't release anything further on social media."

"I'll pass that on."

"And we'll need to speak with her about how she came by the picture."

"Apparently, it just appeared on her desktop with a caption from an anonymous source," Ellie revealed. "I thought that seemed strange but she told me reporters get anonymous tips and material sent to them all the time, sometimes from people who are happy to pass on news items but who want to stay out of the limelight themselves. She thought maybe it was programmed to download automatically from one of the sites she often visits."

"Possible," I commented.

"I still thought it sounded a little odd."

"With technology these days, something odd pretty quickly becomes something normal."

Ellie chuckled. "I think we can all relate to that."

"You're all set for the morning, Ellie?"

"Yes. All set." Earlier, Ellie had received a call from a coordinator at the local field office, arranging for her to take me out to where she and her colleague, Blaine Crawford, had found the boy.

I ended the call, my thoughts drawn to the news item Will had shown me earlier, and I wondered just who it could be that was feeding those details to Brooke Goodman.

I kicked off my shoes and poured a glass of white wine from the motel-stocked minibar. My laptop was on the coffee table. I accessed my Bureau email, clicked on the link I'd been sent, and sank back on the sofa, glass in hand.

What a day.

The video material from the Bureau researchers started playing. I had asked for an overview of the Pied Piper legend, together with detailed background on specific points.

The first segment was from a cable TV documentary, presented by a host I vaguely recognized. It opened with a sweeping view of modern-day Hamelin. Images of the town, nestled in a green expanse of hills and valleys. The host's voice-over:

> *Every legend has a home. And this is the German town of Hameln, known to us in the Western world as Hamelin, the home of what is one of the world's most famous and consistently retold fairy tales, The Pied Piper of Hamelin. It was universally popularized in verse by the nineteenth-century poet Browning. It was one of the many folktales collected in that same century by the Brothers Grimm. But is*

it fact or fiction? Unlike many folktales, this one has its origins in historical fact. A problem with rats was not uncommon in towns in medieval Europe.

The image on the screen cut away to live footage taken of rats scurrying through piles of rubbish.

The image then changed to illustrated depictions of the medieval town, showing a village square, cobbled streets, and then rows of cottages.

The German town of Hamelin, on the western shore of the Weser River in Lower Saxony, called on a ratcatcher to rid their town of a plague of these vermin. This ratcatcher, a charismatic character dressed in multi-colored tunic and coat, hence the term pied, bargained with the town mayor.

Various illustrations and paintings from down the years were shown as the voice-over continued:

Displaying his talent with a pipe, the ratcatcher played music that entranced the rats and compelled them to follow him. He led them en mass out of the town and into the river where they drowned.

For unknown reasons, but most likely greed and the machinations of a corrupt mayor, the town refused to pay the Piper the agreed fee for his services. This is where the story takes a dark turn that has, ever since, seen it told and retold throughout the ages. The Piper threatened that he would lead the children away, never to be returned, if his fee was not met. The town elders did not believe him.

In retaliation for being cheated, the Piper returned to the town again and while the adults went out about their work, the Piper played a new tune. This music enchanted the children and they left whatever games they were playing. Coming together as a group, they followed the Piper out of the town and into the hills.

The images on the screen changed to footage from an old black-and-white movie. It showed a group of children following a pipe-playing man dressed in a long, flowing cape.

> *Some versions of the legend say that the children were led into a cave and that later they emerged from another cave into the Transylvanian countryside where they lived out their lives. Other versions state that the fate of the children remained unknown or that they continue to follow the Piper to this day, on a journey through infinity.*

There was a rap on the door and I paused the program.

"Chinese takeaway," I heard Will's voice say. "One of your favorites, fried kway teow. I've left it at the door."

I raised my eyebrows. I really didn't know how to take Will McCord sometimes. *Most* of the time.

I got up and opened the door. Will was already halfway toward the exterior stairway. "Thanks."

"You're welcome," he called back.

"Oh for Christ's sake, you're here now. You might as well come in and have some of this and take a look at this material."

"I wouldn't want to interfere with your evening," he shot back.

"You are anyway."

He turned and headed back toward me. "I'll admit I'm ready to eat."

* * *

I replayed the documentary while we ate and then accessed the video that had been taken of the interviews with Dietmar. We watched the boy's movements and facial expressions and listened closely to his voice.

"What are we missing?" I said.

"Tomorrow's another day," Will said. "We're not going to solve this tonight."

I got up and walked with him to the door. "Tomorrow, then."

Before he stepped across the threshold, he turned to me. "Ilona, what was that all about this afternoon?"

"What was *what* all about?"

"Today. When we looked at the photo the media published. And when I offered to bring takeout. Your tone."

My voice was sharp. "It's called professional."

"It was personal and you know it."

"Do I?"

"I want us to be able to put the past behind us, Ilona, and work on this case as a real team."

"So do I."

"Can we talk then, can we loosen up and get past this?"

I raised my hands, prepared to concede a point. "Okay, okay, sorry if there was a *tone*. I'm probably tired, I've been up since all hours and that damn photo got my ire up. And you know I need my me-time."

"Okay." He looked as though he was going to add something but then he glanced back across at the video that was paused on a close-up of Dietmar. "If that kid's acting then he should be up for an Oscar."

"He's not acting." My next words were said as much to myself as to Will. "So who on earth is he and how did he get here?"

"Anyway, I should leave you to get that rest we keep talking about–"

"Much needed. And that goes for you, as well." Just saying the word 'rest' had brought it all down on me. I knew the value of getting a good night's rest and tackling a case fresh and reinvigorated the next morning.

"You ever think about us?" Will said.

I rolled my eyes. What was he doing? "How many times have I heard cheap ass lines like that in movies?"

"How many times?"

"I've lost count."

"And you just avoided the question better than any lame movie character."

"There is no *us*."

"There was once."

Tiring of these references to our past, my eyes wandered and I brushed back a loose strand of hair. "No. I don't think about it."

"I do."

"What's this about, Will?"

"Reminiscing." He shrugged. "People do it from time to time."

"I don't."

"Everybody reminisces. Looks back. Wonders 'what if?'"

"What happened to keeping things professional and putting the past behind us?"

"Still the case, but it hardly means we can't occasionally look back on shared memories, does it? We're not machines, at least I'm not despite some opinions to the contrary."

"Your humor hasn't improved." I tilted my head and permitted myself a half-smile.

"Nobody's perfect."

"I don't dwell on the past, Will. I moved on but then you didn't give me much choice." I bit my lip. This wasn't a conversation I wanted to have. I'd been intent on not allowing Will to draw me into any discussions about our old life.

"I'm not sure I ever really put this into words before, Ilona, but the last thing I ever wanted to do was cause you pain."

"Yes, you said it way back then and I get that you meant it," I conceded. "Surely there's no need to dig it all up again. We both moved on, and as you've said, right now we've got a case to solve."

"Agreed. But I never thought I fully communicated with you through the breakup. And I guess that's something I've been hoping for a moment to address. You were rightfully angry. I was out of my depth emotionally and talking a lot of crap."

"Actually, you didn't say all that much."

"And that was wrong."

I showed my surprise. "I didn't know you felt that way."

"I do," he said with a note of regret.

"It may have taken me a while back then, but eventually I understood. You fell for someone else and thought it was time to move on. It's not a crime. It's not even all that unusual in long-distance relationships." I wondered why I was being so damn easy on him.

"Now you're being very reasonable," he said.

"It's an aberration."

He laughed. "Well, I hope this goes some way toward clearing the air, then."

"I never thought it was all that frosty." Actually, ever since we'd teamed up on this case, I had been talking to him like I had ice on my tongue.

"I'll put a lid on the reminiscing," he offered.

"Good." My eyes met his as he gave me a long, appreciative stare. Despite the intensity of his on-the-job demeanor, his eyes had always been a mirror of what was really going on with him. They conveyed the seriousness with which he regarded any given situation, the caring he felt for someone, or the subtle but unmistakable twinkle when he was genuinely amused. I was reminded of how much I'd always liked the man I could see in those eyes.

I couldn't avoid having my mind flash back to our time together. All of a sudden, it didn't seem like two years ago. Time melted. Two professionals. Driven. Ambitious. We thought we could handle a long-distance romance while pursuing lofty goals. Wrong.

What was it he'd said? Do you ever wonder 'what if?'

I hadn't responded specifically to that. Nor would I. But there was a time when I'd lived out a whole 'what if?' scenario in my mind.

I'd never thought of Will as harboring any guilt over our breakup. I certainly hadn't expected him to bring it up, to admit to so much remorse.

I changed the subject. "Is the real reason you brought me in because of my experience as a kid? You figured I'd relate to the boy?"

"It was one of many reasons."

"Ellie Goodman told me when she first saw Dietmar, she was rocked by the fear in his eyes."

Will nodded. "Fear of a piper in a fairy tale."

"Not necessarily a fairy tale according to our Professor Silverstein."

Will cocked his head to one side. "I'm still not convinced about your professor."

"He knows his stuff. And hopefully, he can help us understand what's really going on with this boy."

Chapter Nine

Day Two

"Professor Bernard Reinholdt was a consultant to CARD, now retired," I said to the receptionist as I entered the Poulsbo Agency the following morning. "Could you get him on the line for me?"

"Sure thing," the young woman said.

I was no sooner in my office when the call was put through to the landline. "How's retirement, Professor?"

"Hopefully uninterrupted," Reinholdt said and I could visualize the gentle smile on the patrician face of the man I'd consulted with during my tenure with CCRSB.

I told him everything I knew about this case; the lost boy, who rather than having lost his memories, had memories of a life that could not be possible.

"Yes, I've seen the news items today and I admit to being intrigued, Ilona. But I made a promise to my good wife that retirement really does mean retirement, and I've already broken that promise once before."

"I understand."

"Despite all that, I wouldn't be able to say no to helping out on this. But my lady and I are booked on a three-month European cruise, and we fly out, first stop Rome, tomorrow morning."

"I'm sorry I can't lure you out of retirement one last time," I said, "but your trip sounds amazing and there's no one more deserving."

"Have you crossed paths with my former colleague and protégé?" he asked. "John Sanders?"

"No. I've heard his name, of course."

"He's filled most of my consultancy roles with CARD. Dare I say it, having been his mentor, that John is immensely skilled. He works with a wide range of people but specializes in kids. His insights into young people are like lightning in a bottle. And you'd work well with him, Ilona."

"That's the best endorsement I've heard for a while."

"I'll have him call you," Reinholdt said.

The call came through twenty minutes later on my smartphone as I was heading down to the parking lot. "Special Agent Farris? John Sanders."

"Thanks for getting in touch so quickly," I said.

"Dear old Bernard has recommended me for some interesting cases but I don't think there's anything that could come close to the one he just outlined."

"And that's putting it mildly," I said. "There are several factors to consider. Bizarre memories. Fear, displacement. All seem to be playing a part."

"As I'd expect. I'm just scanning some of the media reports now. Give me an hour or so to contact some colleagues. If I can organize them to take over my immediate workload, then I can be in Poulsbo later today. I actually have another client out that way that I've worked with a few times."

"Who is that?"

"Do you know of the Reverend Thomas Jessway? Various government departments use his services."

"The name rings a bell."

"He was previously a senior pastor with the independent All Peoples Church but it's his occasional assistance to CARD where you've probably come across his name."

"Of course. He runs a youth camp."

"Yes, the SafePlace Youth Retreat over at Port Ludlow," Sanders said. "The rev set up an all-year-round camping, conference, and vacation retreat, providing horse-riding, canoeing, arts, and crafts. He takes a lot of bookings from schools, churches, non-profit and government groups."

"And what do you do with them?"

"I suppose you'd call it motivational speaking. SafePlace teaches physical and emotional health and wellbeing and works on developing team building and leadership skills. Anyway, let me arrange my workload, Agent, and I'll call back to confirm."

* * *

As we'd arranged, Zach met me in the parking lot. We were driving, in one of the Poulsbo Agency's cars, to the Olympic National Forest to meet up with the rangers.

I pulled out of the agency grounds and onto the road. I filled Zach in on my contact with the child psychologist.

The early morning light was strong. It cast its glow across the shopping squares and along Viking Avenue and the parklands around Liberty Bay. In an earlier era, Poulsbo had been settled by Norwegians and the architecture reflected that, with the themed shopfronts and Norwegian flags that dotted the thoroughfares.

We weren't far out of town, speeding along the WA-3 N when Zach snapped his fingers and pointed his right forefinger at me. "That's it. Now I know where I've seen you before. And I'm not talking about that Tacoma case."

"You aren't?"

"You were the lady interviewed on TV a couple of weeks ago."

I shrugged."Oh, that. My fifteen minutes."

"You'd interviewed the kid who tried to commit suicide and the local news quizzed you about it."

"Yeah."

"Wasn't that case somewhat removed from your usual federal jurisdiction?"

"The local police asked for our help," I said. "The boy was fourteen, wasn't known to the authorities, and all of a sudden he was on a city rooftop, ready to jump. They couldn't coax out of him who he was or why he was suicidal."

"And didn't some random urban climber save him?"

"The climber just happened by, saw the boy, and persuaded him to move back from the edge until the police rescue got there."

I was glad Will hadn't called in the chopper for our trip to the Olympic National Forest. I was looking forward to the thirty-five-minute drive to the ranger office in Quilcene. A chance to mull over the details of this case some more and to see the waterways, wetlands, and big sky around Port Gamble and the Hood Canal Bridge.

"And the climber vanished?"

"Into thin air, it seems. Just ahead of the cops reaching the roof. The local police knew about my recent successes with some troubled youths. My unit agreed to consult with them."

"What did you find out?"

"The boy had run away from an abusive family and rather than live on the streets or seek help, he figured ending it was the only way out. He's in foster care now, and doing okay."

Zach remembered some of the details. "And the news segment indicated your team was helping the Seattle Police with finding that climber."

I nodded, keeping my eyes on the road. In the distance, lush green hills were dappled with swathes of alternating sunlight and shadow.

"There was a bit of a craze a couple of years back, with this urban climbing and parkour and freerunning thing. You might have seen reports also referring to it as 'rooftopping,' or 'buildering.' Daredevils putting themselves and everyone around them at risk by dangerous climbs up the sides of high rises, bridges, and state monuments. They don't use safety ropes, and they often dangle from tiny ledges and bars."

"Parkour is the military-style, no-frills movement," Zach expounded on what he knew about the extreme sport, "and freerunning the more random application."

"Yes, but quite often these runners merge elements of the two."

"Along with the crazy-ass climbing?"

"Yes."

Zach shuddered. "And leaping from one ledge to another."

I noticed his uneasiness. "You don't like heights?"

"Not a fan. And this urban climbing or 'rooftopping' is illegal, of course."

"Depends on the area and the building and the risk to the public. But the police and the local businesses definitely don't want it going on. The Seattle Police pretty much cleared it up a couple of years ago, arresting the main perpetrators. Like many of these fads, it petered out."

"Except for this one guy?"

"There's still a few of these rooftoppers being spotted," I explained. "After the incident with the suicidal jumper, Seattle cops wondered if the climber who spoke with the boy was the same guy that had been reported several times before. They lack the staff to follow up on some things, not that the Bureau has people just sitting around…"

"But you agreed to look into it."

"I had a rookie sift through CCTV from the past couple of months."

"I'm guessing your rookie spotted this climber."

"He showed up on a few frames of footage."

"Definitely the same person?" Zach wondered.

"We believe so. Same-colored sweatpants, and bulky jacket with a hoodie covering most of the face."

Zach shifted in the seat. "Doesn't sound like the right outfit for someone bouncing around hard-to-hold, slippery edges and ledges and so on."

"It's not."

"I guess it takes all types."

"I see that understatement is another one of your skills," I said drily.

"Understatement? Oh, I *specialize* in understatement." He raised his arm in readiness to give me a high five.

I stared briefly at his palm, face impassive, then redirected my focus back to the road ahead. "Best we can do is have police and emergency services keep an eye out. If they spot anyone they suspect of being this character, or any others putting themselves or others in danger, they know to call it in straight away."

"Why do these freerunners and rooftoppers do it?" Zach shook his head.

"They're adrenaline junkies, among other things."

"Surely this one climber can expect some leniency from the courts, given he helped save a kid?"

"The law is the law, Zach," I said flatly.

"So you're not helping the cops out on that now?"

"I'm on loan from one FBI unit to another. But when I'm in Seattle, I'll be following up on it."

Zach flashed me a knowing grin. "Because you want to see this climber get a fair deal, given he stopped a teenage suicide?"

"Not really."

"No?" Zach was intrigued. "Then why?"

"These climbers are reckless and they take crazy risks. I want to get to this rooftopper before he hurts himself or someone else."

* * *

Ellie and Blaine drove us to the spot where Dietmar had first been seen in the southwestern perimeter of the forest.

Ellie had grown up in these parts and spoke to me of how much she loved the national park's sweeping landscape. It was nearly one million acres of temperate rainforest, canyons, glacial peaks, and rugged ocean coastline. I smiled. Looking at how the morning light filtered through the wooded hills in this part, I could understand Ellie's passion.

The rangers waited by the vehicle as Zach and I went into the woods, retracing the steps I assumed Dietmar had taken just before the rangers had found him.

We found the cave and going in we scanned the cavern.

"The ground is hard," I observed, "so no footprints."

"Looks like it runs way back." Zach inched forward, deeper into the cavern. "It gets pretty narrow but I think it widens again. There's a pinprick of light back there."

"Another opening?"

"I'd say so. Could be where Dietmar originally entered the cave."

Using our flashlights to counter the darker parts, we pressed on, through the narrow tunnel and then as it widened into a broader cavern with another entry. It led us out onto the middle of a steep incline on the other side of the hills.

There was a trail down the slope that meandered off into the deep woods.

"It doesn't lead anywhere," I said. "Just off into the wilderness."

"Or it's a portal back to the Middle Ages," said Zach matter-of-factly.

I flashed him an exasperated look. "We're going back, to check the area where that picture was taken."

I caught the disappointed expression that passed across his eyes. He took in a sweeping view of the forest below and then turned to follow me back into the cave. "Good plan."

"At least one thing's certain."

"What's that?"

"That ain't Transylvania."

"No. *But* if we'd been following the Piper—"

"Zip it, Prof," I said, suppressing my irritation with a crooked grin.

* * *

We scanned the trees but there was no sign of any photographic equipment. One of the ranger radiophones, which Ellie had given to me, crackled into use. It was Ellie. "Ilona, I've been contacted by the office. They had a call from a guy out hiking with his son, who came across a couple of lost kids less than a mile north."

"The kids didn't say where they thought their parents must be?"

"I'm told they don't speak or understand English."

I stiffened.

Surely not.

Zach, listening in, shot me a glance.

"Did this guy mention how the children were dressed?" I asked.

"Something about weird outfits."

"Any details? Were they medieval-style?"

"He didn't say."

"Zach and I are on our way back."

"More German kids?" Zach asked.

I was already setting off along the trail. Surely this could not be a coincidence. "Starting to look that way," I said.

Chapter Ten

A boy and a girl, holding on tight to each other, their eyes wide with fright.

Blaine had parked the SUV further along the access road, just out of sight of the area where the two children crouched. The hikers who'd found them stood nearby.

It's like some kind of quirky Mexican standoff, I thought, as Ellie, Zach, and I approached on foot. Blaine remained behind with the vehicle. It was Ellie who'd suggested parking the vehicle out of view, so as not to panic the children in case it was a similar situation to that of Dietmar. It was also agreed it would be too overwhelming for all four of us to approach the area.

Before Blaine had pulled up, I had said, "If these two kids are also terrified of modern technology it won't be easy getting them into the car."

"It took Ellie a hell of a lot of coaxing with Dietmar," Blaine said.

Zach glanced at me. "I'm guessing you have an alternative suggestion."

I nodded. "There's a youth camp over at Port Ludlow that keeps horses."

"Yeah, the SafePlace Retreat," said Ellie. "I know of them. A middle-aged couple breeds quarter horses there and they run the horse-riding school."

"Call them," I said.

The forest floor was a carpet of lush green moss and scattered ferns. The hiker and his son looked across as Zach, Ellie, and I reached the clearing. My eyes were drawn immediately to the children dressed in gray tunics and wooden clogs, the surface of the woven fabric burnt and the clogs scorched. The boy was leaner than Dietmar but about the same age, the girl wide-eyed, petite, and a little younger.

There was a cave opening in the cliff directly behind the cowering couple.

I spoke gently to the hikers. "Thanks for your call. Just stay there and stay still for us for a little while longer. We don't want any sudden moves that could frighten these kids into running off."

"Of course not," the man said. He and his son were confused and fascinated all at the same time.

I motioned to Ellie. "You did such a good job with Dietmar that, in this instance, I'm going to follow your lead."

Ellie's eyes acknowledged this. She knelt, waving slowly to the boy and the girl. Zach had told us the German word for 'friend' on the way over.

"*Freunde*," Ellie called out to the children. She pointed to herself, her right finger pressed against her chest. "Ellie." Then she pointed to the children. "Tell me your names?"

Zach chimed in, translating. "*Sagt mir eure Namen?*"

The boy and the girl stared back, shaking, not uttering a sound.

Now I repeated Ellie's moves. I pointed to my chest. "Ilona," I said.

Once again, Zach called to them in their language, his tone soothing, asking for their names.

"Berthold," said the boy haltingly, pointing to his chest.

"Anna," said the girl.

Ellie took a long, deep breath. "Okay, making progress."

"You're doing great," I said to her. I cupped my hand to my ear and whispered into my comms, which were configured to feed to the rangers' radiophones. "Blaine, are the horses here?"

"Just arrived."

"And the riding school couple brought a third, unmounted horse as we requested?"

"Yes."

"And you can ride?"

"Sure can."

"Okay, let's do this. Send them in, and come with them, just make sure they're cantering at a very gentle, very non-threatening pace."

I could see we'd been right to limit exposure to anything modern while trying to get the kids back to the agency.

No SUVs or cars or phones. Not to begin with. Initially, we'd coax these two frightened kids to ride back out of the forest with the friendly, welcoming man and woman who owned the horses.

When the horse-riding couple arrived, they dismounted and I instructed, "Just move very slowly, with the horses, toward them." I noticed that immediately they spotted the horses, the children relaxed a little, looking at one another and pointing to the animals.

I smiled.

Something familiar.

And then when the horses were within easy reach, the girl ran forward and placed her arms around the neck of one of the horses, hugging it.

* * *

Ellie, Zach, and I watched as the children rode off, back-saddle, with the man and the woman. Blaine rode with them, as escort, to ensure safety.

"What now?" asked Zach.

"They'll be taken to the youth retreat. We'll meet them there, and I know we don't have Marcia with us," I said, as she'd remained at Poulsbo with Dietmar, "but if you could manage a few words with them in German, Zach, hopefully, that will help put them more and more at ease."

"Why don't we go one better? Marcia can instruct me in some more difficult phrasing over the phone. And so as not to frighten the kids, I can be listening to Marcia through an earpiece. If there's one with you?"

"There is. And you're already starting to think like a federal agent."

"It's not that hard," Zach deadpanned.

I raised an eyebrow as I shot him a look.

"What's with this raised-eyebrow thing of yours?" he asked, with what I now knew to be his trademark mischief-making grin.

"What raised-eyebrow thing?"

Zach shrugged. "Never mind."

I turned to Ellie. "When Zach and Marcia speak with the children, back at the agency, it will help if there's as many kind, familiar faces – from today – surrounding them as possible."

"You want me to come with you?" she asked.

"Yes. We can arrange it with the Park."

"I want to help any way I can." She brushed her fingers through her blonde fringe. "Have you any idea what's going on with Dietmar, and now with these two?"

"We're working on it."

"Their clothing…" Ellie's voice trailed off. She was overcome with emotion and she sucked in a deep breath.

Zach guessed at what she hadn't been able to finish saying. "More fire damage."

"Yes. The children didn't seem to be harmed but how could their clothing be burnt like that?"

"The same as Dietmar's was." Zach glanced at me. "It may mean the clothing can't be accurately carbon-dated."

"Have you had any fires here at the forest lately?" I directed the question to Ellie.

"We get small, lightning-caused fires on a semi-regular basis. And there was one just under a week ago."

"How does the Park respond to these small fires?"

"Sometimes with water drops from helicopters, but not always. On this occasion, there were no campers in the specific region, and the fire presented no threat. Even so, we imposed an eight-mile perimeter, closing the zone to the public as a safety precaution until the fire had run its course."

"Standard procedure," said Zach.

"The perimeter distances will vary, but yes. We don't go all out to stop a fire that isn't dangerous. Those fires are an essential part of the ecosystem out here. They thin the canopy and let sunlight through, and they recycle the nutrients in the soil."

"Which promotes healthy regrowth."

"Exactly."

"We'd better get moving, back to the SUV," I said, "but first, we take a look in the cave back there."

"Do you think you might find something?" Ellie fell into step beside me and Zach.

"Not really but we need to cover all the bases." I threw a glance at Zach. "Sorry to disappoint but I don't think we're going to find any portals through to Transylvania."

Zach grinned. "But you can't be sure."

"Transylvania?" Ellie was perplexed.

"Don't ask," I said.

We reached the cave. It was small and dark, with a cramped space at the back leading to an alternate side entry.

"And to cover all the bases," I said to Ellie, "do you have aerial imagery of the recent fire?"

"Yes. We'd have a MODIS image from NASA's Terra satellite. The MODIS is what gives us early-warning fire alerts when these flash lightning storms occur."

"What's a MODIS?" Zach asked.

"Moderate Resolution Imagery Spectroradiometer."

"I see why you prefer calling it MODIS."

"We'll stop off at the ranger office on the way through to Port Ludlow," I told Ellie. "I want to take a look at that imagery."

"By the way, I spoke to my sister about what you said on the phone last night, about not exploiting this story any further."

"She understood the reasoning?"

"She does now. And she knows you need to speak with her about that photo of Dietmar."

"Where would she be now?"

"Working from home today. We could stop off there afterward."

"Great, but no mention to her of what's happened here today," I cautioned.

"No, of course not."

"Good, but first, let's take a look at that fire imagery."

* * *

Ellie led me and Zach into the Fire Watch Command Room at the ranger station in Quilcene. She introduced us to the ranger on duty at the console. "Could you call up the image on the recent spot fire," she said to the ranger.

The young man brought the radio image up.

Ellie pointed to the map. "The area marked green is the fire zone."

"Where is the cave Dietmar came from?" I asked.

Ellie motioned to the appropriate spot on the map.

"And the cave from which Berthold and Anna came," I said, "is reasonably close to the north of that spot?"

"Yes."

"Those caves are close to the fire zone perimeter," Zach noted.

"It's entirely possible," I said, thinking out loud, "that those children did run through a forest fire. *That* fire." My right forefinger stabbed at the air in front of the green zone on the screen.

"That fire was almost a week ago," said Zach, "and Dietmar, Berthold, and Anna have only just been found. If they did run through that fire, where have they been in the meantime?"

Chapter Eleven

The Golden K was a horse-riding and guest ranch, backing onto green hills. It was part of the larger estate that was the SafePlace Youth Retreat. In a tranquil setting, away from the main riding school homestead, there was a rustic log lodge, adjacent to the stables.

On a partially roofed patio, with the horses neighing in their nearby stalls, Berthold and Anna were made comfortable. They were given juice and plates of ham and cheese. It wasn't certain if they were familiar with the style of food but they were clearly famished and they consumed the food eagerly.

Sitting with them, and secretly wired for sound transmitting to and from Marcia back in Poulsbo, Zach chatted with the boy and the girl as well as he could manage.

Ellie and I sat quietly, throwing intermittent smiles in the direction of the children. Blaine was nearby, chatting with the man and woman from the riding school. I had phoned Will, and he and Marcia were looking into suitable accommodation for the children.

The more Berthold and Anna ate and drank, the more they opened up to Zach, although I wasn't sure how much of it he and Marcia were fully able to understand.

"Enough to get a decent handle on things," Zach said afterward. While Ellie, Blaine, and the horse ranch couple took the children into the stables to pet the horses, Zach and I reconvened to one of the homestead recreation areas, a wide timber deck with a canvas awning. Zach's laptop was balanced on his knees. "These two kids have the same story as Dietmar."

"How on earth did these kids who can't speak English get here," I said, voicing my frustration, "and why do they believe they're the lost children from a fairy tale?"

"It's not just a fairy tale," Zach pointed out.

"You're back on your soapbox."

He rubbed a spot in the center of his forehead. "Many experts agree that the folktale is based on historical fact. An account of what happened in Hamelin was handed down orally from one generation to another. The earliest known written account was sometime around the 1350s or 1360s. It was a note added to the *Catena Aurea*, a manuscript by a monk named Heinrich von Herford." Warming to his subject, Zach became more and more animated. "His account gives the date of the town's tragedy as June 26, 1284. It describes a well-dressed stranger, playing a silver pipe, who leads the children out of the East Gate of the town."

My curiosity was piqued. "What exactly is the *Catena Aurea*?"

"A *catena* is a series of excerpts from various Christian authors. There are many of them, compiled by various scholars in the early centuries. Herford's *Catena* would have included the Hamelin legend as a moralistic tale, a preaching tool, pointing to the Piper as a devilish figure.

The taking of the children would be seen as retribution for the sins of the adults."

Zach activated a web search, bringing forth a photo of a watercolor painting from the sixteenth century.

"Travelers to the town in the years after the *catena* wrote of an engraving on the glass window of the Market Church that related the story. That window was destroyed in the 1600s, but before that, Augustin von Mörsperg painted this picture, depicting the story on the window."

I looked at the screen. The town, the river, and the cave entrance were all included in the painting. "These accounts are historically proven and correct?"

"Good Lord, no." Zach threw his head back and laughed. "If only they were. There are many different versions of the accounts I've just given you. There are various versions of the legend. But they all tell a similar tale, and they can all be traced to verbal and written retellings. And that's the case with a *lot* of early histories."

I read the translation of the words taken from that church window.

> *In the year 1284, on the day of Saints John and Paul, 26 June, 130 children born in Hamelin were seduced by a piper, dressed in all kinds of colors, and lost at the calvary near the koppen.*

An afterword on the website explained that the *calvary* was an execution point beyond the town and that the *koppen* was the nearby mountain.

"You know some weird stuff," I said.

"It's what makes me so lovable."

I frowned. "None of this explains where Dietmar, Berthold, and Anna are from. And every kid at some time encounters the Pied Piper legend."

"Yes," said Zach, "but, as I said before, when it comes to the medieval world, they don't instinctively know the kinds of everyday facts and details that Dietmar, and now these two, know. What's more, it's interesting to hear

Berthold and Anna say that when they heard the Piper's tune, they felt joy, were compelled to follow and that they wanted to dance. Similar to what Dietmar told us."

"Okay, an unusual thing to say. Especially given how terrified they are now."

"Maybe not." Zach's fingers flew across his keyboard and he brought images from the period up on his screen and tilted it further toward me. "If you read various histories of the Middle Ages you'll find references to something called the dancing sickness. It affected men, women, *and* children."

"What was it?"

"That's never been established. Historians have never really known whether it was a physical illness or a psychological phenomenon. What we do know is that it occurred in several countries over many centuries. Groups of people began to dance frenetically, running off, seemingly joyful but making no sense. In some extreme examples, this went on for days, weeks, even months, with the medics being unable to find a remedy to stop it."

"What happened to these people? Did they disappear?"

"Not clear. Some would have. But many thousands died."

"What?"

"One of the biggest recorded outbreaks was in Strasbourg in 1518," Zach explained, raising his hands and spreading them for visual effect. "A small group of dancers expanded to four hundred over a month, many of whom died from heart attacks, seizures, or physical injuries from manic behavior. There are dozens of recorded incidents from the seventh to the seventeenth centuries, throughout Europe and including Germany in the same period as the Hamelin legend."

"You think this has some relevance to what these children have said?"

Zach scratched at his dark curls. "Not sure. There must have been *something* affecting people in those times. It could in effect be similar to what we now refer to as mass hysteria. We've seen that sort of thing in popular culture. Adulation for rock stars. Beatlemania. The youth in the mid-1960s is probably an extreme example of that."

"So these kids could have been suffering from mass hysteria?"

"One possibility. But hysteria over what?"

I asked Zach for his laptop and he handed it to me, and I browsed to another site. More images of the folktale.

"In the legend, the children were entranced by the Piper playing his music. They followed him. They felt like dancing. Sixties youth went hysterical over rock 'n' roll stars. They danced and wanted to follow them." I clicked to old black-and-white footage from the 1960s, of throngs of young people dancing and leaping at crowded, open-air concerts. "What caused Dietmar, Berthold, and Anna to believe they were lured away just like the children in the legend?"

"You really won't consider the possibility that they actually are those children from the legend, will you?" Zach said.

"I know that's what you want to believe."

"It's not that I *want* it. It's just that there is so much that is unexplained, in legends, and in history as it's been written."

"You really are convinced there's more to the natural world than we know."

"Yes. And one day, it will be proven."

"Dietmar, Berthold, and Anna all have the same, genuine memory of following the Piper." I was thinking out loud again. "But even if the legend has its origin in fact, and even if these kids *did* have that same experience, then what *really* lured them? A tune played on a pipe isn't going to do that."

"Isn't it?" said Zach.

"I hope it's a good time, not a bad time, to interrupt," came a voice from behind us.

Zach and I turned to see a broad-shouldered, dark-skinned man, middle-aged – the silvery streaks in his hair adding to his statesman-like demeanor. He came up the rear steps and onto the patio.

"I'm the Reverend Thomas Jessway," he said, offering his hand. "Welcome to SafePlace, or as I like to call it" – he swept his arm out, gesturing to the wooded hills that surrounded us – "God's Little Corner."

* * *

The reverend took us on a tour of the premises. Around the edges of the property, woodlands swept down to a long strip of sandy, gently sloping beach. Sunlight sparkled across the waters of the lake.

Adjacent to the riding school, the SafePlace compound consisted of a large, sprawling main building with a conference hall, study rooms, relaxation areas, and a cafeteria. It was ringed by the guest rooms, which were rows of log-style cabins of varying sizes.

The mountains of the Olympic National Forest could be seen in the distance.

God's Little Corner indeed, I thought.

"We offer full accommodation, sporting and study facilities, and we run a range of programs for young people and families," Jessway told us.

"I've spoken with Dr. John Sanders about consulting on our case," I said. "I understand he occasionally lectures here."

"Yes. We have several professionals whom we engage for our programs. We use guided meditation, movement, and group discussions. Our programs teach young people to value and understand the emotions within themselves and others."

"I have to especially thank you," I said, "for enabling us to use the horses from your riding school."

"I'm honored to have been able to assist. And Dr. Sanders will be a great help to you, I'm sure. Do you have a suitable place to look after these children, now that it seems you have three of them?"

"Well, clearly we weren't expecting today's events," I said. "And I don't want to keep Dietmar in the Bureau office any longer than necessary. We'll get something organized as soon as possible."

"You're welcome to keep Berthold and Anna here," Jessway offered, "and of course to bring Dietmar to be with them. We don't have any bookings for the next few days and we can make a large cabin available. I have highly experienced youth workers here to spend time with them. Dr. Sanders can meet with them here, and of course, there are cabins available for you and your team, as needed."

I considered this. "It might be the best short-term solution, and a local police officer can be stationed here tonight."

"After we've been to see my sister," Ellie added, "I can stay here with them, as well."

"I must say," the reverend said, "that in all my years dealing with young people, and with all kinds of personal situations, I've never encountered anything remotely like the story these children are telling you."

Chapter Twelve

The home that Ellie shared with her sister was at Port Townsend, a thirty-minute drive further along the coast.

Ellie introduced Brooke to me and Zach.

"The photo appeared on your desktop," I said to the young woman, "along with a caption stating that the boy claimed to have followed a piper from his home in Hamelin." I noticed that Brooke was like a younger version of her sister, except that whereas Ellie had fair hair, Brooke was dark-haired and wore it longer.

"That's right."

"And Ellie tells me you believe it was from some random person who saw your earlier article and sent it to you anonymously."

"Not unusual," Brooke said. "Some people want to report news or do what they can to help, without drawing attention to themselves."

"And here I was thinking everyone wanted their fifteen minutes," said Zach.

"A random couldn't have known the boy's story, that he was from Hamelin," I pointed out.

Brooke shrugged. "I can't explain that, although…" Her voice trailed away.

"Although what?" I pressed.

"It wouldn't be the first time, especially in this day and age and the current climate, that someone's got their kicks spreading fake news."

"Do you think a random hiker with a camera made up the Piper connection because of the boy's language and clothing?" Zach was incredulous. "And added it as a caption to his photo?"

"Weirder things have been sent to the media, believe me."

"We're going to need access to your computer to trace where that photo came from," I said.

"Of course." Brooke ran her fingers through her dark hair. "For how long? It's just that I need it for my work."

"We don't need to take the unit. With your permission, our IT people can access your computer remotely and run their searches."

"Okay, sure. Do you have any idea how the photo was sent to my PC?"

"The IT team will find out."

"I hope you can sort it and help that boy," Brooke said and she exchanged a hopeful look with her sister.

* * *

Zach and I drove back to Poulsbo and shortly after we arrived I breezed into Will's office.

"You got my message about using the SafePlace Retreat?" I asked.

"Yes. And background checks on the staff confirm it's safe until we have something more permanent."

"Marcia will take Dietmar out there this afternoon and stay on. And Ellie Goodman and a local cop will be staying there, as well."

"I've had a team member in Seattle remotely checking Brooke Goodman's computer this last hour," Will told me. "Zoe Marshall, one of our super tech-heads. She's been on it since you got the girl's permission."

"Great. I'll give her a call."

"How'd you go with your child psychologist?"

"He's retired, but he's referred a colleague, a Dr. John Sanders. I just had a text saying he's cleared his schedule and will be here this afternoon. He has previous links to SafePlace so I'm having him meet us there."

"Let's hope he can get inside these kids' heads."

"What's the latest on the news front? Or shouldn't I ask?"

"I was hoping you wouldn't," Will said.

"Meaning?"

"There's a Twitter feed, @weirdnewsjunkies, a group who jump on anything unusual in the general news and then sensationalize it. So this story suited them down to the ground and... ah..."

"It's gone viral. You can say it."

"It's gone viral."

"Feel better?"

"No."

"So, what are they saying?" I asked.

"As you'd expect, they've jumped on the Pied Piper angle, suggesting there's been many more of these occurrences through the years that governments have kept hidden. It's had two thousand retweets, and God knows how many Facebook, Instagram, and Pinterest posts."

"Instagram and Pinterest?"

"The Dietmar photo from the mainstream media is right up their alley."

I breathed out my frustration. "Do any of these people have real lives?"

"Apparently not." Will accessed one of the syndicated TV news segments and played the clip for me.

"…and on to the story, first reported yesterday, of a German-speaking boy in a medieval-style tunic, found wandering in the Olympic National Forest," said the news anchor, a perfectly coiffed, Armani-suited, thirtysomething woman with a distinctive voice. "Local police and a National Forest spokesperson have declined to comment further, citing the boy's privacy. They have issued a statement that confirms a lost boy is being cared for, and that a search for his family is underway through the official channels." The photo of Dietmar, face obscured, emerging from the cave, appeared on the screen. "However, we are receiving unconfirmed reports that federal agents have arrived at the National Forest, raising suspicion that something else is going on with this boy."

"How could they know we're here specifically for this case?" I wondered.

"I expect they don't specifically know anything. They're speculating. Making a bigger story out of it."

"Unconfirmed reports? And they call themselves journalists."

Will laughed. "That's what they call themselves."

"The big bosses won't be happy about this explosion of media coverage."

"They're not smiling," Will admitted. "But at the same time, it's the perfect example of why this team is needed. A baffling, high-profile case that needs to be roped in sooner rather than later."

"Then we're just missing one thing."

"What's that?"

"The rope."

Will's phone buzzed. "Just give me a sec."

When he'd finished the call, he said, "Grab your conspiracy nerd and meet me in the comm room. We've got our radiocarbon guy on the video line."

Chapter Thirteen

Zach and I joined Will in the communications room.

"Let me introduce the gentleman who carbon-tested the clothing." Will motioned to the wall-mounted screen.

"Quick result," I said.

"As soon as Dietmar was out of those garments last night, I had them flown to our Seattle lab."

The man on the screen was the Seattle Field Office's science advisor, a lanky, stringy-haired fortysomething with a solemn expression. I knew the man and I knew the expression. "That's not your positive-vibes face," I said.

"We've done a thorough pre-test exam, which is the reason we're coming back to you this soon," the advisor said. "Sorry, but we can't deliver a result."

"The fire damage," Zach guessed. "Carboxylation occurs."

"You know a bit about carbon dating then?" said the man on the screen.

"I'm a history, science, and criminology professor and I've got more than a passing interest in archaeology, anthropology, and radiocarbon dating."

"The scorch marks aren't deep and they don't cover the whole of the tunics or clogs," the science advisor said. "However, fire-affected garments have greatly increased levels of the $_{14}C$ and $_{13}C$ atoms in the textile cellulose structure. Which in turn leads to wide variations and errors in the dating process. Similar problem with the wooden clogs."

"So garments fire-affected could present as older than they are," Zach said.

"Most certainly. And sometimes vice versa. Look, we ran several prelim tests and the clothing's been severely smoke-affected. We're not going to get anything remotely conclusive with full testing."

"Damn," I said.

"I notice the scorch marks are surface-level, no severe burning," said the advisor. "The boy wasn't burnt?"

"No," said Will.

"The condition of the clothing's consistent with the boy's account of being caught in a forest fire," Zach told the carbon man, "and running through columns of smoke and ash."

"And then what?" asked the advisor.

"He made it to a cave."

"He would have died from smoke inhalation in there."

"The cave led him through to a safer place," Zach said.

The stringy-haired man was incredulous. "How?"

"That's what we're trying to establish," Will answered. He ended the video call. "Disappointing but to be expected."

"I think the clothes were deliberately burned to interfere with any carbon dating," I said.

Will nodded. "I'm inclined to agree."

"But these kids have told us they were caught in a forest fire," Zach pointed out, "and we now know, as well, there was a fire near those caves just days ago."

The landline phone on the desk rang. Will answered it and then handed it to me.

"I've got a Detective Paul Radner from Seattle on the line for you," the front desk receptionist said.

"Put him through." There was a click on the line. "Hello, Detective Radner?" I pictured the detective in my mind. A career law enforcement officer. Fit and vital-looking for a man approaching middle age.

"I hear you're cleaning up the crime rate over in Poulsbo," Radner said.

"Helping out on a case."

"Are we talking about the news reports of a lost German kid from the Middle Ages?"

"You know I can't say, but I *am* in Poulsbo."

"Put two and two together? That's about as good as my math gets," the detective joked. "One hell of a cold case."

I didn't explain that I was working with a different unit. "Not the first time I've heard that comment."

"Ilona, I misplaced your cell number so I called the office there. I hope it's not a bad time."

"It's fine."

"You asked to be kept informed on the case you were assisting us with."

"There's been a development?"

"Not as such. But there's information that may come in use down the line."

"I'm listening."

"We've had one of our consults, a body language expert, look at the CCTV," Radner said. "Like the rest of us, he commented on the heavy-duty jacket and gloves, not the usual gear for these parkour and urban climber nutjobs."

"Not ideal for speed or agility," I agreed.

"Our expert examined blow-up prints. He's pointed out that the climber is wearing workout gear with a hoodie that looks cumbersome but the actual material is far more lightweight than its appearance. And the gloves are tactical climbers' gloves with exposed fingers for grabbing handholds."

"So more flexible than it seems."

"Yes. And the sports sneakers. There are brands with traction soles, ideal for running and climbing, and our man believes that's what we're seeing here."

"All good points. But you said this guy's a body language expert?"

"Yeah, getting to that," Radner said in his laid-back drawl. "Our guy showed us that there's a particular hip movement in some of the footage, combined with less extension of the knees when landing from a jump – all very subtle body movements, you understand – that are commonly attributed to females."

"He thinks our climber is a girl?"

"At least a fifty-percent probability," Radner said. "And, in his opinion, that fits in with the wearing of that particular clothing. It obscures gender. We've assumed the climber is male up until now. Anyways, it widens the parameters in what we're looking out for."

"I'll let my colleagues in Seattle know."

"You got a view on our guy's opinion on this?"

"I think he's on to something," I said. "I'd already thought, with the hoodie pulled low, that this climber was protecting their identity. Obscuring their gender makes perfect sense."

"Good luck catching that Pied Piper." Radner made light of the media reports. "I hear he plays a pretty mean tune on that flute."

"Pipe."

"Whatever."

I didn't laugh. I wasn't in the mood for humor, neither Radner's nor anyone else's.

"There's one other thing," Radner said. "There's an urban explorer group on Twitter. They saw the clips of the climber talking to that suicide kid. They're singing this mystery person's praises, claiming the climber is a hero."

"You're not going to tell me it's gone viral?"

"That's precisely what I was going to tell you."

"So there's a whole Twitter community thinks we should be thanking our rooftopper?"

"Yeah. And not just Twitter."

"That doesn't help when you're calling on Joe Public to come forward if they have any information on this person."

"We'll deal with that," Radner said.

"Thanks for the update, Detective. Keep me informed."

I ended the call. I'd never liked having to move away from any investigation I'd become involved with, and that was certainly the case here. It was why I'd asked to be kept informed and why I intended to confer with the Seattle Police when I was back in town.

"What was that about?" Will asked.

"An investigation my old team was assisting with."

"The urban climbing dude?"

"Yeah. Except *he* may not be a dude."

"I know you were consulting on that but, Ilona, you're going to have to put any work with the Seattle cops aside."

"You don't need to worry, Will," I said dismissively, my voice cold. "I'm one hundred percent focused on these kids."

Chapter Fourteen

I was back in my office. The discovery of Berthold and Anna had dramatically changed the nature of the investigation. We were no longer dealing with one lost, delusional boy. This was something much bigger. As a result, I didn't feel anything had been achieved today in advancing the investigation.

Who were these children?

Zach stuck his head through the doorway. "There's something else on my mind."

"About what?"

"About the legend, of course."

"Which is?"

"According to legend, not all the children of Hamelin were taken," Zach said.

I nodded. I remembered this from the Brothers Grimm storybooks. "Two children were left behind."

"The number differs depending on the version, but in the Grimm fairy tale there were two. One was mute and one was blind. So they couldn't tell the villagers anything about which initial direction the Piper had taken." Zach took a moment, sorting through his thoughts. He came into the office, pacing, his speech speeding up as he talked. "Dietmar says he and his friends followed the Piper out of the village. He wouldn't necessarily have known two of those kids were left behind."

"I guess not."

"Legend tells us that one hundred and thirty children disappeared from that town. Dietmar woke up to find himself on his own in that cave."

"You're still focusing on the fairy tale," I said.

Zach seemed oblivious to my comment. "Dietmar was looking for the others."

"Okay, I'll play along. You're saying the two children in the legend weren't the only ones left behind at some point. Dietmar, and now Berthold and Anna, were left alone at a later point in time."

"Yes. Why? And what happened to the remaining one hundred and twenty-seven? It's just got me wondering if any more children are going to turn up."

"That's all we need."

"You think I'm on to something?" Zach asked.

"No."

He made a face. "You know, you haven't taken any of my hypotheses seriously."

"I'm listening to all of them."

"But always hell-bent on proving them wrong."

"Which I will."

He shrugged. "Not absolutely certain, then, precisely why I'm here, apart from the lovable thing."

"There is *that*."

"Then why, Ms. Special Agent, have you got me involved if you think I'm nuts?"

I gave him an appreciative smile. "Zach, I don't think you're even remotely nuts," I said quietly. "Simply put, you just have a very different way of looking at things. And I think that's a good thing even if my perspective is light years away from yours."

Zach took that in and then responded with his speech slowed down from its usual pace. "And that's why I'm here?"

"Each time you come up with one of your... *theories*, I'm even more determined to prove otherwise."

"Which you haven't done."

"Yet."

He scratched at his straggly hair. "I've no idea whether I've just been complimented or insulted. Or both."

"Seriously, Zach, you've provided a wealth of information on the Piper legend and thirteenth-century village life and it's all part of the mix. Right now, it's raised more questions and no answers, but it's pointing up the questions we need to tackle. And ultimately, I believe, answering *those* questions will help us solve this."

"Thanks. I think."

I flashed a mischievous grin. "Maybe every agent needs a devil's advocate to keep them on their toes."

"I'm a devil's advocate?"

"One of the best."

"Not sure Agent McCord sees me that way."

"Don't worry about Will."

"So, what's the deal with you and our illustrious leader?" Zach asked.

I stiffened, averting my gaze back to the laptop on my desk. "Who says there's a deal?"

"I caught a whiff of some tension before."

"We used to be together. It's not a secret."

"Okay. *Used* to be."

"Yes. Used to be. You need me to write it down and italicize it?" I didn't hide my irritation.

"No need." Zach took a step back. "Touchy subject."

"Nothing touchy about it."

"Even so, don't think I'll bring it up again."

"Good choice."

"Unless it's something you ever want to–"

I cut across him. "Want to what?"

"Nothing." Zach edged further to the door. "I'll be heading off."

"Even better choice." I glanced up briefly.

"We're heading back out to the Retreat?"

"Yes. In a half-hour or so. We'll join Marcia. She'll have arrived there, by now, with Dietmar."

"Okay, see you then."

I ignored him as he left.

I had to stop being so defensive about anything concerning Will and me.

I realized my response would make Zach think I harbored resentment. And that was the last thing I wanted anyone to think. Especially after Will and I had broken the ice the night before at the motel, delving into the research, discussing the case, putting the past to rest.

A brief, simple answer was all that was required and wouldn't have given the wrong impression.

Stupid. I bit down on my lip.

* * *

My next call was to the agent running the search on Brooke Goodman's PC.

As I placed the call, I brought up Zoe Marshall's profile on the FBI internal website. I hadn't met Zoe but recalled seeing the young black woman with the intense, inquisitive eyes around the Seattle building.

I introduced myself when the call was answered.

"Do we have any joy on the source of that photo download to Brooke Goodman's computer?" I asked.

"I've trawled through her PC's recent history," Zoe Marshall said. "She visited over one hundred websites just in the past two weeks. Sites on writing and journalism. Subscriptions to sites with news and opinion pieces, social media; all the kinds of places you'd expect a journalist to be accessing."

"All legit?"

"I'm running background checks on all of them as we speak. The auto-download has to have come from one of them."

"As soon as you have anything–"

"You're number one on my speed dial," Zoe assured me.

* * *

Later, after we'd returned to the SafePlace Retreat, Marcia and I joined the professor in his cabin as he scrolled through pages of data on his laptop. "So, Zach, have you convinced anyone of your theories yet?" Marcia asked with a lopsided smile.

"You're a tough crowd," he deadpanned.

"We're FBI, we're the original tough crowd," I said, matching Marcia's smirk.

"You say I'm a good devil's advocate and I'm still trying to figure whether that's a good or a bad thing."

"Ilona is a pragmatic, no-nonsense agent, as are most of her colleagues," Marcia told him, with a sideways glance at me. "Unlike most of the others, she wants to work with consultants who think freely without the constraints that the rest of us live and work by. People who don't just think outside the box, they live in a whole different box."

"I live in a box?"

My smile widened. "Stop it with the poor, misunderstood professor routine, I've seen that movie before. You know exactly what Marcia means."

82

"I guess I do." There was a crafty glint in his eyes. "That's why I'm sitting here speed-reading through as much as I can on the Pied Piper tale."

"So you can prove those children are from another time?"

"If I can prove it, that would be groundbreaking and epic. If I uncover evidence to the opposite, *dis*proving it, then so be it. Either way, I'm here to get a result as much as you or any of your pragmatic, no-nonsense cohorts are. I've just got a broader mind, like, infinitely broader mind."

"And that's why Ilona wants you on her team," Marcia observed.

My phone buzzed. I answered it then said to Zach and Marcia, "Our psychologist is here. He's ready to meet."

* * *

John Sanders had a winning smile that drew you in but it was his eyes, I noted, *those eyes* that held your attention, at the same time making you feel you were the only person that mattered. A handy characteristic for a psychologist.

I could see that his easy, affable manner would immediately make people of all ages comfortable.

He extended his hand. "Pleased to meet you, Agent Farris." Dark hair, dark eyes, a rugged charm. I wouldn't have been surprised if there was a dash of South America in there somewhere.

"It's Ilona," I said, shaking his hand. I motioned to the others. "And this is our German-speaking history professor, Zach Silverstein, our translator, Marcia Kendall, and the National Forest ranger, Ellie Goodman."

"Marcia knows far more German than I could ever manage," Zach quipped as he shook the psychologist's hand.

"And the professor knows his medieval legends better than the Brothers Grimm," said Marcia.

Sanders nodded and grinned and the five of us moved to the chairs in the SafePlace recreation area.

"Thanks for making yourself available," I said. "Though there has been an unexpected development I need to bring you up to speed on."

"Oh?" Sanders eased his lanky frame into one of the wicker chairs.

"We no longer have just one boy we need your expertise with. Two more children, a boy and a girl, were found in the forest. Berthold and Anna. Both German-speaking."

"Telling the same story?"

"Yes."

"I expected this was going to be an intriguing consult," Sanders said. "But it's certainly gone way beyond that now."

"Caught us all by surprise," Zach offered.

"I expect you'll be wanting to speak with each of the children separately?" I asked the psychologist.

"What was the reaction when Dietmar was brought here and joined with the other two?"

"They threw their arms around each other. Overjoyed."

"Then let's not upset the happy reunion," Sanders suggested. "I will speak to each of them individually later on. But first, I'll sit with the three of them together."

"Yes, it's important to reinforce that they aren't going to be on their own again," Marcia said.

"Exactly. We keep instilling confidence in them that everything can be returned to 'normal,' whatever that 'normal' turns out to be."

"Okay, we'll let you get settled in—" I began.

"No need. There'll be plenty of time for me to get settled later. I'm very keen to have a talk with these three. And there's no time like the present, eh?"

* * *

John Sanders looked through the glass at Dietmar, Berthold, and Anna. They were seated together, facing away from the window through which the psychologist was watching.

The children were dressed in T-shirts and jeans.

"First thing," said Sanders, "is I'd like them dressed in their own clothes, or if they're not available – I know Dietmar's clothes were sent for testing – then clothing that's identical to the garments of their era."

"We can arrange that," said the reverend, who'd joined us briefly.

"It will put them in a more relaxed state of mind," Sanders said. "I think any of us feel more like our real selves when we change into the gear we're most comfortable in."

"What will you wear?" Zach asked.

"Certainly not this suit," Sanders said, threading the gray flannel with his fingers, "but at the same time nothing medieval. That would confuse them further. No, something casual, non-threatening."

"Similar to the sort of T-shirt and jeans they're currently in?" I asked.

"That should do the trick nicely."

* * *

Sanders sat and spoke with the children, Marcia on hand to translate, and Ellie sitting quietly to the side – a friendly, familiar face. Zach and I watched through the window from the adjacent room.

"The three of them seem relaxed," I said.

"I know I can't speak with anyone about the case at this point," Zach said, leaning back in the wicker chair, "but Jessie is not going to believe it when I tell her about this, three kids who say they're from thirteenth-century Hamelin."

"Who's Jessie?"

"My girlfriend. Well, my ex. We're still good friends."

"You have an ex-girlfriend?" I raised an eyebrow.

Zach stared at me for a moment. "You just did that eyebrow thing."

"There's no eyebrow thing."

"Is it so strange I have a girlfriend? An ex-girlfriend?"

"It's just that you haven't mentioned her before."

"We've been somewhat preoccupied here," he pointed out. "And besides, you haven't asked."

"And what does Jessie do?"

"She's a doctor, sometimes volunteers with Doctors Beyond Borders. She's currently doing a stint in South America."

"I'm sorry to hear she's your ex."

"So am I."

"I have to say you're full of surprises."

"And I do it without even trying." Zach grinned and launched his hand into the air for a high five.

I stared for a moment at the palm of his hand, then diverted my gaze back through the window.

"What about you? Family?" Zach asked.

"I expect you know about my father. He was Bureau."

"Yeah. An AD."

I looked toward him again. "I miss him. And my mom. She went a lot earlier."

"Sorry to hear that."

"Sometimes I have a whole lot of things I'd like to say to them, share with them."

"It's never easy losing parents," Zach said. "There's a part of you that always expects them to be around. I've been through the same thing."

"I have a good friend back in DC who's like a sister." It was a while since I had opened up to anyone about personal matters. I hadn't thought that, whenever I did open up, it would be to a Bureau consultant whose favorite pastime was trying to prove the existence of the supernatural. "She thinks I do everything on fast-forward." I smiled at the thought. "I should introduce her to you.

Once she sees your mile-a-minute routine, she'll start to view me as moving in slow-motion."

Zach shrugged, smiling. "Happy to meet her if you think it will help out."

We were both jolted by the sudden sound of a scream.

Chapter Fifteen

The young girl was shrieking.

Zach leaped to his feet but I grabbed hold of his arm. "We go racing in there and we'll make things worse. We have to leave this to Dr. Sanders."

Zach nodded. "Of course."

I could see that Anna's screams had unnerved him.

Through the window, we watched as Marcia and Ellie comforted the girl. Sanders spoke in his gentlest tones to Anna and the two boys, Marcia translating after each sentence.

"We can hear better from right outside their doorway," Zach said.

I walked with him into the corridor. We positioned ourselves at the doorway to the other room, just out of sight but able to hear and catch a glimpse of what was happening.

Marcia was sitting with Anna. She spoke to Sanders. "When you asked Dietmar what he was so scared of, his answer was the Ratcatcher."

"And it was the mention of the Ratcatcher that caused this reaction in Anna," Sanders observed.

"Yes. Just the mention of him terrifies her. All of them, actually."

"They know the man they followed played a musical pipe," Sanders said, "so can you tell the boys that we call that man the Piper. Ask them to use that term instead."

"Less confronting for them," Ellie said, moving back to her chair.

"Yes."

Marcia relayed the suggestion to the children.

"I'm going to address my next question to Berthold," Sanders advised Marcia. "He seems a little calmer than the other two."

"Okay," Marcia said.

At the mention of his name, Berthold looked directly at the psychologist.

"Berthold," Sanders said calmly, "would it be okay if I asked you something about the man we call the Piper?"

Marcia translated.

The boy's eyes didn't move from Sanders. "*Ja.*"

"Okay, good. Berthold, you and your friends said the Piper was playing a tune. Did you know this tune?"

After listening to Marcia's translation, the boy said, "*Nein.*"

"Okay." Sanders thought on this while glancing across to Marcia and then back again to Berthold. "Are you able to hum any of this tune?"

Marcia translated.

There was a long silence and then Berthold hummed a few bars. The other two nodded their heads at this.

Sanders looked across to Marcia again. "Not the melody from any songs I know of. Is it anything you recognize?"

"I've never heard it before."

Sanders returned his attention to the boy. "Another question, Berthold. Last one for now. What is it about the Piper that frightens you and your friends so much?"

Listening to Marcia's translation, the boy began to tremble. He, Dietmar, and Anna clutched each other's hands again, Marcia with her arms still around Anna.

Berthold's breathing deepened and then he spoke quickly. "*Der Pfeifer kommt für uns zurück.*"

From the doorway, I saw Marcia's eyes widen as she focused on Berthold's reply. She turned her attention slowly toward Sanders.

He reacted to the alarm on her face. "What did he say?"

"The Piper is coming back for us."

* * *

The three children huddled closer to one another, hands clasping even tighter. Dietmar and Anna repeated Berthold's answer. "*Der Pfeifer kommt für uns zurück.*"

"Tell them they are safe here with us," Sanders instructed Marcia.

She relayed the message.

"I want to ask them why they say he's coming back," Sanders said, "and what it is he wants, but they need a break from this."

"I agree," said Marcia. "Let Ellie and I take them for a walk in the gardens."

"I'll get the reverend to have a couple of his youth workers join you," I said, standing in the doorway, "maybe they could play some games, have something to eat."

"That would be great."

Zach and I returned to the adjacent room, Sanders joining us.

"Strong reaction," said Zach.

"Stronger than I anticipated for our first session," Sanders admitted. He exuded an air of confidence, and I found myself connecting with those wide, blue, expressive eyes of his. "But no harm done; in fact, quite the opposite, I'd say."

"In what way?" I asked.

"I've established straight away that this is no imaginary tale to them, Ilona. They're genuinely terrified of someone they've been with, someone they identify as the Ratcatcher."

"So far everything, including Ilona's voice test analysis, confirms these kids aren't lying," Zach said and I could see he'd shaken out of his distress and was once again consumed by the children's story. "What do you make of it?"

"It's going to take a few more sessions to delve into their minds, find out exactly what it is they remember, not just about this journey with a stranger, but about their own lives. That, I believe, will help us understand who they are and where they belong. Clearly, the story they are telling us can't possibly be true."

"Not by any currently known science," Zach pressed the point.

Sanders acknowledged the comment with a gentle smile. "I know of your work, Zach, on historical legends and the unexplained. Somewhat outside my area of expertise. What I can do, is to get these children to open up, to talk about themselves, and to tell me as much as they know about this apparent journey."

"Is it possible, John," I asked, "that these children recently heard the Piper fairy tale, and that after becoming lost in the wilds, hungry and exhausted and frightened, they began to identify with the children in that story?"

"Yes. More than possible. You're describing a shared delusion that became more and more real to them."

"Or a shared mania? Like the hysteria of groups of young people over pop idols?"

Sanders grinned, shaking his head. "Not quite, but it could be a variation of that. The curious thing about the human psyche, Ilona, is that a person's delusions or hysteria can spread like a virus to others."

"Which was a possible explanation of the dancing mania in the medieval period."

"Now we're really stretching but that is Zach's area, not mine."

"None of this explains the medieval German speech or clothing," Zach reminded us.

I felt a throbbing in my temples. Like Zach, I'd been impacted by the children's terror. "They seemed even more afraid today."

The reverend walked into the room. "Our young guests are in a much more relaxed frame of mind," he told us. "They're playing ball with my counselors. And a sumptuous dinner is on the way for them."

My phone buzzed. I glanced at the ID on the screen. It was Will.

"Ilona, we've had a call from the Quilcene Ranger Station. A couple of campers out there reported seeing a young girl alone in the wilds. She froze like a deer in headlights when she saw them but when they approached her, she took off."

"Let me guess," I said, "she was wearing—"

"Medieval garments," Will completed the statement.

"They haven't been able to find her?"

"A couple of rangers are out there searching, but so far, no."

"I'm on my way."

"Keep this confidential until we know more. And take the professor and also Ellie, you can use her knowledge of the terrain."

My head felt like it was going to explode. I pushed the avalanche of thoughts aside, and said to Zach and Ellie, "Something's come up that needs our attention."

"Something more important than what's going on here?" It was the first time I detected any irritation in the usually genial professor. And I understood.

"The people who need to talk with the children are all here," I said, avoiding his question. "We'll check back in later." I fixed him with a knowing stare, raising my right eyebrow, hoping he would pick up on my inference that something else, equally as important, was unfolding.

Ellie looked on but I sensed that she already suspected what might be happening.

"I'll keep you informed on our progress here," Marcia said.

"I've got a strong team," the reverend added. "We'll make certain the children are looked after."

I turned to Sanders. "Sorry, but–"

He waved away my explanation. "We're not going anywhere and I've several more sessions over the next day or so with these kids."

"Call me or Agent McCord, or let Marcia know if you need anything else."

He flashed his magnetic smile. "Done," he said.

* * *

From the Quilcene Ranger Station, we took an SUV. Ellie was behind the wheel, I was alongside, and Zach sank into the sheepskin cover on the back seat. He yawned. "When you first called me in and we were dealing with just one boy," he said to me, adopting a serious tone, "I was fascinated but I have to admit that no matter what I might've said, I never thought for a moment you wouldn't find a rational explanation. But *then*" – he leaned forward, gesturing excitedly – "when Berthold and Anna were found, I thought there's way more to this. Is this going to be the proof that the Hamelin legend is real and that something otherworldly is happening? But I guess I still expected you to somehow find a reasonable explanation."

He paused, sucking in a deep breath, his eyes alive. "But now, with this fourth child, I'm starting to believe we could be on the verge of uncovering something incredible. A whole other reality to the one we know." He shot me an almost manic stare. "Surely, this time, you must be thinking the same."

My face remained impassive. My thoughts were consumed by this latest development. Despite this inexplicable chain of events, I couldn't allow myself to be swayed by my devil's advocate.

Something else is going on here, I thought. But what? And how?

"Let's stay calm," I said. "Jumping to conclusions isn't my style. You know that. Let's find this girl and get her over to SafePlace to talk with John."

"Okay, okay, I know, I know."

"One thing that does seem certain."

"What's that?" he asked.

"Someone out there is playing mind games. Testing us."

"Okay. But who?"

"Someone who is far more dangerous than we thought."

Chapter Sixteen

Reaching the area where the girl had been sighted, Ellie, Zach, and I drove further north along the access road.

The campers had moved on but the two rangers conducting the search were returning along a track, having completed a circuit of the hiking trails.

"We haven't found any sign of a girl," said the older of the two men. It was late afternoon, a day of heavy cloud cover and intermittent bursts of rain. The fading light darkened the forest floor with its moss-covered weave of ancient tree roots.

"Many caves in this sector?" I asked.

"Not many. We checked those."

Thinking out loud, I said, "Berthold and Anna were found in a different spot to Dietmar, and had been in a different cave…"

Zach nodded, tugging at the curls at the back of his head. "Yeah, I've been wondering about that. They'd sought out somewhere they thought they'd be able to hide in, maybe?"

I turned to Ellie. "Any thoughts on where she might've gone?"

Ellie was staring off, deep in thought, scanning the woods. "There's a little-known place nearby but way off the tracks…" Her voice trailed, her eyes drawn southwest, her gaze now upturned as though she was seeing over and across the treetops. "I think I know where the girl could be."

* * *

This was a small, hidden, shallow cave, embedded in the rock behind a spectacular waterfall that dropped from a clifftop high above.

Regardless, it was accessible, an easy climb and short walk along a series of ridges that ran between the water and the cliff face. At least, it *was* an easy passage, Ellie told us, in the daylight. It was twilight now and the deepening shadows meant we had to watch each step with added caution, taking it slow and steady. Birdsong came and went in bursts, as though one group was singing to another, telling them of the tale that was unfolding below.

The girl was inside, her back pushed up against the rear of the cave wall. She cowered, arms folded across her chest, her eyes wide with distrust.

Zach had remained further back so that just Ellie and I advanced to the cave opening, hopeful that a warm, smiling feminine presence might be less threatening to the girl.

"Perhaps if you do your thing," I said quietly to Ellie.

"Okay," Ellie whispered back. Kneeling at the mouth of the cave, she pointed to her chest and then gestured to the girl. "*Freund*," she called out, recalling the German word. That was an easy one. And then she pointed again to her chest and said, "Ellie."

Neither Ellie nor I expected what happened next. The child launched herself away from the wall and ran forward, throwing her arms around Ellie and nestling her head against Ellie's stomach. "*Hilf mir!*"

From further back, hearing this, Zach called out, "She said 'help me.'"

I saw that the girl's clothes weren't just scorched, they were ripped, hanging in shreds in places, partly exposing her left arm and the upper left side of her tiny body. She was trembling, and rambling.

"She's saying a man was hurting her," Zach translated, concentrating hard. "She was warned to stay where she was."

"How did he hurt her?"

Zach did his best to frame the question to the girl's understanding. Instead of an answer, she began to shake uncontrollably, her head lolling back and forth, a guttural moan escaping from her lips.

"How do I tell her she's safe?" Ellie called back.

Zach thought for a moment. "*Du bist sicher.*"

Ellie repeated the words to the girl, hugging her close. The girl calmed and as she did, my eyes were drawn to a tiny bronze medallion that the girl was wearing around her neck.

Ellie looked across at me. "It's almost dark and it's a fair way back to SafePlace," she said. "A long drive, we wouldn't be getting there until late, and the girl's distraught, exhausted."

"You don't want to be waking her up later when we get back there." I saw the point.

"Or trying to settle her there in a large complex in the dead of night."

"What do you suggest?"

"There's a couple of very basic log cabins near the ranger station. They're used partly for storage and sometimes as temporary overnight accommodation if required by one of the staff."

"Sounds perfect," I said.

* * *

Ellie tucked the girl, whose name we'd learned was Hilde, into the covers of one of the bunks. She stroked the girl's silky, reddish-brown hair. Earlier, the girl had become agitated when I tried to remove the medallion so I'd left it hanging around her neck.

"It's like a comfort to her," Zach noted. He managed to angle in close enough to take a look at the small object and his eyes widened at the sight of an engraved six-pointed star with slightly curved edges. "A hexagram," he said quietly to me.

"Relevance?"

"Common for ornamental use by religious groups throughout Europe at the time of the legend." He narrowed his gaze further on the medallion. The words 'Marktkirche St. Nicolai, Hameln', were inscribed beneath the hexagram. "Market Church of Saint Nicholas, Hamelin," he translated. "That's one of the oldest churches in Hamelin, dating back to the thirteenth century."

Although her eyelids were drooping, the girl was watching us closely. Kneeling alongside the bed, I referred to the German word Zach had scrawled for me on a piece of paper. "*Schlafen*," I said to the girl. Sleep.

Looking back drowsily at me, the girl said, "*Du bist derjenige, der meine Mutter und Vater findet?*"

I glanced across to Zach, who was by the door. "Something about you being the one to find her mother and father," he translated.

"Tell her that I will."

Zach moved slowly across the room. Catching the girl's eye, he placed his pointed finger against my shoulder and he said to the child, "*Mutter und Vater finden.*"

Once the girl had drifted off to sleep, Ellie, Zach, and I, leaving the bedroom door open, retreated quietly to the living area.

The other three children hadn't been physically harmed, at least not in any way visible. But they'd been deathly afraid.

What was different with Hilde? Why had she been hurt, and how? My mind reeled at the possibilities. Had the Piper been interrupted or called away? Was that why the girl was out here in the wilderness, as the others had been?

"The medallion didn't appear to have been fire-affected," I said to Zach. "But what's involved in time-dating a bronze item?"

"The age of a bronze artifact is usually determined by a foundry mark or the artistry and, of course, physical signs, like corrosion, and then there's natural oxidation."

"How definite is it?"

"It isn't." He shrugged. "There are methods of dating by the composition of the metal but that's a rare craft, takes time, and is best tested against other similar items from the same time period."

"And also not one hundred percent accurate?"

"No. Dealers in antiques and ancient artifacts are ultimately making educated guesses based on testing combined with chronological and historical research. What's really unusual here, Ilona, is that the craftmanship matches the specific artistry of that time, there's nothing like that being done now, and the inscription is of the church, an earlier construction of which dates back to Hamelin in the 1220s." He breathed in deeply and exhaled slowly and I could imagine the wheels spinning in his mind. "I don't believe there are any thirteenth-century Hamelin artifacts remotely like this, in existence." His voice was ragged and I saw that a shiver ran through him. I realized he was still visibly shaken by the girl's terror, as was Ellie. "What on earth are we dealing with?" he blurted out.

Silence hung in the air. When I spoke, my voice didn't sound to my ears like my own voice at all but instead like the voice of someone haunted. My mind flashed with images of my childhood trauma. "Something vile."

* * *

After calling Will to update him on our progress, I walked out onto the cabin's deck. The cool night air felt good on my face.

I would send the medallion for expert analysis once I was back.

At least the poor child was safe.

Who is she?

How is any of this possible?

The surrounding forest was dark and unwelcoming. Rising from the moss and tinged by moonlight, swirls of mist encircled blades of grass and fallen branches. An owl hooted a warning. I looked up at the sky. The cloud cover had large breaks in it and I could see a smattering of stars.

My mind was overflowing.

Was the eccentric, motor-mouthed history professor on the right track? Was there some basis in fact to the legend of a vengeful, pipe-playing ratcatcher? After stealing the Hamelin children, had he turned up now with the lost children? How had these four children escaped him?

I shook my head.

Impossible.

I'd never been one for conspiracy theories. I applied a healthy dose of skepticism when it came to reports of UFOs, ghosts, and other supernatural phenomena.

I was a stickler for facts. For evidence. And it irked me that in this instance the evidence stacked up in support of the impossible. The lie detector. The analysis of language and dialect. The fact that the children hadn't been identified or reported missing. The ongoing reappearances, four as of now, but how many more might there be?

Zach had raised all of those points in his assertion that we were possibly dealing with something unnatural.

Time to switch off until the morning.

I needed a total break. I wanted to let loose. Indulge myself.

My hidden passion. My escape.

I needed to be closer to the city for that. Regardless, it was the one thing I could not do tonight.

Not here. Not now.

Chapter Seventeen

Dietmar sat up and swung his legs over the side of the bed. It took just ten seconds for his eyes to adjust to the darkness.

The moonlight that filtered through the window gave the room a faint glow.

He stood up and walked across to the bed where Anna lay asleep. He looked down at her inert form and then placed his hand firmly on her shoulder.

She opened her eyes and seeing him, she smiled.

He whispered to her that it was time. "*Es ist Zeit.*"

"*Ja.*" She too rose from her bed, pulling on her tunic as Dietmar went to Berthold's bed, repeating the process.

It was quiet, but looking out the window at the darkness, Dietmar heard the night sounds. They merged into one that was like a low hum in the distance.

Berthold rose from his bed.

Dietmar waited, still staring at the moon in the night sky. He felt that if he could walk toward that sound then the closer he got, the more he would be able to distinguish exactly what it was.

It was calling to him and it was the most natural, most exhilarating sensation he had ever felt.

Anna and Berthold followed him as he opened the door. He peered out. The policeman in the cabin alongside theirs, who had been looking in on them at regular intervals, was currently inside his cabin. They needed to make their move before the man came out again. Dietmar pressed his fingers to his lips, signaling the need for silence to Anna and Berthold. The three of them then moved like night spirits across the leafy grounds of the SafePlace Retreat, through the gate near the coastal side of the property.

A rolling green hill stood beyond the perimeter. Dietmar strode forward, Anna and Berthold beside him, no fear, and that was when they saw the figure up ahead, silhouetted by the moonlight.

* * *

The man woke to the shrill ring of the landline telephone.

He glanced at the bedside table clock. 3 a.m.

Who was calling at this hour? It could only be bad news. Something to do with his daughter or his grandkids in New York?

As his wife stirred beside him, the man rolled out of bed and went through to the phone in the living room. He picked it up but there was only a dial tone. A hang-up. Wrong number?

Before he'd replaced the handset, there was a bang on the window that looked out on the hills. He went to the window and peered out. In the distance, caught momentarily in the moonbeams, moving through the forest at the rear of his property, was a figure, garbed in a tall hat and long coat, with what appeared to be a long pipe raised to his mouth. It's like something out of a movie, he thought. Who's out there in the hills at this time of night, dressed like that?

He blinked and the figure was gone, painted away by the darkness.

He went to the back door, which opened onto the balcony. He stepped out and stood against the timber railing, scanning the hills where the slope led to the shoreline. No sign of any movement.

He looked over the balcony near the window to see what had caused the bang. There was a rock and some clumps of weed scattered on the balcony deck, not unusual when there was a strong wind blowing off the coast. But there was only a light breeze tonight.

His wife, pulling a robe around herself, came to the doorway. "What are you doing out here? Who was on the phone?"

"No one was on the phone," the man said, "but the damnedest thing, there was someone out there in the woods."

Chapter Eighteen

Day Three

Will McCord had always been an early riser. As an SSA his days started before those of most agents but even so, he liked to have an hour before that, time for himself, to relax and reflect, and then to plan. Once his day was underway there was little time for reflection and none for relaxing. He launched into the work all systems firing, his energy rising higher as the day progressed and often into the nights. Whether he was in Seattle, Poulsbo, Washington DC, or New York, he relished this time, always finding a window or a balcony from which to watch those first slivers of dawn snaking their way over the horizon. Always there was a moment when he sensed the presence of his late uncle, watching him with pride. Depending on the movement of the soft, early light, Will sometimes imagined that he caught just a fleeting ghost-like glimpse of him – a caring, hardworking man who'd been taken too soon in a robbery gone wrong, a shattering event that had triggered in Will, then just a boy, his interest in law enforcement and his hunger to see justice done.

This was a morning when that reverie was interrupted by an unexpected call. Marcia. And he knew she wouldn't be calling this soon after dawn unless there was a problem. His body tensed as he answered his phone.

"Will, we can't find the children."

"What?"

Her voice was hoarse from stress. "The officer here made his half-hourly check on the children, expecting them to be asleep. The cabin was empty. We've taken a quick look all over the grounds, thinking maybe they're accustomed to early morning walks, but there's no sign of them. They're gone, Will, the children have vanished."

* * *

Morning came with a partly clouded sky and swirls of fog touched by sunlight. After feeding Hilde a breakfast of oats mixed with fruits, Ellie, Zach, and I led the still-drowsy girl to the SUV.

The moment Hilde was tucked into a blanket on the back seat, she was asleep again.

Before I stepped into the vehicle, my phone buzzed. I wasn't expecting a call so early. Glancing at the phone screen, I saw it was Will. "What is it?"

"Big problem," he said. I knew that Will, another early riser, would have been brewing and savoring a coffee in his motel room before heading over to the Poulsbo office. "I've just had a call from Marcia out at the Retreat. All three children have gone missing from their cabin sometime in the night. She, John, the reverend, and the police officer are out scouring the grounds and the surrounding streets right now and I've contacted local police for backup. They'll have half a dozen officers there in minutes to mount a broader search."

"How the hell could this have happened?"

"Damned if I know. No one outside of our inner circle knew these children were at the Retreat. In fact, no one even knows about Berthold and Anna. We figured they'd be safe, feeling comforted to be together in a room with our team in the immediate cabins around them, and an officer doing regular checks."

"This doesn't make sense."

"No, it doesn't."

"We were about to drive over to the Retreat right now with Hilde," I said.

"Still proceed. And don't worry. I'm making certain there's an army of minders and round-the-clock surveillance to ensure we don't lose this girl. We'll speak further when you're over there." He ended the call.

"What is it?" Zach asked.

I had only just begun to outline what Will had told me when my phone buzzed again.

This time it wasn't showing Will's name on the screen.

Unknown caller

I swiped the screen to answer. "Hello?"

I didn't recognize the voice that replied. It had an unusually deep tone. "Are you still wondering how I took photos of the boy leaving the cave?"

I sucked in a breath but rapidly regained my composure. "Who is this?"

"You didn't really think there'd be any equipment left behind, did you?"

I suspected that there was a mechanical modifier being used to disguise the voice. "I'm going to ask again and I want an answer. Who is this?"

"I think you know who I am."

Zach flashed a worried expression as my tone darkened. "*Who-are-you?*"

"You didn't find photo equipment because I don't need your technology. There is so much you will never know, Special Agent Farris. I can make things appear as I want them to appear. I can make people see and hear what I want them to see and hear. I only need to view something and I can transmit its image. As I did."

I ignored his swagger. "Kidnap is a federal crime and we will find you."

"I didn't kidnap the children. They followed me. They belong to me which is why I've taken them back and I won't stop."

The line went dead.

I stood frozen for a moment. I hit redial but the number was blocked.

Unknown caller.

I stared at the screen, my breath caught in my throat.

There is so much you will never know, Special Agent Farris.

"What was that about?" Zach asked.

"Someone claiming to have taken that photo of Dietmar."

"You called them a kidnapper," Ellie said.

"He said that the children belonged to him and he's taken them back."

"What?" said Zach.

"It seems I've just been talking to the Piper."

* * *

This wasn't anything like the morning Will or I had anticipated. By today, we'd expected John Sanders to make progress with the three children. We'd expected feedback on whether the photos sent out established any ID.

Instead, three children had vanished on the FBI's watch. And now there was a fourth child.

I made an immediate return call to Will. "I've had a call from someone telling me he'd taken the children back," I said at lightning speed.

"Ilona, slow down. Did this caller identify themselves?"

"No. But he claimed to be responsible for the anonymous photo of Dietmar emerging from the cave. He knew there was more than one child, information which we haven't released. And as the children were taken rather than having wandered off themselves, then it means this caller also knew where we were keeping them."

"I expect it was a blocked call?"

"Yes. Will, there has to be more to this call and the hacking of Brooke Goodman's computer."

"Granted." I heard him take a breath, absorbing the information. "We know for certain now that we're dealing with a kidnapping rather than children who got themselves lost. Disregarding their story about Hamelin, what we don't know is where they're from and why they haven't been reported missing."

"Unless the parents themselves are also being held somewhere," I said.

"If that was the case then we'd have whole families reported missing. And that hasn't happened."

"At least we now have this new girl, Hilde, for John to speak with."

"I'm wondering why this kidnapper felt the need to call the FBI to gloat?" Will said.

I could hear the unease in my own voice. "And why did he call me?"

* * *

Ellie drove, with Zach in the front passenger seat, and myself in the back with the sleeping girl. I felt bewilderment over this case and it wasn't a feeling I was used to. Twenty-four hours ago I believed, despite the bizarre circumstances, that I would find a rational explanation. Now I wasn't so sure. Not that I would reveal that doubt to Zach Silverstein. That was absolutely not on the cards.

I glanced at him. "I read that historians, exploring the possibility the Piper fairy tale is based on fact, have lots of theories about who The Ratcatcher might really have been. One of those theories is that children from all over Germany were being recruited to train as soldiers."

"Yes, and that was certainly going on in that era in Europe. But" – he raised his hands expressively – "if that was the case, then why aren't there dozens of stories of entire townships of children being recruited and led away? Why just this one mass event in Hamelin?"

"If the kidnapper we're dealing with is your Pied Piper of Hamelin," I speculated, "and he stepped through some time portal, then he wouldn't be hacking computers and comfortably making calls on smartphones now, would he?"

"We don't know who he is or what he's capable of," Zach protested. "He could have been living from that day to this."

"An immortal?"

"I know it sounds ridiculous—"

"It is ridiculous."

"Hey, you're the one who asked for my thoughts. You wanted devil's advocate, you got devil's advocate, right?"

I shrugged the comment off.

"Some countries have legends of a soul that wanders the timelines, abducting people along the way."

"Okay, so referencing those kinds of legends," I said, "the wandering soul would be the Piper, and the Hamelin children his abductees, and – what? – there are others?"

"Stands to reason," Zach said seriously. And then he allowed the hint of a grin. "We'll make a conspiracy theorist of you yet."

"No, you won't. But what I'm trying to understand is, what kind of kidnapper are we being confronted with, and why is this happening here, in Washington?"

Zach shrugged, offering a question of his own. "And why now?"

"*Was ist das?*" The girl had woken up and was looking incredulously out the window.

Zach turned in his seat, looking back at her. "A landscape flashing by outside a car window will be a totally alien experience for her," he said to me and Ellie. "Let me see if I can convince her she's safe." Narrowing his gaze on Hilde, he said, "*Du bist in Sicherheit*, Hilde."

You're safe, Hilde. I wasn't certain he was getting the words right or that with her limited understanding of the language, she would understand him.

He placed the palms of his hands together, a mock pillow, and tilted his head against it as if to sleep. "*Schlafen*," he suggested.

The girl didn't respond immediately, she stared back at him, and then she said, "*Sicher?*"

"Yes, *sicher*, safe," Zach reassured her.

"Ask her if she followed the man playing the pipe?" I said.

"Is that a good idea?"

"Just don't say the German for ratcatcher and it should be fine."

"Even so, we're going to need Marcia's expertise to properly attempt a conversation."

"Then just keep it as simple as you can manage. I want to confirm that we're dealing with the same situation as the other children."

"Fair enough."

"Just say something like 'man playing pipe.' I want to see if it means the same to her as it did to the others." I extended my hand and stroked the girl's forehead, smiling gently at her. "I'll make sure she doesn't get distressed."

Zach caught the girl's attention again, pretending to play an instrument, and then he asked the girl, "*Mann spielt Pfeife?*"

The child gasped and then she began to shiver. "*Der Rattenfänger.*"

Zach recalled Sander's direction that they should encourage the children not to use that term, the Ratcatcher. "*Der Pfeifer,*" he stressed.

I embraced the girl, hugging her. "It's okay, sweetie. You're safe. *Sicher.*"

Zach shot an exasperated look at me. "You satisfied?"

I felt the girl's body relax a little as I hugged her close. "Let's see if we can get her to sleep again."

"*Schlafen,* Hilde," Zach repeated to the girl.

Ellie chimed in from behind the driver's wheel, trying to be helpful. "*Ja, schlafen, eh?*"

The girl was looking out the window again, wide-eyed, and then she looked at the three of us, from one to the other, and she said, "*Der Pfeifer kommt für mich zurück.*"

We didn't need a translator for what she had said.

"The Piper is coming back for me."

Chapter Nineteen

A search command point had been established in one of the cabins near the perimeter of the SafePlace Retreat. The irony of the camp's name had not been lost on Will.

Over a dozen police officers and Forest Service rangers, the latter group contacted by Ellie Goodman, had spent the morning scouring the property. They'd also searched the surrounding hills and coastline, and the nearby streets of Port Ludlow.

There was no sign of the three children, and no indication of where they might have gone, or why.

There had not been any sightings of the children by locals, but there had been a sighting of a different kind.

Questioned in his home by local police, the elderly man, who lived in a hilltop home near the Retreat, had been woken in the middle of the night by a phone call and a bang on his window. From the rear of his property, he'd briefly seen a strange figure on the hill, playing what appeared to be a musical pipe.

Another bizarre detail, Will thought, on a case that's becoming littered with them.

Up until now, he'd been organizing everything remotely, working out of the Poulsbo office, communicating with the on-site officers about the search, following up on the attempts to identify the three children, and the source of the cyber breach on Brooke Goodman's PC.

Now it was time, with more of the Poulsbo agents accompanying him, to head out to the SafePlace Retreat, armed with one unexpected piece of information that his investigations had turned up. Something that both surprised and troubled him as much as he knew it would Ilona.

* * *

On our arrival at the Retreat, Ellie, Zach, Hilde, and I were greeted by Sanders, Marcia, and the reverend. Sanders and the counselors began a process of putting the girl at ease and speaking with her, with Marcia translating, while the rest of us returned to our workspaces.

Later, when Will arrived, I spirited him away from the others to a quiet spot for a brief discussion. I noticed that he looked exhausted, the hollows under his eyes deeper than I recalled seeing them. The early start and the mounting of the search operation didn't account for it, as I knew Will was no stranger to either. It was the sudden damning turn this case had taken that was taking its toll. Before I could raise the point I wanted to make, Will told me about the eyewitness who'd seen a piper in the hills the previous night.

"Whoever was out there, he wanted to be seen and to have his presence reported."

"The same person who wanted me to know, from his phone call, that he had taken back those children."

"And, given the cyber—"

"Given the breach," I interrupted, anticipating his comment, "you want to limit the involvement of our consultants. But Dr. Sanders needs to know what's going on if he's to get the most out of his sessions with Hilde."

"Agreed. It's only on the more sensitive issues that we'll need to exclude him. But I'm not sure we need any more from the professor at this point."

"I want Zach involved in this briefing," I said. "I need him to have a full insight, except of course on anything that requires higher clearance."

"Still confused as to what you see in this guy."

"He may have theories that aren't the kind I subscribe to but he's passionate. He can be trusted with confidentiality as much as any of our agents. And I'll tell you why. In his own weird way, he's got as much invested in this as we do."

"He does?"

"He wants to prove there's a supernatural element, but he doesn't want to prove it by clutching at straws and making outrageous claims. He doesn't want to be seen as some nutcase. He wants it to be legit. He wants *real* proof. And he believes an exhaustive, skeptical investigation by people who don't believe—"

"Like you," Will intervened.

"Like me and you," I picked up again on my thread. "He reasons that if we're convinced, that if we prove it beyond a shadow of a doubt, then that is the exact validation he's looking for."

"How is that useful to us?"

"Because he looks at things differently, and because he's clued in on the medieval stuff. He may see something that we miss but, like us, he's only interested in hard facts."

"I still think there are other consultants who would be a better fit."

"I'm overruling you on that." I grinned. I knew he'd always enjoyed our banter and I hadn't forgotten how to push his buttons when we were on a case. I could tell he'd missed that. So had I.

"Only I'm the one with the overruling powers."

"And I'm not listening," I teased.

He conceded with a shrug and we looked across the compound to where the youth workers were sitting down to a meal with Hilde.

"The assistant director has been on the phone every hour on the hour about this," Will commented.

"He'd be furious three kids vanished on our watch," I said, "and he's right. I'm kicking myself. We should have had eyes on these kids at all times, not just a half-hourly check but a permanent night shift posted at the cabin door."

"In hindsight, yes. But regardless of whether these kids were lost or had been kidnapped, we arranged refuge at a safe vacation camp, their whereabouts unknown to anyone outside the immediate team and the staff here. There was no sign they were being stalked. And besides, Ilona, I'm the unit leader. The blame rests solely with me."

"No, it doesn't," I said. "I – *we* – made a classic mistake from the moment we sat down and talked to Dietmar. And that mistake is we didn't believe him. We ruled his story as being pure fantasy. Despite his obvious fearfulness, despite Zach verifying the boy's dialect and knowledge of medieval life, and despite the results of the voice stress analyzer. And then we made the same mistake with Berthold and Anna."

"Okay, we should have given the story more credence" – Will saw my point – "and at least been prepared for the possibility that someone might be coming back for them. Even so, how could anyone have known we'd brought the children here?"

"Somehow, they were being watched." I took a breath, brushing my fingers through my hair. "Something else is going on."

* * *

An hour later, Will welcomed Zach, Marcia, Sanders, and me, into his makeshift office for a briefing. As we entered, Will made an aside to Zach. "I suppose this fourth kid fits in with your theory that a whole town full of children traveled through time?"

"Not necessarily," Zach said, surprising all of us. "She's telling the same story and her clothes are fire-damaged so we still can't accurately carbon-test. And the medallion seems authentic but its chronology may be impossible to prove. It's made me think back to something you said originally, Ilona."

I took up the point. "That the fire damage might be deliberate rather than accidental."

"Exactly."

I could see that Zach was bemused at the shocked expressions on our faces. He knew this was not what we were expecting to hear from him and he grinned.

"No need to look so gobsmacked. I'm the same as you guys, simply coming at things from the opposite direction. To prove the existence of the supernatural, I first need to completely rule out any rational explanations."

I was sure he noticed the exchange of glances between myself and Will to that comment. I was wearing my 'I-told-you-so' expression.

"If the Piper came back for Dietmar, Berthold, and Anna," I said, changing the subject, "then he'll be coming for Hilde as well."

"Hilde will be moved to a safe house in Seattle," Will said.

"*Or* we keep her here," I countered, "make it appear that we're watching her closely, but allow this Piper to succeed in taking her right from under our noses."

"And track her?"

"Yes."

Will's tone sharpened. "Too risky, Ilona. You know that."

"Not if she's chipped. We'd know exactly where she is, where she's taken, and we're right behind."

"We can't chip her without her parents' permission," Will reminded me, "and that can't happen."

"And the process might be simple but it would freak her out even more," Sanders added.

"We could get permission from the courts," I said.

"A court ruling to proceed without her knowledge?" Sanders said.

"Ilona" – Will put his palm up – "this is way beyond–"

"Yes, way beyond reasonable procedure," I said, finishing his thought, "but if we're going to find this Piper, and wherever it is he's taken these kids, then we need to not just think outside the box, but *act* outside it."

"Ilona has a point," Zach offered.

"This Piper is several moves ahead of us, every step of the way." I rose from my chair, walked to the window, and wrung my hands as I looked out on the grounds. "We let him succeed with his next move, but we sneak on board and take the ride to where this psycho is hiding out."

"I know we need to take bold steps," Will said. "But this would be personally invasive to an already troubled girl. And I doubt we'd get a judge to sign off on it. No, we move her in the morning to Seattle. A safe house is being organized right now, and you'll travel with her."

"And tonight?"

"Just for tonight we'll keep her here, but there will be guards posted at the door and special security cams rigged up."

* * *

After the briefing, Will asked me to remain behind.

"What is it?" I asked bluntly as soon as the others had left the cabin. I was still bristling at his refusal to go out on a limb with this case.

"Outside of the team we've assembled," Will said, "the only other people who know the German children were here, are the reverend and two of his young counselors."

"You had the reverend and his staff vetted. And those workers haven't been off the property the past few days, have they?"

"No. Nevertheless, in light of developments, I've had our people take another look, delve further where possible."

I leaned forward anxiously. "You've found something?"

"Something about the reverend."

"How could it have been missed in the vetting?"

"It was missed because it goes back much further than we had reason to be focused on. The reverend's early childhood. I'm sorry, Ilona, but this is a sensitive matter. Something you and Jessway have in common."

Chapter Twenty

I froze.

Will's words washed over me.

Something you and Jessway have in common.

I felt as though the room around me tilted. Reality bending out of shape. Or was it bending into shape? The past coming to life again. Was it ever really that far away?

A flash of memory and I was fourteen years old again.

* * *

Every breath came harder. The sweat on my brow ran in a trickle down the sides of my cheeks and into my eyes. I wanted to wipe the sweat but I couldn't move my hands. They were bound behind my back.

I could scream but I'd given up on that. It exhausted me and I sensed it used up even more of the precious air. My imagination was working overtime. I imagined that my cries for help did nothing but attract phantom things that existed out there, in the earth; in the dark, silent decay that existed beneath.

It was pitch black in the small, narrow box that had become my coffin. I could see nothing, hear nothing except my labored breaths. How much air was left? How much time did I have?

Why is this happening to me?

* * *

Will's voice snapped me back to the present.

"Thomas Jessway was kidnapped when he was just three years old. His father was also a priest and had a brother whose wife couldn't have children. He was jealous of Thomas and in a manic episode he kidnapped his nephew and kept the toddler hidden in his home."

I swallowed hard, finding my voice. "What happened?"

"The police figured it out. Jessway was returned to his parents and the uncle was charged and served time. This may not, of course, have anything to do with *this* case…" Will's voice trailed off, leaving the thought hanging.

"The rev never mentioned this to us."

"Any reason why he would? He was three years old. It was a lifetime ago and not related to his life and his work as a minister. Our background check on Sanders, for instance, showed that his parents died when he was very young and he was adopted out and raised by a good family. And Zach's parents divorced when he was a boy and he was largely raised by his maternal grandmother. Personal stuff, not the sort of thing anyone is bringing up when you first meet them."

"Fair point."

"It's just that, in light of a kidnapping occurring here—"

"You'd think Jessway *would* bring it up," I said.

"Given that you and he have common ground on this—" Will began.

I could see where he was going with this and I cut in. "I'll open up to him about my childhood and see if he then does the same."

"Yes. But if he doesn't?"

I didn't answer. I mulled the question over in my mind. I wasn't ready to consider that the reverend might have something to hide.

* * *

Before I headed over to see the Reverend Jessway, I stuck my head into the cabin that Ellie had been sharing with Marcia.

With Dietmar, Berthold, and Anna missing and the search continuing with the officers, there was no reason to keep Ellie at the Retreat. Blaine had left the previous afternoon. "Go home and get some rest," I said to her. "And thanks for stepping in and helping us with those kids."

"Call me the moment there's news. I can be here in thirty minutes."

"The moment I have news," I promised.

Waving to Ellie, I headed over to the main building.

I stopped in the doorway to Thomas Jessway's spacious, bookshelf-lined office. He was seated at a coffee table with two young female counselors.

"Agent Farris, come in," he said in his rich, baritone voice. "We were just finishing up here." Turning his attention back to the two women, he said, "Thank you, ladies. Let's get together for another update in the morning."

They left the office and Jessway motioned me to one of the chairs. "I was bringing the ladies up to date on my planning. We did have a youth group booked to arrive in two days, but given the situation, I've canceled that and hope to reschedule."

"I'm sorry for the inconvenience this is causing."

The reverend waved away the apology. "No, no, not at all. Happy to be helping any way we can." He took a moment, and I followed his gaze out the window at the bluish hills in the distance. In the foreground, there was a strip of coast where oystercatchers skittered over the rocks. "I call this SafePlace, but it was anything but safe for those three youngsters. I feel… somehow responsible."

"You couldn't have known what would happen. The children were the FBI's responsibility and we stuffed this one up big-time. We were all blindsided by this."

"Is there any further news, Agent Farris?"

"No luck with the search this morning," I told him.

The reverend's features took on a crestfallen appearance. "No clues on how this could have happened or which direction they could have been taken?"

"No."

The reverend gazed out the window again.

"I can identify with how those three must be feeling," I said, subtly shifting the conversation as Will and I had planned.

"You can?" The reverend's focus was still on the landscape beyond the Retreat.

"I was kidnapped and held captive when I was fourteen." I watched closely for his reaction.

He shifted his attention back to me, making eye contact. "I didn't know that."

"It was a long time ago. I wasn't harmed. Not physically, anyway. My father was FBI, and that played a small part, my ordeal playing a much bigger part, in my becoming a federal agent myself."

"Then, if I may say so, at least some good came of it," Jessway offered. "You're the kind of law enforcement officer that this good country of ours is fortunate to have." He spoke with such warmth and understanding, such an air of calm authority, that I couldn't help myself feeling a sense of pride. But the reverend did not raise his own kidnapping as a child.

Why not?

The question preyed on my mind.

* * *

I left the reverend's office and took the cobbled pathway that wound its way across the grounds.

The memories were always there, lurking somewhere along the back channels of my mind.

Sometimes, like now, they erupted center stage and they might just as well have been a three-dimensional, high-definition series of images.

It was as though I was back in the past, reliving it.

* * *

My breathing was shallow and I was lethargic. It had taken a long time but I'd finally managed to work free of the binds on my hands. I'd shifted and positioned them so I could place my palms against the lid of the box and push upwards. I'd felt some movement but the tiredness overcame me, it was like a lead weight, pressing down.

Too late, I thought.

I heard a voice. My mom?

"Ilona, I know you're frightened. I know you're weak. Hold my hand, darling, and squeeze."

I reached out, into the dark, and I felt the warmth of my mother's touch.

"You can do this, darling. You can find strength. You untied yourself. Now you can push the lid on this box away."

I pushed. Some movement, not much.

I gathered my strength and pushed again.

And again.

* * *

This time my reverie was broken when I came upon Sanders and Marcia strolling across the grounds with Hilde. I spied two police officers following, watching from a discreet distance.

"Deep in thought there, Agent Farris," Sanders remarked.

"You should be calling me Ilona as Hilde does."

"As long as you call me John."

"Done."

"Hilde likes it out here in the gardens," Sanders said. "I think that out here, with the view of the hills and the rustic style of the cabins, it's an environment she can relax in."

"How are you, Hilde?" I asked.

Marcia translated and the girl replied. "*Danke, mir geht's gut.*"

"She says thank you, she's good," Marcia said.

"Have you learned much more from her?" I asked.

"Identical story to the others," Sanders said.

"*Bist du immer noch derjenige, der meine Mutter und meinen Vater findet?*" the girl asked.

"She's asking if you'll still be the one to find her mother and father," Marcia said to me.

"Tell her I'm doing everything I can." To Sanders, I said, "It's good to see her so relaxed and conversing."

"As with the others, it's important not to rush her. I think we can make some good progress, but it would be best for her to remain here and not to unsettle her again with a further move."

"I see your point," I said. "Let me raise that with Will."

"I asked Hilde about the tune she says she heard the Piper play."

"It wasn't something she'd heard before," I guessed. "Did you ask her to hum it?"

"Yes," he replied. "It was the same melody that we heard from Berthold. Not that there was any doubt but we can at least be certain their accounts are genuine and we're dealing with the same kidnapper, the same MO."

"We just don't know how they came to be separated. Unless it was because of a forest fire that they may have run through."

"And I'll be trying to ascertain that, once I've got her speaking more freely," Sanders said.

I then waved and smiled at Hilde as the girl strolled off, Sanders and Marcia by her side.

I watched them for a while as they inspected the gardens, making their way around the perimeter of the main building.

Something nagged at me. What was it?

I had been making small talk, conscious not to be bombarding the girl too soon. Sanders would broach the necessary questions diplomatically once he continued his talks with her, drawing out as much information as he could.

But there was something about the girl's reaction to me. *'Bist du immer noch derjenige, der meine Mutter und meinen Vater findet?'*

Hilde's question repeated itself in my mind as I turned and headed to the cabin to meet up again with Will.

Chapter Twenty-One

Will was staring at his computer, with a concerned expression, when I walked in. He looked up from the screen. "How did you go with the reverend?"

"He didn't share, despite me opening up about my ordeal."

"Did you press him on it?"

"No."

"Good."

"Good? Why good?" I edged around the corner of his desk to see what had his attention.

"I pulled the CCTV from the nearby streets," Will explained. "It took a little time to get it in."

"I take it there was no sign of the children?"

"No, and as to be expected not much at all on those Port Ludlow streets in the early hours. Just a few cars, but one I recognized. The reverend."

"He was heading off somewhere that early?" I said.

"He was returning."

My eyes locked with his. Something wasn't right.

"The timestamp on the footage for his returning car," Will said, "was not long before Marcia discovered the children missing this morning. And there was no footage from the hour before showing Jessway's car heading out. So I pulled the CCTV from the whole previous evening and I've been trawling through it."

"The reverend's living quarters are at the rear of the main building," I said, gazing out the window at the center of the Retreat. "I understood he'd been there all night and came outside when Marcia raised the alarm."

"Except he'd only just returned. Jessway drove out at 10.30 the previous night and returned just before first light. He wasn't in his quarters last night when Dietmar, Berthold, and Anna vanished."

"I need to speak to him again." My heart was pumping, my thoughts swirling.

"No. Not now. Not today."

"Why?" I asked, my impatience showing.

"The rev knows we have surveillance in place for Hilde's cabin and the area around it," he said. "He doesn't expect us to be watching his living quarters around the other side of the Retreat."

"You want to observe if he leaves again tonight."

"And if he does, to see where he goes."

* * *

As I was leaving the room, I looked back. "Oh before I forget, could you print off our photos of Dietmar, Berthold, and Anna. John will get Hilde to look at them later to make certain she recognizes them."

"Of course. I'll have Marcia get them to him."

"Thanks."

I walked across to my cabin. At any other time, I could have enjoyed the view of the surrounding hillside. But today my mind was far away.

For the moment, I had to let Sanders spend time with Hilde, and for the searchers to keep scouring the area. I opened up my laptop and began reviewing everything we knew so far.

Why were these children coming out of random caves, at staggered intervals, in the Olympic National Forest?

I'd been reviewing the case history for a while when there was a knock on the door.

"Had a feeling it was you," I said as I opened the door to Will.

"Why's that?"

"I thought you had that look, when I left your office, that there was something else on your mind."

"Can I step in for a moment?"

"Of course."

I stepped aside and Will walked in but didn't pull up a chair.

"Take a seat," I said.

"No, I won't be here that long. I know you need your me-time, your alone-with-the-case time." He smiled.

I returned the smile.

"I just wanted to make sure you were okay. I know this must have devastated you…" He left the rest unsaid. I knew what he meant.

"I had a duty of care to those kids, Will." There was a fragile edge to my voice that I didn't like, but I wasn't making any attempt to appear stronger than I felt at that moment. An unguarded moment. What the hell, I thought.

"*We* had a duty of care," Will corrected me.

"We failed them."

"We'll find them, Ilona."

"They're out there with someone or some *thing*, and we have no idea who or what we're dealing with." My eyes bore into his with uncharacteristic helplessness. "These kids are frightened, separated from their families, and in the hands of some kind of... *what?*"

Will placed his hand firmly on my shoulder, a sign of support. "It's a some*one*, not a some *thing*," he assured me. "Someone we didn't know existed and who is more dangerous than we could have expected."

"And now there's this... odd behavior, with the reverend."

"We'll get to the bottom of that," Will said. "And we will find those kids. We will reunite them with their parents, whoever and wherever they are."

I nodded my agreement. "Sorry, I was having a moment."

"Moments are allowed, even for otherwise steely, hard-nosed FBI agents."

"Hard-nosed?"

"Okay, bad analogy," he admitted. "I know it's devastating that we let this happen under our noses. I feel the same. But we'll make it right."

"I know."

"As for Hilde, I've organized those extra precautions. Agents posted at the front and the rear of the cabin, and special cams rigged up. Those agents will check in to the command room on their comms every half-hour. I need you to get some sleep tonight, we have a lot to tackle tomorrow. Agreed?"

"Agreed."

* * *

Returning to the command cabin, Will reflected on his 'performance'. He'd seen the hurt and the frustration in Ilona's eyes at the meeting, that was why he'd gone to her cabin. He'd seen her like this before, not often, but he knew it to be one of those moments when even the very best agents needed a strong shoulder from a leader.

The thing is that he hadn't actually felt that inner strength in himself. He'd felt exactly the same as she had. He was furious with himself that he'd let Dietmar, Berthold, and Anna down. He was beyond frustrated that he'd been blindsided by this blasted 'Piper.'

And at that moment, he hadn't just wanted to show Ilona his professional support.

He'd wanted to put his arms around her, draw her close and reveal the way he was feeling about her.

He reached the door to the command cabin. Marcia was inside and Will didn't want the translator to pick up on any of these raw feelings of his. He had to be careful. Marcia Kendall was one of those highly sensitive, insightful human beings. Hard to hide anything from her.

He swiveled his shoulders, shaking off the emotion. He couldn't allow himself to be distracted. This case was too important. Finding those kids took precedence over everything.

He, Marcia, and one of the Poulsbo agents on loan would be taking it in shifts to man the command post through the remainder of the afternoon and night. They would respond to the half-hourly check-ins from the agents posted outside Hilde's room, and they would monitor the CCTV for anyone who approached.

"Sanders is giving Hilde a break now until the morning, and the counselors are keeping her relaxed and amused as best they can. I've got first shift this evening," Marcia said. "I know it's a short while before it gets dark but you'll be up a good deal of the night, why don't you get some early rest?"

* * *

124

He could not sleep. He knew he needed to, and he didn't believe there was anything to be concerned about with Hilde this evening. He was wide awake nevertheless and as it was still early evening he knew Ilona would be as well.

Will wasn't sure what was going on with him but he felt as though his heart had been exposed. His inner shields were down.

Ilona Farris was in every corner of his mind.

Chapter Twenty-Two

I closed the laptop, my head buzzing. I needed some cool evening air.

Satisfied that Hilde was safe inside her cabin now, with the counselors keeping her company until she was asleep, and officers stationed outside, I strolled down the slope to the beach.

I wasn't alone.

I was surprised to see Sanders seated on the sand, looking out across the water.

I sat down beside him. Further along the loop of the coastline, I could just make out a gazebo atop a bluff, silhouetted against the fading orange and gold of a sky at sunset. "I'm not the only one who needed some fresh air."

"It's beautiful out here. Definitely underrated."

"Sorry if I'm intruding on your quiet time."

"It's a welcome intrusion. Actually, I'm glad for the chance to chat. I hope my reasoning on keeping Hilde here at SafePlace was clear." He spread his hands as he expanded on his point. "We've managed to get her to relax here, despite her fears. The more settled she is, the more I can get her to open up."

"Makes sense."

"However, I wouldn't want to be keeping Hilde here if it's putting her at greater risk." The lines around his eyes accentuated his tiredness. "I hoped, with all the added security measures, that wouldn't be the case."

"We're not letting the kidnapper get anywhere near her, regardless of whether she's here or in a Seattle safe house," I assured him.

"You said 'kidnapper'. Solo. You don't think there's more than one person involved?"

"We don't know but that's certainly a possibility given the complexity of what's been happening."

Sanders ran his fingers through his hair. "I'm worried for these kids."

"We all are."

"They were terrified, to begin with. They told us the Piper was coming back for them. And now…" He cleared his throat and sucked in a deep breath.

His sudden emotional drop was palpable. I could feel it. I had been holding it together but the psychologist dropping his guard touched me and punctured my own defenses.

I placed my hand on his shoulder. "I'm glad we've got you here, John. Those three kids barely knew you – Hilde barely knows you – but you've instantly been like a rock to them, to all of us actually."

"Part of the job description, though there's something I want to confess." He hesitated. "Actually, I probably shouldn't be saying this to you."

My brow furrowed. "You can tell me. And anyway, the cat's already halfway out of the bag."

"You can keep a secret?"

"Whatever it is, it doesn't go any further than the two of us."

"Inside, I don't feel like a rock. Although sometimes I feel like I'm sinking like one." He managed a faint grin.

"It doesn't show."

"Good." His grin grew stronger. "Then my professional reputation as a strong shoulder remains intact."

I returned the grin. "Our lips are sealed."

"Isn't that a song?"

I laughed.

We sat quietly for a moment, looking skyward. We watched as the last shimmering line of the sun slipped beneath the horizon. Sanders pointed to the first faint glow of the stars as they twinkled across the darkening expanse. "The endless cycle. Fascinating."

"You spend much time stargazing?" I asked.

"Not so easy in the city but yes, I sometimes seek out the solitude away from the metro lights. Breathing in clean air, watching the stars; it's the perfect meditation for me."

"Helps you keep being the rock."

"I suppose it does." He averted his gaze from the sky and looked at me. "And what about you, Ilona?"

"I could get used to this."

"Your job would not be without its stress," he remarked.

"You could say that."

"I hope you have your ways of unwinding, of unbottling all those pent-up emotions."

If only you knew, I thought. I flashed a gentle smile. I liked the way his gentle tone and naturally caring nature put me at ease. "You think I have pent-up emotions?"

"They're like a neon sign around your neck."

I wrinkled my forehead, fixing him with a curious stare. "I'm that transparent?"

He laughed. "Not when you were with those three children. Not when you're with Hilde. I admire the way you can shift into a very different mode when you're nurturing and communicating with young people."

"But I'm not fooling you?"

"Hey, I'm a professional. I'm trained to see past the hard shells that people build around themselves."

Normally, I would have felt confronted by someone being this insightful when sizing me up. I'd never been comfortable when I'd had to have sessions with the FBI counselors. Few of the agents were. But I didn't feel any of that where John Sanders was concerned. It felt totally natural with him. "And what do you do to unwind when you're not counseling others?"

"My work, as you can imagine, is quite sedate. So I like to get away for a few days every now and then, blow off some steam."

"How do you do that?"

He shrugged. "Jogging. Biking. Whatever gets the adrenaline flowing. Maybe I should get you to join me sometime."

"Maybe I will."

We were silent again for a few moments, enjoying the peace.

"You know what, I'm thinking I could use a drink right about now," I said.

"Why don't you wait here? I have a bottle of white wine in my cabin. I'll fetch it."

"White wine on the beach, under the stars," I said. "I like your methodology, Doctor. Should I consider this a professional consultation?"

"I'm not on duty," he shot back, his manner playful. "Consider this a man simply having a friendly drink with a woman." He pushed himself to his feet and walked toward the cabins. "Don't go anywhere," he called back.

"I can't stay out here for long. I need to stay close to the cabin."

"It's still early. One drink."

"Okay. Sounds like a plan."

A man simply having a friendly drink with a woman. I liked John Sanders and I felt a lift inside that came as a pleasant surprise.

* * *

Will wasn't sure if it was because of the heightened emotions over the kidnapping, or maybe it was the bizarre nature of this case that had taken a sudden dark turn – whatever, there was a time when a man's resolve to be honest about his feelings was pushed to the fore.

It didn't matter that he and Ilona were working together, or that they were in the midst of a difficult assignment. Perhaps it was because of all that, but he needed to stop pretending, not just to Ilona, but to himself.

He needed to let her know he was serious about wanting to give the relationship they'd once had another try. If she was willing.

Crazy? Maybe.

He left his cabin and knocked on the door to hers.

What am I doing?

Everything he was feeling right now was the total antithesis of how he'd expected he'd be, just twenty-four hours ago. Even just half an hour ago.

He'd brought Ilona onto the team because he knew she would be brilliant and because he believed they could work well together. He had not expected to be doing *this*. Secretly, he may have hoped that working together for many months, maybe longer, perhaps a moment would come when they would rediscover what they'd once had.

Now he was doing a complete one-eighty. Throwing caution to the wind. Hoping there was a part of Ilona that felt the same.

Perhaps he shouldn't have gone to her cabin earlier, giving her a strong professional shoulder for just that moment.

It had brought on a torrent of feelings and now he was acting on them. Telling himself it didn't need to impact their work on this case. Just a private moment where he talked freely, letting her know that… what? He hoped there would be a time, not now, but a time when they could start again if she was prepared to give it a try?

No answer. *Damn.* He didn't want to lose this momentum. Where was she? Taking a walk around the grounds? He knew she wouldn't be far.

He wandered across to the edge of the main building, from where the coastline came into view. Twilight, the moon making its appearance as the darkness took hold.

He saw her down the slope, on the sand, hugging her knees, looking out across the water.

He was halfway toward the beach when he spotted another figure, emerging into view from behind a tree.

* * *

Waiting for John to return, I gazed out across the Sound. The first shards of moonlight gracing the water were beautiful.

Even so, I couldn't stop the case from winding its way back into my mind.

I visualized the photo of Dietmar emerging from the cave – that damn photo – and all of a sudden it was as though a three-dimensional world exploded around me, images of Berthold and Anna in the forest, the horse riders cantering in as I watched Ellie coax the children forward, Hilde's chilling words about the Piper returning, a kaleidoscope of everything that had happened, like a spinning vortex, faster and faster.

My heart was thumping, I struggled to breathe and there was a ringing in my ears. *What is this?*

I felt a hand on my shoulder.

"Hey, you okay?"

I looked up as John crouched beside me, a bottle and two glasses on the sand beside him. My voice was a croak. "…yes."

He sat beside me. "You don't seem okay."

"I felt a little weird for a moment."

He handed me a glass. "Panic attack?"

"I don't have panic attacks."

"Okay, but you came out here to switch off, commune with nature, recharge. Correct?"

"Yes."

"And you did that to shake off the stress. No matter how professional any of us are, losing those kids last night, and in your case receiving an anonymous call from the kidnapper, is traumatic. So call it a stress attack if that sounds better, but either way, there's nothing unusual in having all this crowd in on you when you're letting your guard down." He poured the wine into my glass.

"I think I've spoilt the serenity of the moment." I managed a faint smile.

"That's in the FBI job description, isn't it?"

I laughed. "I think it is."

He clinked his glass against mine and leaned in, whispering in my ear. "Here's to having a drink and reclaiming that serenity. Is that Zen enough for you?"

I felt the tone of his voice calming me. "Zen enough," I said.

* * *

Will squinted and he realized the figure that came into his view was John Sanders. The psychologist sat down beside Ilona and a minute later Will heard the tinkle of glasses.

Not long after that, he heard their laughter.

What the hell am I doing?

Maybe I'm the strong shoulder she needs.

He stood, watching them for a moment, and then he turned and strode back up the slope and through the gardens to his cabin.

It was just as well that Sanders had been approaching Ilona ahead of Will.

It had given him the jolt he needed to regain his senses.

He was here to lead the trial run of a team tasked with solving potentially unsolvable crimes. He needed to concentrate one hundred percent on that. It was important he maintained a totally professional relationship with every member of the team.

He knew this, he'd known it all along, so what the hell had he been thinking?

It wasn't like him to let the powerful emotions that came with some cases, usurp his inner feelings.

This wasn't the time or the place to open up further to Ilona.

There would be a time and a place, he hoped, for that. But not now.

And Ilona clearly wasn't ready for any such development, regardless.

He wondered if she was getting close to John Sanders and whether something might develop there. She barely knew him and it was early days… but still. When people met in their line of work and there was a spark, something could always develop.

He winced. If that happened, it happened. Nothing he could do about that.

Right here, right now, the only thing that mattered was this case, this team, and those missing kids.

Chapter Twenty-Three

The adrenaline wouldn't stop pumping and I knew I wouldn't be able to sleep.

At the same time, I knew I had to. There was so much to follow through on in the morning, and I had to be on top of my game.

I'd felt like this before, more times than I cared to remember. For that reason, I decided to sink back into the sofa, book in hand, and try to read. If anything could help me to doze off, this might work. It had helped on other occasions.

I found my thoughts turning to the time I'd spent with John Sanders, earlier in the evening. At my lowest ebb, distraught by the plight of Dietmar, Berthold, and Anna, I'd found not just comfort but I had actually laughed in his company. *Just a man having a friendly drink with a woman.*

I wouldn't mind getting to know that man better. It was ages since I'd dated. Maybe it would be time after this case was closed. If it was closed.

Of course, I was being presumptive that John would be interested. He seemed to be, on the beach, but maybe that had merely been professional courtesy.

The minutes ticked by.

It seemed to me I spent more time glancing at the time on my watch than I did reading.

At 11 p.m. I rose from the chair and peered out the front door. I had a clear view of Hilde's cabin on the row opposite and a few doors along.

Two agents stood at the front of that cabin, alert and ready. All was quiet. The moon was bright, illuminating patches of the wooded hills that rose in the distance.

I went back inside, sipped a glass of water, and then eased myself back onto the sofa.

All is quiet.

After a while my eyelids began to droop as I read.

I slept.

My smartphone rang, ripping me back to the waking world. I'd been asleep for less than an hour. I answered the call, the name on the display screen jumping out at me.

Will McCord

I heard several vehicles screeching to a halt outside.

In that split second my mind didn't want to accept the reason Will would be calling me at this hour. Now, when he was only a few doors away.

"Ilona, you need to get over here."

"Will? What is–?"

"Now, Ilona."

I raced out the front door, glancing across to Hilde's cabin, my heart thumping and sinking at the same time.

* * *

In the command cabin, Will activated the screen on his computer as Marcia and I looked on. "The CCTV was hidden in the trees, with a clear view to both the front and the rear of the cabin."

An image flickered to life. I watched as the two men posted at the front of Hilde's cabin suddenly became faint, slumping back against the wall and sliding slowly down as their heads lolled.

The door to the cabin then opened and Hilde walked out. She did not seem aware of the two unconscious men on either side of the door. She did not look left or right but walked at a steady pace down the front steps. Avoiding the rear of the cabin where another man was posted, she strode along the front path toward the point where she could veer toward the edge of the property.

Will manipulated the camera angle to show a further point along the path. Hilde was heading toward the junction where the hills sloped and met the shoreline. And then she was out of view of the camera. It occurred to me that Hilde was still wearing the medallion. It had kept her calm, and the intention was to coax it away from her in the morning, before sending her to another location.

"What happened to those men?" I asked.

The cars I had heard had been the medical team arriving.

"They're fine. I've just had word they were hit in the neck by tranquilizer darts that were too small to be seen on that footage."

"Which means that the dart shooter was far enough in front of them to be clear of the camera."

"Only a very few people, including our camera tech, knew about the CCTV," Will said in sheer frustration and anger, "which means it's looking more and more like a breach from someone on the inside."

"What about Jessway? You had local police watching his quarters."

Marcia responded. "I was on shift and took a call that Jessway drove out at 10.30 as he had the previous night."

"Our people followed him?" I asked.

"Yes. To a residential address in Swansonville," she said.

"The area is outside the range of the CCTV we've pulled," Will said.

"Did they go in?" I asked.

"Whoa!" Will raised his palm. "We can't go barging in without a warrant, no probable cause, and as it is I don't want Jessway alerted that we're watching him."

I pursed my lips. I knew I was overreaching.

"At least we know he's in that house and there's no sign of Hilde there," Marcia said.

We all heard the sound of more vehicles pulling up.

"Right now," Will said, "extra men are arriving from the sheriff's office. We need to organize them to join the search."

"There's something else I need to raise with you both now," Marcia said, and she directed the next comment to Will, "something urgent you'll need to check on first thing."

I didn't like the expression on her face. "What is it, Marcia?"

She turned to the side desk and picked up three prints. "Just before this happened, I went to the photo file of Dietmar, Berthold, and Anna that was sent out to all agencies. I printed them out. You wanted John to show them to Hilde but of course, he never got the chance." She fanned the photos out on Will's desk.

I felt a jolt, like a deep stab to my chest, as I gazed at the photos. I did not recognize any of the pictures. "What's this?"

"The wrong photos were sent out."

I exploded. "How could this happen?"

"That's what I can't understand," Marcia said. "These are the only photos in the system of those three, so I also printed the picture we've taken of Hilde." She slipped it from her folder and placed it alongside the others. "Same thing. That's not Hilde."

Will intervened. "I'll have our tech guys check it out. We need to get this fixed asap. Doesn't make sense that the wrong pictures got accessed from the correct file."

"They're not just wrong photos," Marcia said, her gaze meeting mine. "I ran a search and those four faces don't appear anywhere else in the FBI database."

My mind was cast back to the call I'd received from the Piper. 'I can make things appear as I want them to appear.' I looked from Marcia to Will and back again, voicing what we were all thinking. "So where the hell did those pictures come from?"

Chapter Twenty-Four

Before

The boy looked at the back of the man leading them, the long coat billowing out behind, and then he looked behind at his village, becoming smaller and smaller, his parents now just stick figures in the distance.

The forest thickened as they climbed the hill. He was thirsty, his legs ached, and some of the other children were crying.

Where were they going?

The sun was hot, blazing down.

The boy couldn't recall if he'd seen the face of this man, but he knew he hated him, hated everything about this.

He shook off his lethargy, broke momentarily out of his fear, and he raced forward, pushing past the other children, screaming at the man to take them back.

He reached the man and he grabbed at the tails of the long coat, tugging them, and yelling at the top of his voice.

The man turned, swiping away the boy's hands. His eyes locked on the boy.

The boy whimpered. He could not avert his gaze. He had only seen dark, soulless eyes like these once before, on the face of a black crow that had swooped on the carcass of a forest animal.

This man's presence, like the swoop of that crow, chilled the boy to the bone.

PART TWO

Chapter Twenty-Five

Brooke Goodman arrived home late and decided it was a good night to get to bed early. Early for her was 11 p.m.

Except she didn't turn in.

She was at the corner desk in her room. She succumbed to her regular late-night ritual, scanning the internet for news that might be breaking on the other side of the world. And then she'd finish off by watching a few music videos on YouTube.

She was getting sleepy, lounging back in the chair, and halfway through one of the music videos when the screen was suddenly directed to a private web page.

Hello, Brooke Goodman.

Those words flashed and then dissolved to show a long-distance photo of a girl in a medieval tunic and leg stockings being escorted from the forest by Ilona and Ellie and another man whom she couldn't quite make out.

Underneath that, a photo of a medieval-garbed boy and a different girl emerging from a cave.

Her breath caught in her throat. *How can this be?* The FBI had remotely checked her PC and discovered the bug that had previously downloaded the Dietmar picture. They'd removed that bug.

The page on the screen began automatically scrolling down revealing further information.

Your proactivity in publishing the story about Dietmar, and the photo I sent you, have won you professional kudos as a reporter. So, congratulations. There is more.

Two more German-speaking children from Hamelin were found by the FBI but they have kept this from the public. Now a fourth child has also been found. Doesn't the public have a right to know?

Brooke wondered why this anonymous source was contacting her again. She shivered. She had to let Ellie, who was in her own bedroom, know. She had to alert Agents Farris and McCord.

She rose from the chair and as she did the phone rang. As she pressed to answer, her eyes fell on the phone's display screen.

Unknown caller

* * *

Ellie was in her room, reading through ranger reports on her PC. She could hear gusts of wind ramming the side of the house. That wasn't uncommon in this spot, on the hill, not far from the higher point where the cliff and the tourist lookout faced out over the ocean.

She heard Brooke's phone ring and Brooke answer.

Ellie concentrated on the reports, which were updates on ranger duties, rosters, and general forestry information.

She was tired.

I should turn in.

The gusts of wind were stronger. Storm coming in.

She was vaguely aware of the front door opening but she didn't pay it any particular attention, probably her sister was removing some garbage or pacing in and out, something she did when thinking or talking on the phone. The girl had always been hyper.

After a few minutes, she felt the cold rush of air as another strong gust blew in the open front door. She heard the hinge on the door groan.

What was her sister doing?

She got up from her desk and went out to where the front door off the living room stood open. Through the doorway, she saw the treetops across the road shaking as the gusts rattled them.

She went out to see what was taking Brooke so long.

No sign of her.

She walked to the front fence, looked up and down the short, narrow road that led up to the lookout and the clifftop. Rain began spitting.

And then, illuminated by the moonlight, she saw Brooke up ahead, in her light blue jacket and hoodie, walking off into the area beyond the fenced lookout.

Brooke passed out of sight.

What is she doing?

Ellie headed up the road, reaching the higher point, and glanced off to the side.

And then she saw Brooke further along at the exposed part of the clifftop.

The wind whistled around Ellie, the crashing sound of the surf on the rocks, far below, louder than she had expected.

She ran forward. "Brooke! What are you doing?"

Her sister turned to look back at her. There was a vacant stare in her eyes. "I'm so sorry for what I've done."

"Brooke, what are you talking about? What are you doing out here?"

"I never care whom I might be hurting when I'm chasing stories. And I lied to you. I really don't deserve… to go on." She turned back to face the cliff edge.

God, no, thought Ellie.

"Brooke, look at me."

Her sister teetered on the edge.

"Brooke, before you do anything, there's something I need to tell you. Please, just turn around and look at me. Let me at least tell you this one last thing."

Brooke turned.

Ellie fixed her gaze on her sister and managed to establish eye contact with her.

Got to keep her engaged.

"Brooke, I know you've always been the ambitious one, the pushy one. And that's okay, really, it *is*." As she spoke, she inched forward, keeping eye contact and hoping her sister wouldn't notice that Ellie was edging closer.

Just a little further.

"The world needs investigative reporters like you," Ellie said, "people who aren't afraid to dig deeper, run with their gut instincts, ask the hard questions, push for the truth. I just wanted you to know that, from me…" She was near enough but Brooke was perilously close to the sheer drop.

Ellie lunged. She grabbed hold of Brooke's sleeve, instantaneously stepping back at the same time, pulling her sister with her.

Just need to get her far enough away from the edge.

They fell to the ground. Ellie clutched Brooke close and stared into her sister's eyes again.

Brooke stared back. Lost. Confused.

What's happened to you? Ellie thought.

"Let's get you back inside." She helped her sister to her feet, her arms around Brooke's shoulders.

As they walked slowly back, Ellie's mind flashed to the phone call she'd heard Brooke receive a little earlier. Whom had it been from?

Whilst still holding on tightly to her sister, Ellie managed to free her right hand. She slid her smartphone from her pocket and hit the number for Ilona.

The call was answered, and Ellie said, quietly but urgently, "Ilona, I need your help. Something's wrong with Brooke."

Chapter Twenty-Six

Day Four

Will and I drove to the Goodmans' house.

The search for Hilde had been underway for a short time when I had received the phone call from Ellie Goodman.

I told Ellie I'd arrange an ambulance to head over there, so the paramedics could check Brooke's vitals. I told Ellie to stick by her sister's side and that Agent McCord and I would call on them as soon as possible, early morning. "We're just in the middle of something here right now."

"Now? In the middle of the night?"

I didn't want to elaborate, not until I saw Ellie in person. I promised we would be there as soon as we were able and I ended the call gently.

We had found no sign of Hilde, nor which direction she might have ultimately headed.

Dawn broke as we arrived at the Goodmans' house.

Ellie took us through to the sunroom at the back. The large wraparound window afforded a view of the surrounding woods and the clifftop. The early morning sun streamed through the treetops.

Brooke Goodman was on the sofa, draped in a blanket, clutching a mug of coffee. She looked up as we came in. "I'm so sorry," she blurted out.

"Before I found Brooke up at the clifftop," Ellie said to the agents, "she had posted pictures to social media and sent links to the local and national media."

"So she bypassed her editor," Will said, picking up on her point.

"Yes. Something Brooke would never normally do."

There were tears in Brooke's eyes as she looked at us.

"The paramedics were here earlier and Brooke is fine physically," Ellie advised.

"Can you tell us what happened, Brooke?" I asked.

"I don't really know." Brooke was staring at a spot on the floor. "I remember my laptop being hacked again, with pictures and information downloading. I don't remember writing a caption and posting it with the photos and yet I knew that I had done it. I vaguely remember going out to the cliff, and I felt… so bad…" Her voice faded and she sobbed.

"She was babbling about being sorry and not wanting to go on and she was about to jump," Ellie said, her voice breaking.

"You wanted to end it all?" I asked Brooke.

The young woman raised her head and stared at me, as though afraid to answer.

"I heard Brooke take a phone call," Ellie said. "This was sometime after eleven. A little later I heard her go out the front door and when she didn't come back in, I got curious and went outside looking for her."

"Do you remember the phone call?" Will asked Brooke.

Brooke shrugged. "Not really… it's all so hazy."

"I'm afraid the morning news networks have already run with it," Ellie said, handing the TV remote to Will, "if you haven't already caught it…"

There was a widescreen TV in the corner of the sunroom. Will aimed the remote and the screen flickered to life.

"Four days ago in Washington State," the reporter, a wide-eyed young woman, announced, "a junior reporter on a Poulsbo newspaper broke the story of a lost German-speaking boy who claimed to have followed the Pied Piper from Hamelin over seven hundred years ago. The FBI confirmed they were assisting with the boy and searching for his real identity and family. A bizarre story and one that, as you might expect, has gone viral with theories on social media."

The cave photos of Dietmar and also of Berthold and Anna appeared as inserts at the side of the screen. They were followed by a photo of Brooke. "In breaking news this morning," the newscaster continued, "that same reporter, Brooke Goodman, has revealed that three more German children were found, telling the same story. Brooke Goodman's post states there are unconfirmed reports that all four of those young people have since vanished while under FBI care."

The studio news anchor could be heard as a voice-over. "Those photos do not show the children's faces. Do we have anything more identifiable?"

"Not at this point," said the on-site reporter, "and it is also unusual that the FBI has not released any photos for ID."

"Something else appears to be going on," said the news anchor from the studio.

"We have not been able to reach Brooke Goodman or the FBI for comment this morning," the reporter said, "but we are following this breaking story and will bring further updates as they come to hand."

Will switched off the TV. He motioned for me to step aside, into the adjoining living room, and he lowered his voice. "We're going to have to front a news conference."

"We?" I said. "How about just you? I hate those things."

"Show of force. We need to reassure the public that the Bureau is working with local authorities, that we're dealing with a kidnap scenario, and that we will keep them updated."

"Brooke is going to need a psychiatric evaluation so we can make sure she's okay," I said, "and so that we can find out more about that phone call. It has to be the Piper sending her that information."

"We'll arrange that," Will said. "And given that Dr. Sanders has been consulting to us, I'll also ask if he can give Brooke a phone call later on. Perhaps he can help her remember."

* * *

We were outside the Goodmans' home, just reaching the car in the street when Will took a phone call.

He paced back and forth, agitated, while he was speaking. I caught a couple of words, 'cyber' and 'photos.'

Ending the call, Will slipped into the driver's seat, as I entered the passenger side.

"Was that about the photos screw-up?" I asked. "How does an error like that happen?"

"Seems it wasn't an error."

"What do you mean?"

"They've detected a serious security breach."

I could hardly believe what I was hearing. "Another breach? This was deliberate?"

"The pictures were tampered with." Will's voice betrayed his sense of frustration. "We need to keep this strictly between ourselves, Ilona. Neither our consultants nor agents without clearance are to know of this while our cyber team investigates."

"You think this could be internal?"

"Unclear."

"Good God." I sucked in a deep breath and exhaled slowly. "Who's running the investigation on the breach from the cyber end?"

"Zoe Marshall."

I recalled my earlier conversation with the tech who ran the remote search on Brooke Goodman's laptop. "I spoke to her earlier. Will, she sounded very young to be our go-to girl for something on the level of this breach."

"She's older than her years."

145

"Okay, but it's not like we don't have far more experienced tech guys in Seattle."

"For now, leave the photo breach thing with me. We're heading to Seattle later this morning for the press conference and we're meeting with Zoe after that. She can bring us up to date on what she's learned and how we're going to handle it. Zoe's part of this new team, Ilona. The big bosses have given me the go-ahead to have Zoe show you in person what our new unit is all about."

* * *

The previous night, the search party had covered the surrounding areas using high-beam flashlights, before calling a halt. From first light, they'd reconvened and were expanding the search.

"The search leader reported in," Marcia said to me and Will as we walked back into the command cabin. "They haven't turned anything up."

Zach was already in the room, seated to the side. Bloodshot eyes. Stifling a yawn. None of us are getting any sleep, I thought.

"Same result as when Dietmar, Berthold, and Anna walked off," said Will. "It's as though they all vanished into thin air."

"And I've just received a report back on that Swansonville address that the rev went to," Marcia added. "It's the home of a local area psychiatrist, Dr. Moana Nessman."

"Has the reverend returned to the Retreat this morning?" I asked.

"Yes. Exact same routine as the previous night."

"Then we confront the reverend," I said, "but before we do" – I glanced at Will – "I think first we need to pay Dr. Nessman a visit."

Chapter Twenty-Seven

"The Reverend Jessway was sighted entering your home at 10.45 last night," I said to the middle-aged woman, who had a captivating appearance, her blue eyes striking against her ochre skin. She had ushered us through to her counseling room, adjacent to a courtyard where the cobbled pathway and potted plants could be seen through the glass of a double doorway. The room itself was airy and filled with sunlight, conducive to a safe and welcoming environment.

"May I ask what this is about, Agent Farris?" Dr. Moana Nessman asked. She sat behind her desk and gestured to the other chairs but Will and I remained standing.

"We need to know if the reverend was here the whole night, and also the night before that."

She clasped her hands against her stomach. "I'm afraid I wouldn't be able to help you with that, Agent."

"Why is that, Doctor?" Will stepped forward.

"The reverend is a client of mine. Therefore, I am bound, as you would know, by doctor-client confidentiality."

"Dr. Nessman," I pressed, "we are investigating crimes occurring in Port Ludlow the past two nights, at the SafePlace Retreat. We need confirmation of the reverend's whereabouts."

"I'm sorry that I can't help, really I am." Dr. Nessman was apologetic, but I also detected a frosty distance. "I'll certainly assist in any other way that I can but unfortunately, I'm going to have to ask you to leave as I have patients waiting."

"The reverend led us to believe he was on his premises the past two nights," Will told the psychiatrist, "and he is one of the few people with inside knowledge on the matter we're investigating. If you cannot confirm his whereabouts for us, we have no choice but to take him in for questioning."

"You're arresting him?" the doctor said, alarmed.

"I'm afraid it may come to that."

Dr. Nessman rose from behind her desk. "I can assure you that Thomas Jessway is a good and honest man."

"And I can assure you, Doctor," I said, "that anything you tell us is confidential. It could result in us not having to detain the reverend. As I'm sure you're aware, an arrest will put an unfortunate stain on the reverend's reputation, something we would all prefer to avoid if it isn't necessary."

Moana Nessman considered this for several seconds, knitting her brow. "It isn't just Thomas's reputation at risk here. It's also…" She stopped herself, her inner turmoil reflected in her eyes.

"Yours?" I ventured.

She nodded resignedly. "Yes. Mine."

I waited for the doctor to open up further. I knew that Will had no intention of taking Jessway to a station for questioning, let alone arresting him. Not until we had hard evidence of wrongdoing. At this stage we had none. Only suspicion, and we were yet to confront the reverend himself. Until now, I'd kept at bay the thought that Jessway could be involved in the children's disappearance.

"I don't know if he has informed you of any of this," Dr. Nessman said, "but Thomas was himself kidnapped as a very young child. As a result, his earliest childhood memory is a confusing, frightening one, despite the fact it was his uncle who took him. He experienced separation anxiety as well as the trauma of seeing police arrest his uncle."

"He hasn't spoken to us of that," I said.

Dr. Nessman met my gaze. "But I can see the FBI was aware of it."

"Yes, we were," Will confirmed.

"It has been a repressed memory all these years," the doctor explained, "but just recently it resurfaced. He's been having nightmares, and reliving that traumatic experience."

"We didn't know that," I said.

"It was the reason he was coming to see me. He had a series of counseling sessions with me for a few months."

"Late at night?" Will queried, frowning.

"No, of course not. They were one-hour daytime sessions."

I wasn't surprised when Will decided to reveal the nature of the investigation to the doctor. "There have been kidnappings from the Retreat these past two nights," he said, "during the same hours that the reverend was away from the premises."

The shock registered immediately on the psychiatrist's face. "Oh my God."

* * *

The shock on Moana Nessman's face was not for the reason Will or I expected.

"You think Thomas is involved with kidnapping those poor children?" She put her face in her hands. "Oh God, what have I done?"

"You need to tell us exactly what is going on," I said.

"Thomas had completed his sessions with me. He was doing well; he was in a much better place mentally."

"And?" I queried as Will looked on.

"We've been seeing each other," she revealed. "And as it's nowhere near the twelve months since his sessions, which is what the medical board requires, it's unethical for me to be involved with him romantically." She stifled a sob. "That's why Thomas has been coming over during the nights and keeping it secret."

I looked at Will. "It also explains why the reverend didn't reveal his own kidnap to us. He didn't want us delving into that side of his life and finding out about his relationship with Dr. Nessman."

I wasn't surprised by the edge in Will's voice. "It means we've wasted precious time following up on something unrelated to the kidnappings."

I felt exactly the same. I turned my gaze back to the psychiatrist. I could see the regret in the woman's eyes and the tears forming at their edges.

"And those poor children are still out there somewhere," Moana Nessman said.

Chapter Twenty-Eight

"The search party and my team will be moving out," Will said to the Reverend Jessway, shaking his hand.

"You'll let me know the progress?" Jessway asked.

"Absolutely."

"I spoke with Moana just a few minutes ago," the reverend offered. "I understand you're aware of our relationship."

"It would have been better if we'd known beforehand," I said, fixing the reverend with a disapproving expression. "It would've saved us having to eliminate your night-time visits from our inquiries. And as you can appreciate, every minute is crucial."

"There's not much I'm ashamed of," the reverend admitted, his tone flat, "but my silence is one of them. It's not nearly enough, but all I can do is apologize."

"We appreciate the help you and your counselors have given us," Will said, "and the use of the rooms here. We will leave it at that, for now."

Jessway also offered his hand to me and I took it. "You and I are birds of a feather," he said to me. "I very much hope we can get together another time."

"Another time," I said, suppressing my disappointment in the man.

The police officers and the Poulsbo agents who had made up the search party had packed up, and their cars were pulling out of the parking area.

Together with Marcia, Zach, and John, Will and I headed across to the federal vehicles that would take us to Seattle.

"I'll be in touch, once we're back in town, for a full briefing," Will said as we reached the cars.

Zach attempted to lighten the mood. "What, no special transport for me?"

His quip fell on deaf ears, attracting only a disapproving glare from me. There was no lightening of mood wanted or needed at this point. Everyone's focus was solely on the rapidly deteriorating situation.

"It doesn't feel right, moving on without those children found," Marcia said, sliding into the back seat. She was in the same car as me and Will. We adjusted our seat belts as the driver maneuvered the vehicle down the long entry road and out onto the main street.

"We can achieve more from the field office," Will said. "We need to establish who this Piper really is and where he's likely to have spirited those children away to."

"And to do that," I said, "we have to adjust our brains and start thinking the way he does."

"Ilona and I are at a press conference this afternoon," Will added, "but first up I'm having each of us dropped off at our homes. Change clothes. Take a little time to refresh. Then we regroup." And glancing at me, he said, "Marcia has agreed to stay with the team, for now, as both analyst and group coordinator."

* * *

Stepping from the car, I wasn't ready to head straight into my building. There was something else I wanted to do. Just for a quarter-hour or so but it could make all the difference, given that this wasn't the right moment to fully indulge myself in my hidden side.

I made my way around the block to an internet café, not one I regularly used – it was too close, but once in a blue moon was okay. And given my nerves were on edge, my anxiety on the rise, this moment had 'blue moon' written all over it.

I entered my online alias and password and within seconds my secret cyber spirit was roaming the web, visiting the select group of bloggers that helped make my senses soar. I read through the latest post from one of my favorites, his descriptive text and accompanying images both exciting and strangely calming at the same time.

> *It is like a dream that has morphed into reality, a montage of beauty that has taken shape around me, beckoning me, reaching out.*

Soon, I thought.

* * *

It always felt good to step back into my apartment.

I stripped off, stepped into the shower, and felt my body revitalize as the steamy water gushed over me.

Pulling a bathrobe on, I headed for the kitchen. A coffee and a sandwich before dressing and driving over to the Bureau offices for the damned press conference.

My phone rang. I reached for it and my breath caught in my throat as my eyes fell on the display screen.

Unknown caller

I drew in a deep breath as I answered.

"The last time we spoke I told you there was no photo equipment in that forest." This time I knew that voice.

Deep, guttural. As before, I guessed it had been electronically interfered with.

"So I'm speaking with the famous Pied Piper, am I?"

"That's *your* name for me."

"For a man from the Middle Ages, you seem very comfortable with our phones and computers."

"You think the technology from this or any other era is a challenge for me, Special Agent Farris? I've seen all this and far more than you will ever know."

"I don't believe you."

There was something deeply unsettling in the ready laugh I heard from him. "And what do you believe?"

"I know you're a man. And a criminal. And I'm going to find you."

"You're making threats?"

"I call them promises."

"Then I will promise you this, Ms. Farris." Before the line went dead, he said, "I can and I will find you, wherever you are and whenever I want. But no matter how far or for how long you search, you will *never* find me."

Chapter Twenty-Nine

I phoned Will and told him about this new call from the Piper.

He would have their tech people attempt to trace it. Standard procedure, but I knew the result would be the same as before. I tried to shake it off. But the call had unnerved me as much as the first one had.

He's always one step ahead of us.

I took a bite of the sandwich but I was no longer hungry. I pulled on a conservative outfit for the conference, a white blouse, and a dark blue pantsuit. I headed out, opting on this occasion to make the short trip to the office by public transport.

Just weeks before, I had been called to the Seattle city rooftop where a young boy had been stopped from jumping by the mysterious urban climber. I played a part in coaxing the boy's identity from him and getting him to safety.

I'd been interviewed by the TV networks. I hadn't liked it but at least they had been prerecorded for later broadcast.

This was a whole different experience, a live press conference to a horde of reporters hungry for updates about the so-called lost children of Hamelin.

"Agent Farris, why is the FBI involved in a local-lost-children incident?" Under the glare of camera lights, I hadn't even seen who'd asked the question.

And why was the question aimed at me? Will was right beside me and he'd been introduced as the supervisory special agent. I was supposed to be there for backup only. "The FBI was asked to assist by the local authorities. And I've been involved with child cases before."

"You're referring," said another reporter, this one a young woman in the front row, "to the rooftop jumper saved by an urban climber?"

I realized that was the reason the newshounds were focused on me. A familiar face from a recent news story. "That was one of them," I answered.

"Can you confirm," another voice in the crowd called out, "that there were four children, all telling the same unusual story, and that all four have since gone missing while under your duty of care?"

I winced. And then realized that wouldn't play well on camera. *Duty of care.* I didn't need some jumped-up media asshole reminding me of that.

"These children were believed to be lost and to be suffering some form of memory loss," I said. "We now believe that they were the targets of a serial kidnapper and we are working closely with all law enforcement agencies to find the children."

Lights flashed and a chorus of voices erupted. One of the louder male voices cut across the rest with a series of questions that captured everyone's attention. "You say you're dealing with a serial kidnapper. But why were there four German-speaking children in the forest, all with no understanding of the modern world? What sort of kidnapper plays a musical instrument and is called the Piper? What kind of danger are all our kids in?"

Will leaned forward to his mic to address the onslaught. I wasn't sure what he was saying and I felt my anxiety spiking. I felt as though I was trapped and I wanted to get up and run. Escape. I'd felt the same when I'd faced the media barrage after my teenage kidnap.

Deep breaths, I reminded myself. You can get through this.

* * *

As the press conference wrapped up, Will and I retreated through the back door of the media room.

In the area behind this, we were approached by a tall man with a long face and tired eyes. His dark hair was graying at the temples.

"Detective Radner," I said, surprised but not sorry to see a familiar face.

"I was at the conference, up the back," the detective said. "Dropped by to see if I can lend some support but I think I got lost in the mob." He smiled. "Sorry to say, it looks like you've got a media frenzy building up around this case of yours."

"That's because our kidnapper has found a way to leak information to the press," Will said.

I introduced the two men and they shook hands.

"You handled it well," Radner said to us.

Will thanked him, reminded me that we were meeting with Zoe Marshall in half an hour, then excused himself and left me to walk with Radner to the front lobby exit.

"You've got a major investigation on your hands with this," Radner said, "so I don't expect you to give us any more help on the urban climber thing. But I did want you to know how much my team and I appreciated the help you've already given."

"Thanks for that, Detective. Just let me know how you get on."

"The fact that this dangerous climber might be female only makes me even more determined to apprehend them. Not that I need any more reasons to be determined, given my story, but you know all that."

"Your story?" I queried.

"Yeah. My daughter."

"Actually, I don't know your story."

"My daughter was an urban climber," Radner revealed.

I didn't like the use of the word *was*. "I didn't know that."

"She was enticed into it by a group of friends. Met them at college. They call themselves urban explorers, rooftoppers, and freerunners. Whack jobs are what I call them."

"What happened, Detective?"

"They were into running and leaping in all sorts of dangerous places like building sites, underground tunnels, and of course scaling the sides of monuments and skyscrapers." He paused, choking back emotion. "She fell. Forty feet. Never stood a chance."

"I'm so sorry, Detective. What happened to the other climbers, her friends?"

"Friends?" Radner didn't disguise the contempt in his voice. "There was no hard evidence linking anyone else to the incident. And not one of the selfish, cowardly so-called daredevils stepped forward to accept any responsibility."

I felt an enormous lump in my throat. My heart poured out for this grieving man. At that moment he wasn't a detective with the Seattle Police Department, he was just a father who had suffered an unimaginable loss. "When did this happen?"

"Two years ago." He produced a photo from his wallet and showed it to me. "Her name was Sarah."

"If there's anything I can do, at any time, to help..."

"You've already done plenty and your kidnap case is far more important," Radner said. "As a senior detective, my focus has to be on serious offenses, whether it's acts of violence or organized crime. Not on a small number of daredevils who run and climb on restricted properties. That's been made very clear to me by my superiors. Even so, if you come by any information that's helpful, I know you'll pass it on. As you can tell, my commitment to cleaning up this urban climbing fad that puts others in danger is as personal as it is professional."

* * *

I watched Radner leave and then I walked to the windows that afforded a view of the city and its skyscrapers. I hadn't been able to get the image out of my mind of Radner's daughter up there among the towering columns of steel and glass. I visualized the girl's hand slipping as she reached for a handhold, and her plummeting toward the city street.

It wasn't just Radner's daughter I was seeing. It was myself, climbing out of the tunnel where the kidnappers had buried me. Scaling a largely sheer wall face with no experience, no idea of what I was doing, desperate to find a way out. Terrified of the death that waited if I slipped or miscalculated a move.

I'd often had nightmares of a different outcome, of slipping and falling.

My nightmares. Sarah Radner's reality.

Chapter Thirty

My father, Clayton Farris, was an assistant director of the FBI at the time of my kidnap. After my rescue, I remembered him telling me how he was in the study of our home in Mount Pleasant, Washington DC when he received the anonymous email. The sender advised him to click on the link in the email if he wanted essential information about his daughter.

She's not at a friend's place as you currently believe.

I recalled my father describing how his heart thumped as he watched a video of me in a confined space. He'd listened to my raspy breathing and the fear rose in him.

He'd called his office and put the finest minds in law enforcement to work. In the following hours, they made no progress in tracing the transmission. I could hear my father's words when he explained the email had been routed and rerouted around the globe like a ball in a digital ping-pong match.

He'd admitted to me that strange thoughts zig-zagged through his mind. He'd always grieved that his late wife, Cordelia, had not been around to see me on stage in school plays, trying out for the junior cheerleaders, achieving distinctions in science and math. But he was glad she wasn't witnessing this.

He'd told me how the video feed had ended and a dialog box appeared in the center of the screen.

Clayton, I know your people have tried to locate me. Waste of time. But I guess you had to try. Human nature.

He told me how sickened he'd been that this monster was communicating with him by his first name.

I'd asked to see the email, I knew he'd kept it, but he'd said no. I needed to concentrate on recovering from my ordeal, he said. Years later, when I graduated college and began my training at the FBI's Quantico Academy, I'd pressured Dad to show me that email. I said it would bolster my determination to be the very best agent I could be. I knew my father hadn't wanted me to follow in his footsteps, I knew he thought I'd never been the same person since the kidnap. And I hadn't been. He'd relented, though, and showed me the email.

> *It's time to act on my request, Clayton. No more playing Mr. Big-Time. Forget that now. Your daughter has ten minutes of air. Act now, and she lives.*
>
> *I'm prepared to make it a little easier for you to decide. I'll provide a little countdown so that you know precisely how much time your daughter has left. Your daughter or your career. It's tough making the big decisions, isn't it?*
>
> *Nine minutes now, and counting…*

At the same time my father had been reading those words, I had freed my hands. Empowered by my mother's voice and my mother's hand, I had pushed on the lid of that box over and over. In a fit of unnatural strength, I'd shifted it enough to create a handhold. I'd pushed and slid it further and further until there was just enough room for me to slip through.

Over the years I'd looked back and wondered whether my mom's spirit had actually been there or whether it had all been in my imagination. I'd decided that even if Mom had only been there in my mind, it was still my mother's voice and strength reaching out to me from my memories of her.

I barely remembered being taken. I was walking to a friend's house in the early evening when a car pulled up on the quiet street alongside me. At the same time a man stepped up from behind, his hand enclosing my nose and mouth with a cloth and I remembered the strong smell which I later learned was chloroform. I woke in the box from which I later escaped.

I found that the box in which I'd been imprisoned was itself at the bottom of a deep, narrow shaft. There was a locked, concrete door. I stood, leaning against the rock-hewn wall for support, and looked up. The tunnel seemed to rise forever. I could make out the tiniest pinprick of light far above. Where was I that there was a hole with a drop of such incredible depth?

Could I climb out?

The walls were rough but regardless, fairly sheer. There were cracks and tiny crevices but would they provide a handhold? Could I even reach far enough from one to the next or even see them properly in the near darkness?

The distance between one side of the tunnel and the other was almost the length of my body. Placing my back against one side and my feet against the other so I could shimmy up would only work for brief moments before my foot or my back would slide. I wouldn't be able to prevent myself from falling and scraping down at breakneck speed.

There's no way out.

I'd sat, contemplating the hopelessness of my situation for a long time, but I didn't know how long. I didn't have my watch or my phone, and time had no meaning, no measurement, down there.

* * *

"What's Themis?" I asked. Will had told me that I would be learning about it in the meeting with Zoe Marshall. I tapped my ID card against the scanner and followed Will through the frosted glass sliding doors.

"Welcome to the UCU, Unsolvable Crimes Unit," Will said. It was a large, open-plan room, with several offices and conference rooms skirting two of the walls. In the center was a series of large, wide screens, positioned to form a T-shaped column, with a bank of desktop screens and desks beneath.

"Themis is artificial intelligence software," Will elaborated, "but not just any ol' AI program; this one has over fifteen hundred terabytes of memory. I sometimes can't help thinking of it as an entity. And don't think this is all old hat to me, either. I've only been exposed to this newly constructed command point a few times recently."

"And Themis does what exactly?"

"Themis sifts through data on all reported crimes, collected hourly from all state and federal law enforcement organizations. It's constructed with multiple levels of data mining tools. It cross-references that data against the data from every crime, solved or otherwise, from our archives. Themis can also access CCTV from various sources. It contains a complete database, updated daily, on forensic and medical science, psychological profiling, and technological advances."

A young woman rose from the main console and turned toward us. I recognized her from the online FBI profile. Mid-twenties. Cyber and information technology projects. Someone I'd seen around but never met in person. I was reminded that this girl seemed young to be the senior tech guru called on by Will but it wasn't the only thing about her that drew attention. Intense green eyes were set off by her copper-brown skin, her smooth cheekbones a contrast to her black curls.

Will introduced her. "Zoe Marshall, one of the few FBI employees I've worked with" – and he grinned – "who isn't here for the salary."

I wasn't sure what he meant by that. Was this young woman independently wealthy?

"I wouldn't be so sure of that," Zoe responded with a secretive grin, "money is like chocolate. Before you know it, you've devoured the block."

"And too much can be bad for you," I said drily.

"I'm afraid I had to learn that the hard way." Zoe winked, holding out her hand at the same time.

A hint of attitude just beneath the surface. A rebellious kid in the not-too-distant past? I wondered.

"I've been looking forward to meeting you, Ilona, just sorry it couldn't have been before you were yanked out of bed and thrust into this sudden assignment. Themis, which has been in testing mode these past few weeks, rang the alarm bells on this. Our pesky higher-ups thought it was the right kind of case to trial with a 'live' team." She rolled her eyes. "I didn't think it needed a trial run – it's already been run through simulations to the nth degree – but hey, what do I know?"

"Zoe can fill you in, better than I can, on Themis," Will said.

"The object of the software," Zoe said, moving to the rows of desktop screens, "is to analyze newly reported crimes, against the database of all recorded cases. It uses a sophisticated set of algorithms to predict those crimes with the highest probability of remaining unsolved."

"I'm surprised it isn't called Nostradamus."

Zoe laughed. "This machine doesn't foretell the future, but it does give us the chance to impact it for the better."

"By sending in a strong team with special skills," Will added, "to focus on, and solve quickly, a crime that might otherwise never be solved."

"Why Themis?" I asked.

"Themis was the Greek goddess of divine justice," Zoe explained, "usually portrayed holding the scales of justice, armed with her sword for delivering that justice. She had prophetic abilities, which led her to become one of the oracles of Delphi."

"A fitting name, then."

Zoe nodded. "With a fitting set of symbols."

"What made the system red-flag this case?" I asked. "I know that a lost German-speaking kid in medieval clothing is odd but surely that alone is not what prompted Themis to highlight it?"

"Themis identified various John and Jane Doe amnesiac cases where the victims never discovered who they were. No trace of their previous lives could be uncovered. Admittedly, most were in the days before the internet and social media but there are also more recent examples. In each of these cases, the amnesiacs adopted new names and began new lives."

"No one reported them missing, no one was looking for them," I said. "Okay, I'm aware of such cases…"

"We don't know for certain these children have amnesia, but the memories they do have, of another time and place, are not that dissimilar to total amnesia cases. In fact, in *this* situation–"

I jumped in. "It's even more bizarre."

"Yes. But I'll let Themis herself tell you more about her process."

I cocked my head toward Zoe. "It talks?"

"Of course," Zoe responded with a wry smile. "I always figured that if everyday gadgets could give digital voice responses, then Themis should do that, and more. She's programmed to 'conversational' mode, understands natural speech, and can respond accordingly using inflection and emotion."

I was curious. "I'll think I'm speaking to a human?"

There was a gleam in Zoe's eyes. "It's good but perhaps not quite that good. But it's close."

"Eerily so," Will added.

Zoe directed her attention to the bank of screens. "Themis, I'm with Agents Ilona Farris and Will McCord. Could you give us some background on your identification of the Hamelin case?"

"Of course, Zoe," said the machine. It was a feminine voice, soft, smooth, and confident with an easy but professional manner. And something else.

"Greek accent?" I said to Zoe.

"Just a touch, a nod to her namesake. Synthesized from an actual human recording as a sample."

"Welcome, Agents Farris and McCord," the machine said. "In answer to your question, Zoe, I cross-referenced the case details with the well-known Barnum & Bailey Circus fire in Hartford in 1944, which killed over one hundred and sixty people. Just one of those was a six-year-old girl, to this day never identified, never claimed. Another well-known mystery involving children happened a year later in West Virginia. The Sodders, a large family, two parents, nine children." Zoe indicated the monitors where Themis projected images of old newspaper reports from that incident. "On Christmas Eve," Themis continued, "the mother received a mysterious phone call from a voice she didn't recognize, asking about a person she'd never heard of. When the family house burned down that night, the parents and four of the children escaped, but the five children on the upper level couldn't be reached. And yet when rescue workers combed the wreckage the morning after there was no sign of any of those five, or their remains, or their clothing. No clues to whether they survived, or where they were, no explanation."

"And no one ever traced who made that call." I knew of these well-documented historical mysteries. I turned to Zoe. "Are there other cases out there that are a closer match to this, to children not missing, but found alive, and with strange memories?"

"Not exactly but" – Zoe snapped her fingers – "that's where Themis surprised even me. Over the years there have been hundreds of children who vanished in national parks across the United States. There are a few bizarre situations, where clothing was found, neatly folded and abandoned. Those cases–"

"Unsolved," I completed the sentence. "Themis pulled in all that data and drew similarities with these lost children."

"You got it…" Zoe's enthusiasm reminded me a little of Zach's hyped-up passion for his subjects. But only a little. I sensed an edge that kept that side of her in check.

"If I didn't know better," I said, "I'd say that Themis is an AI version of one of our consultants. Professor Zachary Silverstein."

"Oh, I know Zach."

I showed my surprise. "You know Zach Silverstein?"

"He was one of my lecturers back in my university days. I haven't been in touch with him since then, although I did once attend his book launch." Her face lit up. "Gotta love some of those crazy-ass ideas of his."

"You said before," I backtracked, "that Themis surprised even you. Why *even you*?"

"Because," Will stepped in and replied, "Zoe created Themis."

Chapter Thirty-One

Barbara Gauchi was in her kitchen in the exclusive Seattle suburb of Broadmoor, packing away groceries when her phone rang. She answered it without checking the caller ID. She was in a hurry; she was due to leave in a few minutes to pick up her daughter from school.

"Am I speaking with Mrs. Gauchi?" said an unfamiliar voice.

"Yes."

"You won't be needing to pick Bethany up at the normal time, Mrs. Gauchi."

"Who is this, please?" Barbara asked.

"Have you seen the breaking news over the past twenty-four hours?" asked the deep voice. "About the lost children from Hamelin?"

Barbara felt a chill run like a knife up the center of her spine. "Yes, but… who am I speaking with?"

"Your daughter is safe for the moment, Mrs. Gauchi, but the question of whether you ever see her again is something else altogether."

Barbara opened her mouth to speak but no words, only a gurgle, a strangled sound, emerged. She felt as though the knife of fear tracing her spine had stuck in her throat.

"The parents of Hamelin were told that if they did not pay the agreed fee then they would never see their children again. You know this story, I believe. But there is something else they were told, Mrs. Gauchi, something never included in the retellings."

Barbara pushed out a deep breath and managed to speak. "What?"

"Not only would their children never return but there would be no end to the children being taken forevermore. That the debt would never be settled."

"No." Her voice was a croak, and tears welled in her eyes.

"The kidnappings have been taking place ever since. Whenever a ransom is paid the kidnapped children are returned. When it isn't, the children – like the youth of Hamelin – are never seen again."

"Where do you take them?"

"To places and times from which they can never be retrieved."

"What… *happens* to them?"

"That's not something you want to ask."

"Tell me. They're children for God's sake. What… happens?"

"There are others out there who will pay for them."

"Other parents…?"

"No. Why would other parents pay such an amount—"

A chill shook Barbara Gauchi to her core. "Twisted… people?"

"It's not something you want to know. But the others of whom I speak have existed among us through all of history."

Barbara could hardly speak. Her throat was so dry she struggled to swallow. Her heart hammered like a battering ram. She somehow found her voice again and she forced the words out: "We will pay."

"I also require, Mrs. Gauchi, that you do not contact the police or any authorities. Not until after our business is concluded. Then I will want them to know. But not before."

"I understand."

"Some say that and then, of course, they go against my wishes. So I need you to be very clear on one important fact."

"Yes?"

"If you do make contact with the police or anyone else, I will know, and then no amount of money will ever see young Bethany returned. You do *not* want to know what will become of her, believe me, your nightmares would be… impossible to live with."

"No one will be contacted." Barbara did not recognize her own voice. She was not able to comprehend how any of this could be happening to her, to her family, to their daughter. She stared down at her manicured nails, only that morning coated with a soft, stylish hue of pink that now seemed to represent a life that had been erased in a matter of seconds by an unseen hand. "Can you at least tell me if she's close?"

"It's not a question of close or far." There was an air of absolute power and indifference to his voice. "Bethany is beyond the reach of anything that you or the police could possibly understand. It's up to you, Mrs. Gauchi; the return of your daughter is solely in your hands."

"But you will return her? This *is* just a kidnap for money?"

"This is far, far more than that. This is just one small part of the great reckoning."

The chill in Barbara's spine flared, engulfing her entire body. She shivered, the hairs on the nape of her neck rising. "Reckoning? How can my girl be part of any reckoning—"

"The destinies of all of these children lie with me and they always have."

Barbara whimpered, every breath a struggle.

"Listen very closely," the Piper said. "This is what you are to do."

* * *

"I'm going to give you an account number," he said. "You will go to the First Accord Bank on Bay Street at precisely 3.30 and you will transfer two hundred thousand dollars into that account number. Don't write the number down. Memorize it. And afterward, make certain you forget it. The account will be closed and the money laundered elsewhere anyway, but regardless, *forget* that number."

"Okay."

"Absolutely one hundred percent clear?"

Even Barbara Gauchi did not expect the words that came next from her own mouth. "If you're the Piper from the news and you say you're from the thirteenth century then how do you know about modern banking details and transfers—"

"Did you really think I wouldn't know everything there is to know about every time zone, every society, all of the systems and processes and technologies, past, present, and future?"

Silence.

Barbara's mind went blank.

"I'm waiting for your answer. Are we clear?"

"Yes."

"You have your instructions. You know what to do and what not to do if you ever want to see your beautiful daughter again."

Chapter Thirty-Two

"You created Themis," I said to Zoe. "That's a helluva bullet-point on your resume."

"It was a labor of love. She was swirling about in my head long before I began to write the code." Zoe shrugged, a devilish glint in her eye. "I guess you could say she was my first love."

"Then she'll be a hard act to follow."

"That's for sure." Zoe's sudden earnestness could have made me believe she was talking about a much-loved partner. "During my college days, I studied the application of predictive analytics by child welfare agencies, specifically in Florida's Hillsborough County. They had a high degree of success eliminating abuse-related child deaths after making decisions based on their predictive modeling." She paused, allowing a moment for the significance of her words to sink in. "Predictive analytics combines data mining, machine learning, and modeling to make predictions on the outcomes of certain events."

"And of course, it's not just in child welfare," Will added. "It's a science now being applied in many business sectors."

Zoe nodded enthusiastically. "And just as those businesses are dealing with massive streams of incoming data, so too, of course, is anything related to crime investigation. The intention, with Themis, is to analyze specific data at high speed to determine the most likely outcome. It also functions as a highly targeted search engine, which can help us with our investigative legwork."

"Like another agent on the team."

"Exactly."

I was fascinated and wanted to know more about Zoe Marshall and her creation but there would be time for that later.

"What's the update on Brooke Goodman's computer and the photo breach at Poulsbo?" Will asked.

"Brooke subscribes to several news sites, both traditional and indie," Zoe said. "She received an email last week from a new site offering weekly rundowns on local Poulsbo items of national interest. It's a fake site that was taken down just after she'd clicked on their link. Exiting from a rigged site like that one can trigger the download of malicious code and that's exactly what happened. The malware created a backdoor on Brooke's computer through which the photos and text she received could be sent and displayed on her desktop. We thought we'd removed the malware and the backdoor when we went in remotely."

"It wasn't fully removed?"

"There was hidden code in there, triggered to re-download the virus when the original malware was erased. Very sophisticated. And what's more, it was a very similar Trojan horse used to manipulate the photos on the Poulsbo Agency's system."

"How could a virus enter a protected FBI network?" I asked.

"I've had Themis looking into that," Zoe said. "I can utilize my baby to check external networks, so I've had Themis collect every email, every peer-to-peer download, every website access made from the Poulsbo Agency. It then cross-referenced and tested for viruses."

"Anything?" asked Will.

"Nothing, which is not surprising given the security protocols and the firewalls in place."

"Is there any other way to install malware that can edit graphics automatically?" I asked.

"It would need to have been transferred from a hardware device," Zoe said.

"Like a USB?"

"Yes. And that, I believe, is how it's been done. Once an infected USB was inserted into one of the networked computers at Poulsbo, it downloaded the malware into the bowels of the system. It's been activated just these past few days to attack any new photos uploaded into the system."

"Triggered to manipulate the image and change the appearance of a face."

"Yes. Kind of like facial recognition software in reverse."

"But the photos were correct when we viewed them on the Poulsbo computers," I protested.

"The manipulated image takes on its new shape only after it's transmitted externally, which explains why the photos you had printed off were of the altered faces."

"There's software that does that?"

"There is now. This is specially designed, Ilona. I've seen variations on this type of program, but nothing else like it."

"But, Zoe," Will said, "all devices, USB or otherwise, used by our operatives have come from secure sources."

"I'm aware of that. I suspect one of the office devices was replaced manually."

"Which means someone internal is our breach."

"Or someone visiting that office."

"There's something else," I said. "We suspect a breach of some kind was how the kidnapper knew that the children were being housed at the SafePlace Retreat. We couldn't figure out how that could be, given so few people knew of that arrangement. But if someone placed a rogue

USB in the office, then that same person could have planted listening devices that circumvented the regular sweeps for bugs."

"It would explain both of those breaches," Zoe said.

I turned to Will but he spoke first. "We need an immediate sweep for bugs."

"And we need to know who's visited Poulsbo over the past few months." I directed my next thought to Zoe. "Can we still access the original shots from the photo equipment?"

"We've struck out there as well," Zoe said as Will raised his hands in frustration. "When the images were uploaded to the computer, the virus attacking them was also programmed to bounce back via the upload, violating the images at their source."

"Okay, so we still don't have photos of these kids we can use." My tone was defiant. "Has anything further come in from Missing Persons, anything remotely likely to be connected?"

"No," said Will. "What's more, we expanded the search parameters to include all countries going back ten years and we've got Themis running analytics on that as well. Nothing."

Chapter Thirty-Three

Barbara Gauchi stood outside the building that housed the office of Senator Bill Tiernan and nervously addressed the throng of reporters who'd arrived. She'd always been a woman conscious of her appearance but on this occasion, for the first time in her life, she hadn't even stopped beforehand to run a brush through her glossy, wavy black hair. She'd only made the phone calls to local media a short while before. Not many had turned up at short notice and, after all, she was a virtual unknown, the wife of a low-level politician, what could she say that could possibly be of interest?

"Thank you for coming," she said, struggling to find her voice.

"Could you speak up," one of the reporters called out.

"What is this about, Mrs. Gauchi?" another one said.

"I have wrestled with my conscience about this" – Barbara pushed herself to project her voice – "as I believe sometimes we all have to own up to our mistakes. It is… with great regret…" Her voice trailed away and after a moment she found it again, as the media group waited impatiently. Cameras clicked. "…great regret I must confess to an affair this past year with Senator Bill Tiernan…"

Questions were fired at her as she shakily completed her statement. And then, without warning, she fled from the scene, turning a corner just a few doors away and hurrying along the crowded sidewalk.

She glanced back several times. None of the reporters were following. The sky had clouded over and a brisk wind was tunneling up Bay Street from the waterfront. Typical Seattle. Barbara felt almost thankful that there was at least something typical she could observe on a day that was, for her, anything but.

Another half-block along and she reached the First Accord Bank.

* * *

Barbara entered the bank at 3.30 as instructed.

Just before entering the swing doors at the front of the building, she glanced furtively in both directions, up and down the street. She felt as though a thousand eyes were boring into her, from every direction. She shivered, her stomach churning, her hands trembling, but she pressed forward. She had to get through this. For her daughter.

She stood in line for the teller. Heart pounding. That was when her attention was drawn to the line beside her. And one particular man in that line. A customer, just like the rest of them. Except that this man was also a police officer.

She leaned toward him, catching his eye, her voice no more than a whisper. "Officer, my daughter has been kidnapped."

The policeman returned her gaze. "Ma'am...?"

"I received a phone call, I was told to come here, to pay a ransom... or... or..."

"Ma'am, I need you to take a deep breath and slow down," the officer said. "Can you do that for me?"

Her voice was a croak. "Yes."

"Your daughter is missing?"

"Yes."

"How old is she, ma'am?"

"Ten, she's just ten years old."

"And you received a ransom call from a kidnapper?"

"It's the man who... who took those lost Hamelin children."

"Hamelin?"

"It's been in the news. The German children who were found in the Olympic National Forest–"

"He said he was the man who took those children?"

She nodded, her head bobbing as fast as her speech. She wasn't anything like herself. "The Piper."

"Ma'am, I'm going to get you to come to the local precinct with me."

"He told me I wasn't to contact the police." She gasped, sucking in a deep breath. "Oh my God, what have I done? I shouldn't have said anything."

"He's watching you?" the officer asked.

She cleared her throat, breathing rapidly, nodding her head again. "He told me he'd know... everything I said and did."

"You believe he watched you enter the bank?"

"Yes. Oh, God…"

"Ma'am, take deep breaths for me, okay? Try to remain calm. I'll get our plainclothes detectives to come here to the bank, to speak with you."

"But the Piper…" Her voice trailed away. She felt faint.

"He won't know they are detectives," the officer assured her. "I want you to wait here quietly while I make the call." He moved to the side of the room, away from the other customers, not sure what any of them might have heard. He placed his phone to his ear.

Barbara stared after him, remembering at the same time that there was a deadline. She needed to transfer the funds by 4 p.m. She was next in line for the teller and she moved to the counter the second the teller was free.

* * *

"Major problem," Will said to the team as he ended the call. We had moved to his office for a briefing, with Zach and Marcia joining us, and had only been there a few minutes when his phone rang.

It was rare for me to see this level of shock on his face. "Will, what is it?"

"There's a police officer with a woman at the First Accord Bank. She says her daughter was taken by the Piper. She was in the bank to transfer ransom money but believes the Piper is watching. She was told she'd never see her daughter again if she contacted police."

"Which she's done," said Zach.

"By chance, this officer was in the bank and she panicked and told him. Now she's terrified."

"And we don't know if the Piper saw her exchange with the officer?" Zoe guessed.

Will shook his head. "No, we don't."

"Did she transfer the money?" I asked.

"Yes."

"The officer should've prevented that."

175

"She did it while he was on the phone arranging plainclothes detectives to attend the scene."

"Can we get the detectives to turn back? And get a message to that police officer," I said to Will. "Tell him to have the woman pretend to faint and have him phone emergency services. If the Piper saw the exchange and then sees her collapse and the arrival of medics, it creates the impression the woman told the officer she was ill. It reinforces that she hasn't revealed the kidnap because she's sent the money."

"Good thinking." Will made the call.

"The ransom's paid," Zoe said, "so if the Piper doesn't believe the police were alerted then he should release the girl."

"And we try to learn where and when so we can strike," I said.

"How?" asked Zach.

"I'm counting on the Piper wanting to release the girl to the mother in a hidden place."

"Why would he do that?"

"Because I'm hoping that the Piper wants to be seen, from a distance, by the mother."

Zach snapped his fingers. "Of course. He wants her to report that she saw him. Describe him. Another sighting that proves he exists."

Zoe nodded. "Which continues to spread fear."

Will ended his phone call. "It's not just any mother. The woman is Barbara Gauchi, wife of Congressman Joe Gauchi. She'd just come from a hastily organized press conference where she revealed she'd had an affair."

"You think that's related to all this?" Zoe asked.

"I'm thinking it must be, even though she didn't say anything about the kidnap to the newspeople."

"Do we know if the affair is real or just part of the Piper's ploy here?" Marcia said.

"No doubt we'll find out in due course, but I expect it's real. Why Barbara Gauchi's family has been targeted for this, that we don't know."

"And now we hope the Piper leads her to where he'll set the girl free." Zach rubbed his temples, his mouth in a grimace. "It's a hell of a long shot."

I nodded. "But right now it's the only shot we've got."

* * *

Will and I entered the hospital by a rear staff entrance. It was unlikely the Piper had eyes on the hospital but we were way past the point of taking anything for granted.

An officer escorted us to the second-floor wing where Barbara Gauchi was propped up in a bed. Although she hadn't really fainted, I noted that the woman was nevertheless shaken to the core.

"What have I done?" Barbara said, tears in her eyes. "I've ruined our lives. I've destroyed my family and my husband's career and I'll never… see Bethany again."

I covered the woman's hand with my own. "You need to hang in there and be strong, if not for yourself, then for Bethany. I understand you transferred the money as instructed?"

"Yes."

"Even if the kidnapper was watching you in the bank," Will said, "there's every chance he'd believe that you only spoke to the officer to say you needed medical help."

I spied the woman's cell phone on the bedside table. "Now we wait for the kidnapper to call you with Bethany's whereabouts."

"My husband's away on business," Barbara said, "but he must have seen my press conference. Have you heard from him?"

"The police are attempting to contact him, Mrs. Gauchi," Will said.

In the following moment, we all turned to the cell phone as it rang.

Chapter Thirty-Four

Barbara Gauchi expressed her fears to me. The Piper had instructed her to come *alone* to collect her daughter.

"Just follow the instructions he gave you," I told her. "The agents will be watching, and we'll be following you, but none of us will be seen, nothing will be obvious."

Barbara walked to the end of a major platform at King Street train station. She edged past the sign that read 'Public Access Prohibited'.

She stepped down onto a narrow ledge. It led into a disused tunnel that had once been a walkway for workers between one workspace and another.

We'd been told that the walkway twisted and turned through near-darkness. It eventually opened out into an abandoned work area near the far end of an active platform. I'd assured Barbara that federal agents, disguised and masquerading as workers, would be at that end of the platform. They would be ready to pounce when the Piper exited the tunnel.

When she'd taken the call in the hospital, Barbara had been ordered by the Piper to follow the walkway for several minutes. There would be a point where she would see her daughter under the light of a flashlight held aloft by the Piper himself.

Bethany would then be allowed to walk forward to her mother. The Piper would leave and she was not to follow him.

I could imagine Barbara's heart pumping like mad as she pressed forward. The Piper had only allowed her a half-hour to get here.

Will and I were not too far behind her, garbed in black from head to foot to blend with the darkness.

The Piper would be trapped.

As she rounded a corner the path ahead was illuminated and reaching that bend, I saw Bethany up ahead. Directly behind her, a tall figure in a peaked hat and a long coat with strips of color.

"Stay where you are, Barbara," he called out, a loud voice, the tone unnatural.

Bethany began to walk toward her.

I watched as the dark figure raised an instrument to his mouth and played a short tune, something that had a chilling, ethereal resonance.

As he turned away the flashlight was extinguished.

We were plunged into near-total blackness, just a sliver of light emanating from somewhere, maybe the faint residue of light spilling in from the ends of the tunnel.

* * *

"*Now*," I said.

Will and I raced forward, past Barbara and Bethany, the tunnel now completely dark at its center. We activated our mini-flashlights, casting a swathe of light ahead of us. It wouldn't matter now that the Piper would see we were coming for him. He was cornered.

Through his earpiece, Will ordered the agents at the far end to move into position. "The Piper will be exiting at your end any minute."

My breathing was like thunder in my ears. We'd been running for less than a couple of minutes. No sign of the Piper. No sign of the tunnel's end.

Will was in front of me, taking the lead.

"Where is he?" I said to him through the comms.

"Can't be far."

We had to slow down as we rounded the tight corners, making certain the Piper wasn't lying in wait.

Up ahead, I saw a thin shaft of brightness that indicated the exit.

I strained my eyes as we came closer. The light illuminated more and more of the tunnel. "Do you see him?"

"No."

We burst into the open area. Four agents, in place at various points around the opening, stared at us.

"Where is he?" Will shouted.

"He hasn't emerged this end," one of the agents called out.

I whirled back toward the opening, crouching to a defensive stance and aiming my weapon, to ensure we weren't somehow being ambushed from behind.

No one there.

I breathed heavily. "Where the hell is he?"

* * *

As she faced the horde of reporters and news photographers, Barbara Gauchi felt numb inside. She wanted this to be over. She needed this to be the end of it.

"Mrs. Gauchi," one of the reporters called out, "the FBI has issued a statement that your daughter was kidnapped by someone identifying himself as the Piper. The same man who took the four lost German children."

Barbara tugged Bethany close as she replied. "That's correct." Her voice was fragile.

Will McCord and one of the Seattle policewomen were fronting the news conference beside her. Ilona had opted out given the media profile she was already attracting.

"Is it true you paid a ransom for your daughter's return?"

"Mrs. Gauchi cannot comment on the case details," Will interjected. "She is only here to respond to any questions about the emotional ordeal that she and Bethany have suffered."

"Bethany," one of the female reporters at the front said, "are you okay?"

"I'm okay," the girl said. She had a smattering of freckles across a pert, upturned nose, and a tangle of light brown curls.

"Can you tell us what happened?"

"It's... kind of vague." Bethany searched her memory. "I was walking to a shop before school when I saw this man, in the shadows by a laneway."

"Can you describe him?"

"I couldn't see him clearly. He was dressed in black, with a wide hat and a long coat with stripes. He was playing a flute or a whistle, something like that."

"What happened then, Bethany?" the female reporter asked.

"I followed him."

"Why?"

"I... don't know. Can't remember."

"Where did he take you?" called out another reporter.

"I don't know. I don't remember anything until I was in the subway and my mom was there."

"Mrs. Gauchi, did you see the Piper?"

"Yes, I did," Barbara said.

"Was he as your daughter describes?"

"Yes. Exactly like that."

"And your news conference earlier, was that related to this kidnapping?"

"I said what I was instructed to say at that press conference in order to get my daughter back." Barbara was fighting back tears. She felt Bethany's hand clasp hers even tighter.

"Is it true that you and Senator Tiernan have been having an affair?" called out one of the others.

One thing that Barbara had done was to anticipate that question. She'd decided precisely what her answer would be. This story wasn't going to go away, no matter what she said. But she wasn't going to add fuel to an already burning fire. "I'm not going to dignify that with an answer."

"But, Mrs. Gauchi," – the same reporter was shouting now to be heard above the clamoring voices – "we've contacted the senator's office and been told 'no comment.' And just hours ago an anonymous sender began circulating photos of you and the senator at a private dinner, and of the two of you entering a hotel late at night. Can you explain?"

"Mrs. Gauchi won't be taking any more questions," Will said, leaning into the mic.

The newswoman at the front called out a final question. "Mrs. Gauchi, was there anything that the Piper said to you that you can reveal to us?"

There was one thing. The Piper had given her a message that she was to relay at her press conference after Bethany had been released. He'd warned if she didn't make this announcement that he would take Bethany again, and this time it would be forever. She believed him. And even if she hadn't, it wasn't a risk she would ever take. "Yes, there is something."

A chorus of voices called out, "What is it?"

"He wanted me to send a message," Barbara said, "to everyone out there who is hiding an unmentionable secret. He told me those people will know who they are. He said, tell them, *he's the Piper who was employed to rid the villages of the rats.* He said, *let the corrupt know that the Ratcatcher is coming to expose them.*"

Chapter Thirty-Five

The receptionist contacted me to tell me I had a visitor.

"I wanted to let you know," John Sanders said as I joined him in the front lobby, "that I had a very good telephone counseling session with Brooke Goodman. A long chat."

"How is she, John?"

"She's going to be fine but it will take a little time."

"An experience like that is going to shake anyone up," I said.

"She'll be meeting in person with a local Port Townsend counselor and I'll speak with her again, as well. Hopefully that should be all the guidance she needs. There's an inner strength there."

"Do you know what happened? What led her to act that way?"

"Brooke is a very ambitious young woman, strong but with hidden insecurities. And that's not uncommon."

"I know."

"When her sister Ellie told her about the child who was found," John said, "Brooke grabbed the opportunity by the horns, sending an article to her editor and citing her sister as a source. It gave her a name for herself in journalistic circles much sooner and at a much younger age than would normally occur. It was like a drug to a gung-ho adrenaline junkie. Even though asked to hold back if any further info came her way, she received that phone call and the extra material and she couldn't help herself. She acted on it."

"And then she felt remorse?"

"Yes."

"That quickly?" I said. "And to such an extent she was suicidal?"

"Doesn't make sense, granted. And that's what I'll be focusing on with the next session."

"Did you ask more about the call she received? It has to have been from the Piper."

"She doesn't remember. But give it a few days and there's a good chance her memory will come good."

"Thanks for the update." I glanced at my watch. 8 p.m. "Above and beyond the call of duty, I think, calling in person."

"Oh, I know. I could've phoned, but it's not the only reason for my visit." He gave me an appraising look. "I'm concerned about you."

"I'm fine."

"You're still taking it personally that those kids haven't been located."

"And I shouldn't be. I know."

"Maybe you should." His reply surprised me. "You made a connection with those young people in a very short time. It's only natural you're feeling the way you are. I wanted to reinforce that there's nothing wrong or unprofessional about that. And I know you'll be fine because I've seen how strong you are."

"Part of the training," I said, trying to make light of it.

"It also wouldn't be unusual if dealing with those lost children, caused you to 'relive' your own kidnap."

"You know about that?"

"With consults like this, I make a point of looking up the team members' histories."

"Of course."

"And chasing the Piper in that subway is also going to give you flashbacks. Totally normal."

I shrugged.

"I understand," John said, "you were at the bottom of a deep, man-made chasm."

"An abandoned, partially built nuclear power plant." I took my time. "It was started in the 1950s and then put on hold due to political changes and budget shortfalls. A few years back there was even a proposal to turn it into a museum. Either way, it has sat derelict for decades in a remote area."

"You got out," John said.

"The chasm, as you called it, was a deep hole dug by the construction crew to contain some of the pipes.

Unfinished, it had reinforced walls of cracked earth and stone, mostly sheer."

"That didn't stop you."

"To this day we don't know who was responsible for taking me. And my father's career was ruined."

"I read the internal reports on that," John said. "Your kidnapper's ransom demand was that your father release classified data to the public, information on an internal investigation. It outed a senior colleague as being suspected of involvement in organized crime. There was a subsequent media meltdown."

"My father was told I had just minutes to live, and he was being fed video of me in that coffin." My shoulders sagged under the weight of the memory. The worst memory of my life. "But that video was on a loop of the same scene over and over. My dad had no way of knowing I escaped the box. He had mere minutes to decide what to do. No way of getting help in time."

John put a reassuring hand on my shoulder. "He did what any father would do."

"The Bureau didn't see it that way. The rules are firm. They don't give in to the demands of criminals, kidnappers, or terrorists. No agent is to take matters into their own hands."

"But your father didn't have a choice."

"No, he didn't," I said. "The Bureau carried out an internal investigation, of course, and they weren't going to charge my father. They probably would've relegated him to a lesser, back-room role. But he did the noble thing and retired early."

"I'm sorry you and your father had to go through any of that."

"One of the agents my father called in, a colleague and friend of his, managed to trace the kidnapper's video feed. He followed the trail but it took several hours. It led them to the plant, they found the hole and they got a rope down to me."

"You were already quarter-way up that chasm."

"I don't know how I even managed that."

"Sheer determination, Ilona. Something you have in spades. And I expect it's why you joined the Bureau."

"That made my dad proud, at least. He spent several years with my uncle in New Jersey, but he never got over what happened. How could he?"

"I'm sorry that you lost him."

"Just a couple of years ago. Yeah, it was hard. I miss him."

"I expect your own kidnap is one case you really want to solve," John said. "Did you hope that being in law enforcement might one day lead to that?"

"Partly. It's always in the back of my mind."

"Totally natural."

I smiled. "So I don't need counseling?"

"I think a strong drink will suffice. There's an Aussie-themed bar not far from here."

"I know it. Land Downunder. And I'd love to, John, but maybe another night?"

"You're tired?"

"Oh yeah."

"You've had a hell of an afternoon," he said. "I saw the news, saw the conference with Barbara Gauchi. My professional opinion? You're more stressed than you are tired."

"And a strong drink is the doctor's prescription?"

"Just one. Stress-Buster. And a short wander along the downtown waterfront. That's one of my personal favorites for stressy days."

I used my thumb and middle finger to illustrate a tiny distance between the two points. "We were this close to catching him today, John."

"How did he escape?"

"There has to have been another exit, something hidden within that tunnel. Will has got the city plans being sent over and we'll pore over them in the morning."

"One drink, short walk," he repeated. "And tell me all about it. The parts that aren't classified, that is."

"I'll get my jacket."

The classic Men at Work's song *Down Under* was just one of the tracks playing in the background as we chatted over our drinks. A photo gallery of Aussie icons, from the kangaroo to Crocodile Dundee, adorned the walls. John had a beer. I opted for a Scotch on the rocks.

Afterward, we strolled along the waterfront. The cool evening air was refreshing, just what I needed. There had been a downpour just a little earlier and the wet, earthy after-rain scent was in the air. I felt the tension lift.

"When you find Dietmar, Berthold, Anna, and Hilde, and you will," John said, "then promise you'll call me straight away. I'll be there to help with them, no matter the hour, day or night." We stopped by a railing and looked out on the water, shards of moonlight skimming its surface, the Seattle Great Wheel in the distance.

I nodded. "No matter the hour," I repeated.

"My car's nearby. I can drive you over to your apartment."

"Thanks."

"And I'm prescribing more of these walks, with me, when this whole thing is over."

"But not as my therapist?" I flashed my most mischievous grin.

"No, just–"

I cut across him. "A man having a friendly drink with a woman."

"A drink and a walk, actually, but you get the drift."

"I do."

Despite the intimacy of the moment, I didn't expect what happened next. John leaned forward and kissed me.

I kissed him back, my hand moving instinctively to the nape of his neck. I felt the adrenaline kick in, a breath of fresh air, a special, tender moment amid the chaos.

We walked hand in hand to his car, no further words spoken, no further words needed.

* * *

He pulled up outside my apartment building. "Thanks, John," I said.

"You're welcome."

Our eyes locked. "Where do you live?" I asked. "Just realized I've never asked you that."

"Fremont. Not far."

"Do you need a coffee before you head off?"

"I don't want to keep you up. Maybe a quick nightcap."

As we entered my apartment, I said, "That kiss before…"

"Just a friendly–"

"Kiss with a woman," I finished the in-joke between us. In that instant, eyes locked on one another again, we came together, his mouth on mine, a classic, lingering goodnight kiss, my hand once again tugging on the hair at the nape of his neck, his fingers gently stroking my cheekbone.

I began to undo his shirt buttons as he gently slid my blouse from my shoulders. My eyes were drawn to the matted hair on his chest, his gaze dropping to my bra and the swell of my breasts.

The kiss was longer and deeper this time. And then his mouth was on my neck and I arched my back. His fingers trailed my collarbone and then began exploring lower as he cast his shirt aside.

I felt as though my body was being recharged.

What am I doing?

I'd never been one to dive headlong into a relationship like this. I was more the slow-burn type, cautious with my heart at first, and then gradually letting my defenses down as I got to know the other person. That was how it had been with Will. But then what difference had any of that meant in the end?

My mouth found his again and I pushed him back against the living room wall, hungry, those defenses peeling away.

I'm in the middle of a major investigation and this man is one of my consultants.

I stopped, easing back, appraising him. Those eyes. That smile. That deep, comforting, *sexy* voice.

He leaned toward me, whispering in my ear. "I should go."

"Yes."

"It's too soon," he said. "Next time?"

"Next time maybe stay longer."

Part of me wanted to keep going. Part of me knew it was wiser to slow down. I wondered if his instincts were telling him the same.

"Raincheck on that coffee then." John reached for the door handle. "I'll see you tomorrow. Will has asked me to attend your morning brief."

"You might just want to take this with you," I said, reaching for his shirt and handing it to him. He hurriedly pulled it on and we went down to his car.

* * *

I watched John drive away and then I headed back up to my third-floor apartment.

I recognized that I'd slipped into the 'overtired' zone and that had always worked against me in a perverse kind of way. How many nights had I lain awake, tired but feeling more and more awake as the minutes ticked by?

Ultimately, there was only one thing that helped. The very thing I'd craved these past few nights and the one thing that cleared my head and relieved my stress. The very thing I'd had to hold back on while in Poulsbo and Port Ludlow.

Tonight was the night, now that I was back home.

I went into my bedroom. The blue duffel bag was in its place in the corner. Waiting.

I picked up the bag and headed out again, this time by the building's back exit. I walked along the narrow laneway that led to a cluster of buildings on the edge of the city district. My car was in my apartment building's basement parking lot but I wouldn't be needing it. Not where I was going.

There were a number of spots in the immediate vicinity that I used. I called them my 'launch points.' This one was a small shopping complex with some outdated office suites over the top. There was an exterior stair that ran up to the complex's rear balconies and the rooftop.

There was a dark recess under the stairway on the top balcony. From there it was a half-dozen steps up to the roof.

In the recess, I set the bag down, unzipped the cylinder-shaped canvas, and reached in. I stripped out of my blouse and pants.

In their place, I donned the sweatpants and hoodie and pulled on and laced up the sneakers.

I went up the steps and adopting a stealth-like stance, I moved fluidly across the rooftop. There was a short gap between this building and the next. I leaped across that gap, onto a narrow ledge.

The windowsills and the layered, older-style brick design enabled me to scale the walls, up to the next level and then the next – my adrenaline soaring, my blood pumping, the night breeze whispering to me, the clear sky above with its magical streak of stars like a beacon, calling to me with its promise of freedom, of joy, of empowerment.

I hadn't been able to indulge myself in those other towns. I couldn't take the gamble that I'd be seen and that a connection would be made with the mysterious urban climber who was on the police's radar in Seattle.

It was unlikely anyone would join those dots, noting that I was a Seattle-based agent who was on assignment in that other region at the same time. A chance, though, that I couldn't risk.

I'd suppressed the craving.

Until now.

Tonight I was running free, leaping into the unknown, reaching for the heavens.

Weeks ago, when I'd chanced upon the suicidal teenager on a city rooftop, I'd stayed with him, kept him from jumping until the police and rescue services arrived. During that brief but tense period, I'd kept my distance so as not to alarm him. Perched on the edge, the boy had glanced at me just once but hadn't seen my face. With the hoodie pulled low on my forehead, my face averted and adopting a lower, huskier tone to my voice, I'd protected my identity as I always did when climbing. Later, I'd presented very differently as the Fed assisting the police in interviewing the boy.

I'd known that particular spot was on camera. The intense media coverage that followed meant I had an unwanted profile as the mysterious climber who'd saved a life while breaking the law. The media loved that angle.

It also meant that Detective Radner, already intent for personal reasons on arresting any active climbers, had someone to focus on. He had officers running regular checks on CCTV, except that initially because of my bulky, masculine-looking hoodie they'd thought I was a he.

Now Radner wasn't certain.

I thought of what I'd learned today about Radner's daughter. No one should be encouraged to attempt this without being fully experienced, with a lot of practice behind them. Even then, it was dangerous and had to be the considered choice of an adult.

If I ever came across anyone encouraging inexperienced young people to risk their lives up here, I would intervene. If I ever suspected anyone of being responsible for Sarah Radner's fatal fall, I'd find a way to point Radner in their direction.

Sometimes it bothered me that this hidden passion of mine was something the detective would never understand or approve of. It was something that, as an FBI agent, I could never share with anyone, not Will, not even my closest friend from back in my DC days.

I did not doubt that if John Sanders knew of this, the psychologist in him would see it as my teenage self still trying to climb out of that deep tunnel. My way of expressing freedom, my way of searching for the people who'd kidnapped me.

None of that mattered.

This was the part of me that I could never reveal. Just me and the air currents, with the birds and the stars, and the landscapes both natural and urban.

This wasn't one of the multiple camera zones that I often frequented and which I knew the police were monitoring. Even so, I was going to have to find new places to climb, places they wouldn't expect, and I was going to have to change my climbing outfit.

There was a point where a balcony of the building alongside lined up with the ledge I was on. That balcony led in turn to a whole new set of obstacles and scalable walls.

I'd crossed over this wider gap several times before.

I sized up the distance as I approached.

I reached the stepping-off point.

And I leaped.

Chapter Thirty-Six

Day Five

Climbing and freerunning for over an hour, I felt exhilarated. As always it cleared my head and opened my mind to all kinds of mental stimuli about the case I was working on.

Will had requested we all be at the UCU offices at 8 a.m.

As we arrived, he thanked us all for our efforts so far. The disappearance of the children from the SafePlace Retreat had been a massive emotional shock to us all. We moved to the chairs that were ringed in a semi-circle around Will's desk.

I felt a secret surge of excitement as my eyes met John's. He smiled. I returned the smile but just as quickly refocused my attention on the meeting.

Zach pulled up a chair for me but I remained standing. Arms folded across my chest, I shifted my weight from one foot to the other.

"We've got a fair bit to get through," Will said to the team.

"Before we get into it," I said, "could we get the police officer who was at the First Accord Bank on the phone."

"Wouldn't it be better to meet with him after this, in person?"

"No need. I only have one question for him."

I threw Will a determined look as he said, "Okay," raising his eyebrow as he made the call. I knew he'd learned to allow me some leeway when I was playing one of my hunches.

"You're in luck, he's on duty at the precinct this morning." He handed me the phone.

I raised the phone to my ear and introduced myself. "Could you tell me what business you had in the bank yesterday afternoon?"

I listened to his response, said, "Thank you, just clarifying a few points," and then handed the phone back to Will.

"What did he say?"

"You've definitely piqued my interest," Zach said.

"The officer's shift finished at 3 p.m. It was his two-week payday. He was at the bank to withdraw some personal operating cash."

"Let me guess," Will said. "He follows the same routine every second week, same branch, same time."

"And you think the Piper knew this?" Marcia said.

"I didn't think it was coincidence and now we know," I said. "Barbara Gauchi was instructed to be at that bank at precisely that time. The Piper knew she'd encounter the officer and expected she'd tell him what was going on. As a result, the Piper anticipated we'd be with Barbara when she received his instructions about going to King Street Station."

"He wanted us to go after him in that tunnel," Will said.

I breathed in and out slowly. My mind was racing. A wisp of hair had fallen across my cheek and I brushed it aside. "He planned this all along. He wanted us to chase him and be stunned by his disappearance. He'd already studied the station's archived construction plans and knew how to vanish. Just as he knew the routine of the park rangers when they happened upon Dietmar."

"And he knew we'd be in the forest when Berthold and Anna were found," Zach said.

My gaze swept over the others with a piercing intensity. "He's just getting started. That's the reason for the message he had Barbara relay to the world, *tell them the Ratcatcher is coming to expose them.*"

* * *

"Okay, let's run through what we've learned," Will said. "First up, Bethany Gauchi. She was dropped off yesterday morning at the school, as she is every day. Unknown to her mother, Bethany always walks around the corner to a local shop where she buys sweets and meets up with friends. There's CCTV at the school gates and also outside the shop."

"But not along the street in between," I guessed.

"No. I've pulled the CCTV. We can see Bethany heading off but of course, she doesn't appear on the corresponding footage outside the shop." ⎯

"Once again," Zach said, "the Piper knew the routine, and he knew where the camera blind spot was."

"I've had the building and renovation plans for King Street Station sent over." Will tapped on the keyboard and projected the plans to the screen on the wall. "The station was built in 1906. It's been through many restoration projects. These blueprints show some of the now disused and out-of-the-way tunnels, walkways, and workspaces." He moved closer to the large screen, pointing out the place that housed the tunnel where the Piper had been. "There's a latched doorway in the sidewall at the center of the tunnel. It leads to an abandoned electrical supply area. That room sits directly beneath a disused workers area."

"So the Piper accessed that doorway and then climbed a ladder to the area above." Zach adjusted his glasses as he leaned in for a closer look.

"I expect that doorway is flush with the wall," I said, "making it impossible for us to notice it in the dark."

"We would've needed to know, in advance, that it was there," Will said.

I summarized the points. "So the Piper knows where the public and private security cams are, and he knew the hidden and abandoned places around the train station. He knew where the children were being kept. He was able to hack the FBI network and to infiltrate a reporter's PC from a rigged website."

Zach let out a low whistle. "Jack-of-all-trades."

I turned my attention to John. "You've documented that all the children exhibited the same sense of disorientation."

He nodded. "That's right."

"And even when we'd managed to get them relaxed, they'd been easily terrified again when talking about their experience."

"And that's completely normal."

"Before you arrived, Zach and Marcia commented on the difficulty of talking with the children."

"Limited vocabulary," Zach explained.

"And once again," John said, "that would be expected of children from the thirteenth century."

"They have nowhere near the word or subject knowledge a modern kid has of today's language," Zach said.

Will was watching me intently. "Where are you going with this?"

"I've looked back over the video of the interviews. I know that none of us, ultimately, got to spend much time with any of the children." The others waited, expectantly, as I paused, collecting my thoughts. "Most of the questions we've asked the children have been about their homes, their parents, and about what happened to them. And their answers have been consistent – the name of their village, the fact they miss their parents, and their experience of following the Piper on a long journey." I looked from one to the other, the thoughts spiraling through my mind. "But ask anything else and their responses were vague, or they simply stared back vacantly. Supposedly because of limited vocabulary. Except, what if that's *not* the reason?"

John picked up on my reasoning. "No matter what, we kept going over the same ground."

"An endless loop," Marcia added. "That's definitely how it seemed."

"Everything we learned from them was repeated and then they struggled to understand anything further." Zach ran his hand through his thick mop of curls, slicking them down only for them to spring back in defiance. "Reinforcing the idea that they're from another time."

"And then they've been whisked away." I snapped my fingers. "Like that! Before we've had a chance to break them free of that loop."

"You were wondering before," Will said, "about Hilde's question to you. She asked if you were the one that would find her parents."

"Yes." I shifted my weight again. I gestured with my right hand to make a point. "When we first met Hilde, I assured her we could help. She accepted this readily. Later, before she was taken, she asked me if I was the one in charge of finding her family. If Hilde is a ten-year-old girl from the thirteenth century–"

John jumped in. "...then she comes from a world where men run things, where men make the decisions, and the womenfolk do the cooking, the cleaning, and the child-rearing."

"The idea of a woman running an investigation and issuing orders," I said, completing the reasoning, "should have been confusing to her."

"But it wasn't," said Zach.

"Instead, she accepted it as though it was a natural thing," I said. "And now that I think of it, so did Anna in our talks with her. It's the first sign we've had, the smallest clue, that they're not from the past. Sorry, Zach, but it's a definite sign that something else is going on, that there's a part of them that's comfortable with the modern way of things."

"There was something," Will said, taking up the point, "that was impeding Hilde's memories, and like the other children, restricting her ability to converse further." He turned to Sanders. "John, I know you didn't get much time with those kids–"

"Not nearly enough. Even so, I'm working up a psychological report from my sessions. I'll have something for you later today. It will include the point Ilona just made, and something else."

"What's that?" I asked.

"It's more to do with this Piper himself. The kids don't seem to know why they followed him, and they don't remember much else. The Piper's behavior itself is very deliberate. He has made brief, self-congratulatory calls to you. He has appeared ghost-like in the night to that elderly man at Port Ludlow. He's appeared briefly and in the dark to Barbara and Bethany Gauchi, and yourselves, in that tunnel. It's as though everything is a tease."

Zach was nodding. "I'm on your wavelength with this. Everything about the Pied Piper in the legend is enigmatic. We don't who he was or where he came from and he vanished into a cave with the children of Hamelin."

Will's impatience flared. "You're both saying the Piper is acting differently to the one of legend?"

"Yes," said John.

"The Piper of legend," said Zach with a burst of enthusiasm, back to his breakneck speed of speaking, "disappeared, making no further contact. But this Piper is the opposite, teasing us, making calls, spreading terror via the media, and now actively kidnapping another child. But this is different, something has changed."

I saw his point. "This kidnap is of a modern-day, American kid. Not medieval, not German-speaking. And this is a kidnap for a ransom."

"Yes. And why the Gauchi family? The Piper of legend was cheated by the townspeople, that's why he lured their children away. But apart from their wealth, why Barbara and Joe Gauchi's daughter?"

I straightened, my gaze intense. "There's another agenda at play."

"Regardless, this fits the profile of a modern-day serial kidnapper and psychopath," Marcia added. "It's as though he's deliberately *not* trying to fool us into believing the myth."

"He's playing games with us," I said, "because we're not the ones he intended to fool."

Marcia shot me a questioning look. "So who is?"

"Everyone else. The media and the general public. The people out there with kids who could become his next targets. They're the ones he's scaring with the vigilante-like threat of someone otherworldly. He wanted everyone with something to hide to hear the anti-corruption message he forced Barbara to relay, all the while taunting us with a cat-and-mouse game."

Will's phone rang. He answered it, his face hardening as he listened. As he ended the call, he said to us, "It's happened again."

Chapter Thirty-Seven

The CEO of Seattle's leading construction firm accessed his internet banking account. He made a direct deposit to the account number he'd been given on the phone.

From his days as a star quarterback on his college football team and his rise through the ranks of the company, Ed Beatty had always been in control. Always super confident, always the winner.

This was the first time he'd felt as though he had no control over a situation. None at all.

Hands shaking, the CEO adjusted his tie and walked out to the waiting media throng in the lobby. An hour earlier, he'd instructed his secretary to arrange a news conference.

'I have a major announcement to make,' was the message he'd sent to the financial reporters, 'and it involves Congressman Joe Gauchi.'

Reading from a prepared statement, Beatty said, "I have a brief announcement, and I will not be taking any questions. Over the past five years, my company has made bribes to several congressmen, including Joe Gauchi. These resulted in my company winning major government tenders." He ignored the eruption of voices that fired questions. "I am solely responsible for these actions. None of the officers in my firm knew of these transactions."

"Does the congressman know you are making this announcement?" one of the reporters called out.

Sweat broke out on the CEO's brow. Taking a moment, he wiped his forehead with a handkerchief. "I must also inform you that earlier today I received a call to say that my four-year-old son had been taken from a public playground. This happened in a split second while his babysitter was talking with another sitter on the nearby park bench."

"Who phoned you?" another reporter shouted as the babble of voices increased.

"I was given two hours to arrange this conference, pay a ransom, and make this announcement." His voice choked. "I pray my boy will be returned."

"Where is your wife?" one of the reporters asked.

"Was your boy taken by the Piper?" another shouted.

Beatty stood frozen to the spot, staring at the huddle of newsmen and women, until his deputy and his secretary shuffled him away from the clicking cameras and out of the room.

Back in his spacious office, his phone rang. His secretary answered it, and then handed him the receiver, saying, "It's your wife."

The construction chief spoke briefly with her. After ending the call, he said, "My boy is back home."

The deputy CEO confronted him. "Switchboard has lit up with calls from the shareholders," he said. "Ed, is this business about the bribes true?"

The phone was ringing again and the secretary took the call and then turned to face her boss. "The FBI is here to see you."

* * *

Quickly ending the team meeting, and before driving across town with me, Will had a brief word with Zoe. "I need everything there is to know about the Gauchi and Beatty families asap. Can Themis fast-track that?"

"Every new piece of information on this case is fed into the system," Zoe said, "so it will already be compiling those details. We'll have a full report by the time you're back."

In the car, Will said to me, "We have one thing the Piper doesn't know about, one thing he couldn't have foreseen."

"Themis."

"Yes."

"You came back here from DC to head this up," I said, voicing something that had been in the back of my mind. "Why Seattle?"

"Zoe's hometown. She developed Themis here and the UCU project was put together around that. I wanted to come back and you and Marcia are based here." He took a breath, pondering another point. "And–"

I was ahead of him. "And back at head office, the DC bosses would be breathing down your neck." Will liked his autonomy.

"You got it." He pulled the car into a parking space. "So it was Seattle for now, for this trial."

As we were led into the construction boss's office, we were confronted by a broken man. He told us what we already suspected about the ransom call he'd received. A replay in many ways of the account Barbara Gauchi had given us. Just as Barbara had been instructed to front a news conference and admit something secret, so had Ed Beatty. But Beatty's reveal had been something criminal and he'd also been instructed to tell the reporters that his boy had been kidnapped. It seemed the Piper was building his campaign of fear step by step, unveiling a little more each time. I recalled the message Barbara had been ordered to convey. *Tell them the Ratcatcher is coming to expose them.*

From there we traveled to the Beatty home, where we interviewed Beatty's wife and the couple's four-year-old son, Timmy.

The boy had been left at the door. His mother had only learned of her son's abduction minutes before. She'd just returned from a visit to her sick mother and had immediately phoned her husband. The boy's visit to the park with his sitter was part of a routine.

As I expected, the young boy was not able to furnish us with very much in the way of details.

He didn't know where he'd been but it had been "yucky dark." He described the man he'd been with as "scary and he played a song with a stick."

"That's called a pipe, honey," his mother said.

"Why did you follow the man?" I asked.

The boy shrugged.

I tried another tack. "Did you follow him when you heard his music?"

"No," the child said. "He near the tree. He waved to me."

"And then what happened, sweetie? Did he take you by the hand and take you somewhere?"

"Yes," the boy said.

On the drive back to the Bureau office, I said to Will, "Different MO this time. The child wasn't following him because of a tune being played."

"Wasn't any need with a kid that age," Will said. "He only had to gently lead the boy away when the babysitter was distracted. We'll check out the park but it seems the tree the boy described was only steps away from a tree-lined path that immediately obscured the view."

"Once again the Piper knew the family routine, knew exactly when and where to make his move."

As we entered the UCU, it struck me that Zoe Marshall was in her element at the Themis console, her eyes and her fingers darting across the multiple screens and keyboards, her street-smart appearance a stark contrast to the high-tech environment. I wondered briefly what Zoe's story was. What had motivated a young woman like her to create crime-fighting software like Themis?

Zoe rose excitedly from her chair when she saw us enter the room. "Themis has accessed everything on the backgrounds of those families."

"It's found a connection?" asked Will.

"Not directly between the families. Both the Beatty and Gauchi men are directors of investment firms. Not the same firm, but both firms have one thing in common. A financial stake in a fruit orchard called Rain Glow, in Yakima County."

"What do we know about Rain Glow?"

"The orchard provides job opportunities to the unemployed, and for young adults needing work experience. Seems legit."

I turned to Will. "It's the slightest of connections, but it's the only link between Gauchi and Beatty."

"Yeah, and you're thinking what I'm thinking."

"We need to pay that orchard a visit," I said.

Chapter Thirty-Eight

The Rain Glow Orchard had been in the Weatherby family for three generations and would soon pass to the fourth. The current owner, Bill Weatherby, was a man in his sixties, a farmer with a laconic manner and a laid-back drawl. A widower, he ran the farm with his two sons. I scrolled through the Themis document on my phone. I filled Will in on the details as he drove for the two-and-a-quarter hours along the I-90E to Yakima.

I'd called ahead and Weatherby had said to drive in and straight up to the homestead.

As we drove through the front gates of the two-thousand-acre property, I gazed out on a peaceful green landscape. The horizon was a sweeping vista of rolling hills. The Weatherby orchard was a mix of modern and traditional. The vast area surrounding the homestead was lush with short grassland and rows and rows of closely planted, low-growing trees. Further afield, the density of the trees was sparser, the fields dotted with wildflowers and a cluster of cottages.

The Rain Glow Orchard grew apples, cherries, pears, and an assortment of berries.

I saw fruit-pickers working along the nearby grove of trees as we walked up to the front door.

Weatherby ushered us into his office at the front of the homestead and Will explained the reason for our visit.

"I don't know either of those men personally," Weatherby said, "but of course, I know the names. They're directors of investment firms that have a financial interest in our orchard."

"So your orchard is partly funded by investors and partly by financial contributions from community supporters?" Will asked.

"That's right."

"An unusual configuration for an orchard."

"Not really," said Weatherby. "When you think about it, most educational institutions and research organizations function in the same way. We're a commercial farm for sure, but we also provide work to the unskilled and unemployed during our busy seasons. We give them lodgings while they're here. That's the community care aspect that attracts financial donations. As for the other investors, they're purely interested in profits, nothing more. That's the nature of the corporate mind, I guess." He grinned.

"And you're not aware of any link between the Gauchis and the Beattys that could bring about the kidnap and ransom ordeals they've experienced?" Will asked.

"No idea about that. Way outside my area of knowledge or understanding. I must say, though, it does seem like a strange coincidence." The farmer leaned forward, a serious expression etched into craggy features, his voice lowering a tone. "My concern, Agent McCord, is that any mention of this unrelated matter will create unnecessary suspicion of the orchard."

"Understood," said Will. "You wouldn't want it to hurt the financial donations."

"Or the business we do with our fruit buyers."

"Do all of your workers have lodgings on the property?" I asked.

"It varies. Not all, because we have a few shorter-term contractors from time to time. At our busiest periods of the year, we have up to one hundred and fifty workers. Around eighty or ninety of those live in the cottages at the rear of the property. No rent. The lodgings form part of their pay."

"Some of the workers are immigrants?" I asked.

A cloud crossed Weatherby's eyes. "I hope you're not implying anything there, Agent," he said. "Yes, they are. And the immigration auditors have sighted and approved all the documentation the workers provide."

"Perhaps if we could have a word with a few of them?" I was aware of the concerned look that Will shot me as I pressed the point with the farm owner.

"I can assure you the workers know nothing of the commercial aspects of the orchard," Weatherby said. "And speaking with them will only cause them alarm. These are simple, hard-working families who mind their own business."

Will rose to leave. He extended his hand to the farmer. "Thank you for your time. We are committed to investigating every piece of information on this case, however small. So let me assure you the FBI appreciates you answering our queries."

Weatherby's manner lightened as he shook Will's hand. "I only wish I had some information that was of use to you," he said.

* * *

From the parking space outside the homestead, I looked across to the small group of workers in the field. One of them, standing a little to the side, was a woman in her thirties, staring back at me with wide, fearful eyes. "I need to go and talk to that woman."

Will shot me a stern look. "We don't have probable cause to advance further on private property—"

"You're the boss, I'm the disobedient agent," I shot back, "and I'm done with protocols." Before he could respond further, I was marching across the green space.

The female worker, Mexican in appearance, didn't move. She froze to the spot, visibly shaking.

"Hello," I called as I approached. "Would you mind if I had a word with you?"

The woman didn't reply at first. She just stared as I reached her.

"Is something wrong?" I asked.

"Please not take my boy," the woman said. "Please, ma'am."

"I'm not here to take anyone. Why would you think that?"

"You no Immigration?" the woman asked.

"No. I'm nothing to do with Immigration or Homeland Security and I only want to ask you a question. Would that be okay?"

The woman stared, eyes wider than before, saying nothing.

She's petrified, I thought. "Can you tell me what's bothering you, miss?" I made certain my tone was non-threatening.

"A friend from Mexico call me for the first time in a long time. She hear I come here for this job, she tell me to leave straight away. She said she also work here once, came here with her family."

"Go on," I prompted.

"She tell me government people raid property, deport her and her husband but they separate them from her child. She not see her child again." The woman burst into tears. "Please, I will leave, please not take my boy."

I placed my hand on the woman's arm. "I'm not here to take your boy."

Will came up beside me. "Ilona, the manager is watching and he'd have grounds to file an official complaint. We need to leave. Now."

"I can guarantee he won't be making any complaints," I said to him. I spoke again to the woman. "Thank you for talking to me." I turned to leave.

"Can you help? Please?" the woman pleaded.

"Yes," I said, "I promise you I will do everything in my power to help you."

Will and I walked back across the field to the car. "You think they're illegals?" he guessed.

"Yes, and something very strange has been going on here."

Back in Seattle, I spent over an hour on the phone, calling all the federal agencies involved in immigration, customs, and border protection.

I strode into Will's office.

He was getting off the phone, a fan of papers spread across his desk. He knew I had been checking on deportations and he was expecting me. "What's the verdict?"

"There have never been any immigration raids at the Rain Glow Orchard," I said.

∗ ∗ ∗

Will spent ten minutes in an in-depth conversation with the US Immigration and Customs Enforcement (ICE) director.

I waited, listening to Will's side of the discussion.

As he ended the call, I said, "I'd love to be able to see Weatherby's face when ICE agents raid his orchard."

"The director over there is keen to follow up on this," Will said. "They're getting an application for a search warrant before a judge within the hour. But it's shaky ground. You spoke with that fruit picker without the property owner's permission."

"She was within sight as we returned to our car and there's no law to having a conversation. She offered the information that there'd been deportation raids there. Fake raids, as it turns out."

"Let's hope the judge sees it that way. At the very least, it helps that two of the Piper's kidnap victims are from families that have a financial link to the orchard."

"We need to know if there's a deeper connection."

"It also means we need to talk with the Gauchis and the Beattys again."

"Yes," I said. "But we should wait until ICE does its thing, Will. We don't want Ed Beatty or the Gauchis getting wind of our suspicions and contacting Weatherby."

He shifted in his chair. His strong jaw jutted out as it always did when he faced a challenge and was determined to meet it head-on. "Agreed. In the meantime, there's something else we need to look at."

"What have you got?"

"The agents in Poulsbo have completed a comprehensive sweep for bugs." In the palm of his hand, Will revealed a couple of tiny transmitters. "They sent these over this morning while we were out at Yakima."

The first thing I noticed was that they weren't metal.

"Coated with rubber, the center hollowed out so there's minimal metal," Will said. "Specially manufactured to avoid detection."

"But the agency does a regular sweep for bugs. They would have detected the electronic impulses."

"These bugs are wired to operate on a low-frequency modulation," Will explained. "They were planted in or near electronic office equipment which unintentionally hides the micro-vibrations of the bugs. All pretty standard, I know, when it comes to professional spyware operations. But we also believe these transmitters were dormant as well at the time of the last regular sweep."

"Dormant?"

"If they'd been remotely activated in the last week or so, after the last sweep, then that would further explain how we didn't know they were there."

"So, they've been planted at some point in the past and then remotely activated to time in with our arrival."

"Exactly. And planted, I expect, at the same time that the USB was switched by someone in the office."

"I guess it explains how the Piper knew what we were doing."

"Which brings us to the question of *who*," Will said. "An internal investigation will be underway overnight into the agents stationed at Poulsbo. But they are all long-term agents and there's no reason for any of them to be under any suspicion."

"Visitors have always been required to sign in at the front desk," I said.

"Yes. I've just been on the line with the agency head over there. I asked her to look back at the signatures for the past six months, for starters. And I had her read through them for me."

"That would've taken a while."

"Tell me about it." Will winced. "It's the one thing they haven't digitized yet. But short of her scanning all the pages and emailing them, the phone was the quickest way to deal with it straight away."

"You found something?"

"Visiting agents, witnesses, servicemen. The usual. But there was one name that I didn't expect to hear."

"Who?"

"Three months ago," Will said, "Dr. Bernard Reinholdt paid his first-ever visit to the Poulsbo Agency."

"That's not unusual," I countered. "He is — *was* — a consultant."

"Reason for the visit was to interview and analyze a witness on a local case. He had a colleague with him, a young woman. She was part of a mentoring program the professor was involved with. I'm having her checked out but the name doesn't ring any alarm bells. I decided to call the professor for further clarification."

"Good thinking, but the professor—"

"Is on a European trip, I know. Which brings me to the next part. I couldn't raise him on the phone. I had an agent double-check on his travel arrangements, wondered if I could track him down another way."

"And?"

Will's reply unnerved me. "There are no flight reservations for Bernard Reinholdt or his wife. They never left the country to board their cruise in Rome. We're checking whether they even had cruise bookings."

I stared back at him, a tightness constricting my throat. "There has to be some mistake."

Will's phone rang. He answered, listened to the caller, thanked them, and then rang off. "Those were the agents I sent out to Reinholdt's home. No one there."

His eyes connected with me and we were silent for a moment, the information hanging between us, making no sense.

Chapter Thirty-Nine

John and Zach had remained at the Seattle Field Office during the day. They carried out research and John discussed the case with Marcia and Zoe. Half an hour after Will and I returned, we all reconvened in Will's office for another catch-up.

Will brought the others up to date on the visit to the Rain Glow Orchard.

I noticed that Zach was on the edge of his seat, leaning forward, restless. "What have you got, Zach?" I said.

"We've been going over the talks that we all had with the children, focusing on their consistency. They were in a group, following the Piper, they entered a cave."

"We know all that, but go on," said Will.

"They all refer to their long journey, at some point, as climbing or going up a steep rise. Whatever else is going on, I believe there's some truth in their memories of that experience."

"There are hills and mountains throughout the forest where they were found," John said.

I nodded, adding, "And they disappeared from the SafePlace Retreat near the region of that same forest."

Will considered this with unblinking focus. "They've been in the National Forest all along."

"Following this stranger," said Zoe, "trekking up and down hills and at a specific time, hiking to the cave."

"The forest that surrounds the national park covers over six hundred and twenty-eight thousand acres," Marcia pointed out. "That's a lot of hills and gullies."

"Plenty of hiding places," Zach said. "So how do we find those kids out there? They're needles in one of the world's biggest haystacks."

"There's no easy way," Will said. "But we need to be ready for when the Piper makes his next move. I'll get surveillance on major entry and exit points."

"We still need to discover exactly who these children are," I said. "Someone has to be missing them."

"Dietmar and the others didn't speak any English and they had limited German, so what is their natural language?" Zoe was responding to me and thinking out loud at the same time. "What should we be looking for? Maybe German kids, who've only been in the country a short time?"

"Or children whose first language is something else, and who have learned some German as a second language," Zach suggested.

"We'll have to start with a wider search parameter than I'd like," I instructed, "a search for all children in Washington who are learning the German language. We can expand it later to other states if we need to."

The others nodded their agreement.

Zoe was already typing commands on her keyboard. "I'll run a search of all German language teaching institutions and draw up a student list."

* * *

As the briefing finished, Marcia zipped into the kitchen and returned with a tray of cupcakes and coffee. She insisted we could all afford just ten minutes for refreshments, and to relax and recharge before diving back into our respective roles and then finishing up for the day. Thank God for Marcia.

"As always, you make perfect sense," I said by way of support.

As she leaned back in her chair for a moment's relaxation, Zoe threw me a look that was equal parts cheeky and enigmatic. "You know, I didn't expect the professor would recognize me and it seems I was right."

Zach tilted his head, looking at her. "Recognize you? Should I?" His face wrinkled with curiosity.

"I attended your lectures, both in history and science more than a few years ago now," she told him.

Zach shifted the glasses on his face as he appraised her. "I thought the name was familiar." He flashed her a grin, a glint of recognition in his eyes. "And it is. But you're a lot more than just a former student. You're *the* former student who made a name for herself creating a video game, and later started the Virtour company that was sold for—"

"A few dollars."

Zach laughed. "Is that what you call a few dollars?"

"That's all in the past."

"You're too young to have a past," Marcia insisted.

"*The* Zoe Marshall. Seattle Young Entrepreneur of the Year," Zach said. "I remember reading about Virtour. A 3D virtual tour online of several different aspects of half a dozen major US cities. You could select to take a guided look at the restaurant scene in New York, the tourist monuments in Washington DC, or the high-end boutiques in Los Angeles. Dozens of choices. I loved it. You sold up and said you were going into law enforcement. New direction. Wanted to contribute to the nation." He took a breath, nervously fiddling with the glasses. "Sorry. Speaking at light speed again."

"I can keep up."

"I can't," I said.

Zach's attention was still on Zoe. "So you ended up here, at the FBI."

"Doing my bit."

"So what *is* your role here?"

Zoe stole a subversive glance in my direction. I shook my head, my eyes relaying my message. *No.* Only the directors, along with Will, Marcia, and I had been briefed on Themis. Perhaps, if Zach Silverstein became a permanent consultant to the UCU…

"Back-room cyber stuff. Bits and pieces. Or perhaps I should say bytes and pixels."

Zach grinned. "Sense of humor too. I like it."

"I've read your book," Zoe said. "I went to the launch."

Zach blushed. "You're a fan."

"I wouldn't say that," she shot back.

I suppressed a grin. I knew that Zoe had been referred to as 'nothing if not direct.'

"I follow all sorts of things," Zoe said. "I'm no conspiracy theorist, but the pushing the scientific boundaries stuff, I'm into that."

"Good to know."

"Sorry, anyway, that this case hasn't stacked up in terms of proving the Pied Piper was real and that he's still lurking around today."

"There'll be other cases for proving some of those theories. Right now, this one's looking more and more like a modern-day psycho using the legends of old for his own twisted purposes."

"And you would *not* like that," Zoe said.

"Not one little bit."

I had noticed Will's mind seemed to be somewhere else during this. Now he interrupted. "Marcia, I want to pick your brain about language. And believe it or not, Zach, that crazy brain of yours as well."

"Not sure whether to be insulted or gratified," Zach said.

Zoe chuckled. "Maybe both."

Will waved away the deadpan response from both of them. "Something's rattling around in the back of my mind, given what we were just discussing. If the children were to be taught key phrases and basic words in another language, how quickly could that be done? Months?"

"It's possible," Marcia replied, "but learning a second language is a tricky thing. There's a wide variant based on age, number of hours per day of learning, or actual round-the-clock immersion in the language."

"Can you elaborate?" I asked.

"There are several stages of second-language learning, the most basic being what educators call elementary proficiency. That level enables you to use key phrases for things such as travel. Next is limited working proficiency."

"And what does that enable?" Will asked.

"Routine social and work-related comments or answers."

"These children had a very limited vocabulary. How would you rate their skill?"

Marcia thought on this for a moment. "Somewhere around limited working proficiency."

"Then it means they had to have been learning the language for a long time to give us the responses they did," I said.

"And keep in mind," Zoe added, "that even for basic fluency, researchers state that four hundred and eighty hours of learning would be required. Divide that into, say, six hours per day, five days a week, and that alone is several months of nothing else but learning the language."

The others fixed her with surprised looks but I was quickly learning not to be surprised by her. "I read up on a lot of diverse subjects," she said by way of explanation.

"What if they were only taught specific answers to specific questions?" Will asked. "What's the most efficient way to learn that sort of thing quickly?"

"It's generally believed the younger the child, the easier for them to learn a language," Zach said. "Far more so than adults. And repetition is the key."

"As in learning the times tables?"

"Exactly. Rhyming and reading the same set of information over and over, whether it be the times tables, the alphabet, or the words to an anthem."

"What about learning to speak with an accent or a specific dialect?"

"Same sort of thing," Zach offered. "Although speaking with a Middle-Ages dialect is not an exact science. We don't *really* know how speech sounded in ancient times because there are no recordings."

* * *

Will had taken a leaf from Ilona's playbook, drawing on the prof's knowledge to illustrate what was possible and what was improbable. Ilona reasoned that this approach would help determine the direction the investigation should take. Perhaps she was on the money regarding Silverstein being every bit the perfect devil's advocate for that.

If this medieval German was not the children's first language, then the time required to instruct them was unrealistic. And the purpose of such a thing was even more mystifying, especially as the children hadn't been identified and hadn't been reported missing.

Time to switch off for tonight, Will told himself. He was sticking a few papers in his briefcase, powering down his computer, getting ready to leave.

He held his smartphone in his hand and thought about calling Ilona. She'd left before him and was probably back home by now. He could suggest grabbing a meal, talking over the day's trip to the orchard.

He reminded himself they were both tired, and the time for re-establishing anything with her was best left until this case was closed.

His mind flashed to the moment he'd seen Ilona and Sanders, talking and drinking wine on the beach. He pushed the memory away. Will wasn't going to lose her to someone else, not without attempting to draw her closer to him again. Everyone deserved at least one chance to revisit a past regret and to set it right, didn't they? He knew Ilona and he knew that, like him, she would be one hundred percent focused on this case until it was resolved. When that time came, he hoped she would be able to find it within herself to be open to what he had to say.

Frustration gnawed at him. He could only wish for this case to end sooner rather than later. He slipped the phone back into his trouser pocket and headed home.

Chapter Forty

It had been another long day but regardless, as I headed out of the office, I hoped to receive a call from John.

I was also feeling another overwhelming desire to scale the city heights and swing from its lofty edges.

Driving home, I passed the internet café where I sometimes read the urban climbing blogs. Anonymously. On an impulse, I decided to indulge myself for a half-hour.

The café was in a shopping mall. I parked in the underground parking station. Once inside the café, I took a cubicle, fired up a machine, and browsed the site I frequented the most.

My eyes wandered to the latest series of posts and I stifled a gasp in disbelief. One of them was from a user calling himself Outsider.

> *A warning to all of the genuine users on this site.*
> *One of the climbers out there is not who they appear*
> *to be. They are law enforcement.*

Not something I'd ever expected to see. My nerve ends tightened and I felt my heart pounding in my chest. Another poster had replied.

> *'Is this for real?'*
> *'Very real. Watch your backs.'*

'You need to tell us more.'
'I have photos.'
'Post them.'
'Not in your best interests to let the imposter see them. They could be reading this.'
'Who is it? Who do they work for?'
'I have photos I will give to one of you. Just one of you. That person can then distribute the photos privately to climbers they know and trust. You will then know who to look out for when you're up there doing what you love.'
'Who are you?'
'Someone who appreciates alternative lifestyles and who watches out for those who live them.'
'How do you know they're law enforcement?'
'I make it my business. Believe me, I know more than you could possibly imagine.'

Then a user named StarX had intervened.

'You can send me the photos in a private message.'
'How would I know you're not the imposter unless I can see you? I would need to hand them over personally.'
'Then I will meet you.'
'That can be arranged. Check back here later for details.'

I drew in a ragged breath. Was this mystery user talking about me? Or someone else? Did Detective Radner have an undercover climber out there that I didn't know about? But if not, and this Outsider was referring to me, then he knew I was both an agent and a climber. How? The only possible explanation was that someone had been following me and had discovered my secret.

I clicked on Outsider's profile. No details. The avatar was a large, enquiring eye. Someone watching?

* * *

I reached for my phone and called Detective Radner. "I thought I'd take a look at that footage you've been compiling."

"I'm on shift tomorrow," Radner said, "but aren't you preoccupied with this Piper case? It seems to be escalating by the hour in the media."

"Yes, which is why I think a short breather looking at something else, on my own time, would be good for me."

"You call having a breather lending a hand on someone else's case?"

"Therapeutic." What I really wanted was to see if I could detect any of the climbers carrying or concealing a tiny camera. And whether Radner might reveal anything to me about having an undercover man out there.

"I don't know whether you're serious or you're joking. Knowing you, I'm thinking it's both."

"I've got some free time this evening?"

He chuckled. "You don't muck around."

"If it's inconvenient–"

"I can spare an hour. I'll meet you over there."

When I arrived, Radner took me through to the op room where a tech officer was running the CCTV footage. "This is an edit of the runners or climbers captured on video over the past few months," the officer said.

"Have there been many?"

"Not a big number. Four different ones that we've picked up on, including our angel of mercy," said Radner.

"Show me the other three."

The tech officer pulled up a sequence of specific time frames and ran the video.

I focused. Three very athletic climbers, no heavy gear, just sweatpants and hoodies. "Can you freeze images of those three and blow them up?"

"I can try," said the operator, "though the quality is poor."

He zeroed in and enlarged twice. The image quality deteriorated further each time but regardless there were no packages or shapes attached to, or bulging from beneath, the climbers' clothes. Of course, it was likely Outsider wasn't an urban climber, and he could have taken his photos from the ground or a window.

Radner looked at me with sudden, sharp interest. "You seem to be looking for something specific. Something I don't know about?"

"No, I just wanted to see the CCTV you've compiled, stay up to date for when I can get back to helping out." I flashed a smile at Radner but the expression on his face alerted me that he wasn't completely convinced. "The whole climber thing has been playing on my mind, ever since I was called in to talk down that suicide climber. I want to help clear up this dangerous fad."

His expression was solemn. "Believe me, I know what you mean."

"Of course you do." The empathy in my voice was genuine. I hated having to lie but right now, I needed to cut this short and there was no indication from Radner that he had anything else going on, such as an undercover man in the field. "Got to go, Detective, I'm due at a meeting."

"At this hour? I thought you were taking a breather."

"So did I."

Radner nodded as I waved and left.

I had to keep my eye on that site, for when Outsider was back online. Anxiety coursed through me at the possibility that photos of me would be put in the hands of urban climbers and that I could be identified.

I would have to hang around the internet café. And when it closed? I didn't like the idea but I may have to resort to accessing the climber site from my phone.

My cell rang. John Sanders.

I answered it. "Hi."

"Hungry?"

I wanted to grab dinner with him but at the same time, I had to monitor this Outsider situation. "Hungry and tired. Maybe not the best night. Hell of a long day."

"I hear you. Get some sleep. But no excuses tomorrow night."

"Deal." I rang off. I had almost reached my car, in the parking station near the police precinct, when, from the corner of my eye, I caught a glimpse of movement. I turned toward it, looking across to the far end of the space.

I wasn't certain but I thought I'd seen a blur, something darting behind the pylon.

Ever since my teenage self climbed out of that tunnel, I had experienced a heightened sense of sudden movements at the periphery of my vision. If I was ever being followed, I wanted to sense it. I was never going to be prey for a kidnapper. *Ever. Again.*

I moved cautiously toward the pylon, drawing my weapon as I did. Was I being paranoid? *Has this case got me jumping at shadows?*

Or was this the person who had been watching and photographing me?

I put my back against the pylon wall and then, aim at the ready, I whirled around the corner.

Empty space.

And then I heard the bang of the exit door which was just out of sight.

I raced to the exit, flung open the door, and peered in. Coast clear. I ran down the stairs and out onto the street.

Whoever had been here, they were gone now into the deeper, wider shadows of the city.

* * *

It was a short drive over to the internet café. The shopping mall was a small complex, most of the other shops closed.

The café was a late-night venue, its parking lot even smaller and wedged between tall buildings on either side.

I stepped out of my car. My phone buzzed.

This time the incoming call display was the one that sent a chill digging into my spine.

The same deep, muffled voice. The same arrogant tone.

"I enjoyed your press conference. Word of mouth was the original media. It enabled my story to be told over and over. And then came the engravings on church windows, handwritten manuscripts, the Gutenberg printing press, the poets and the storytellers, and oh those wonderful German brothers who included my tale in their collections."

It seemed the Piper was raving and I didn't interrupt.

"Today's media is nothing more than an accelerated extension of all that. Of course, I'm helping it along with my photos, my tip-offs, but then I have always done that, it's simply more obvious with the communications the world now has at its disposal."

"You disappeared at King Street Station because you knew its layout. I don't believe for one moment there's anything otherworldly about you."

"So you say. You think I'm a normal man?"

"I intend to prove it."

"I'm sure you do. But there's another side to you, Agent Farris, deep inside, that doesn't believe that at all. A side of you that knows you're denying all the evidence you have because you don't like its inescapable truth. There will come a time, however, when you will no longer be able to remain in denial. A time when you must face the fact that I am everything I appear to be. And more."

"This is all a game to you," I said. "I can hear that in your voice."

"Is that what you think?"

"Yes. And you're an arrogant player."

"Therefore you think I can be beaten?"

"I will win your pathetic game," I promised.

The Piper sneered. "You haven't even begun to play and you have no idea of the stakes." He ended the call abruptly.

There was something different with this call, I thought.

I phoned Will and filled him in.

"He's boasting," Will said.

"Yes. But there was something else."

"What?"

"An anger that wasn't there before."

Chapter Forty-One

Arriving home, Ellie wondered where Brooke was. Her car wasn't in the driveway so maybe she was still at the office. Or had she gone for a drive to help clear her head? Just for the next day or two, she'd asked Brooke to let her know if she'd be late home, and where she was going to be. But then, had she really expected Brooke – headstrong Brooke – to do that? She tried phoning her but the call went to voicemail.

That was when she heard a muffled female voice, coming from out the front. Distant. "Brooke?" It was like an echo. Someone calling for her sister. She went to the front door and scanned the street. No sign of Brooke or anyone else. She was about to step out when she felt the gust of cold air. She shivered and turned around to grab something warm, catching from the corner of her eye the hooded blue weather jacket Brooke had been wearing the previous evening. It had been left draped over one of the lounge chairs and Ellie pulled it on as she went out and walked across the front garden and onto the sidewalk.

It was quiet, empty, and dark. Had she imagined the voice? Ellie had never felt unsafe here but she felt a sudden chill, not from the cold night air but something else, stirring deep inside her. Something was different, she wasn't sure what, maybe it was simply the imagined voice, if, in fact, it had purely been her imagination, or maybe it was the whispering thrum of strong wind through the trees. She shrugged off the disconcerting feeling and turned, heading back up the garden path to the front door, stepping back inside. And then she heard it again, quite distinct this time, a voice in the distance, muffled, the sound no doubt fragmented by the wind, calling out Brooke's name.

She turned again, this time striding out into the middle of the road, scanning it from one end to the other, taking in the forested reserve opposite and the higher ground at the end of the cul-de-sac beyond which was the bluff. Ghostly shards of light appeared and disappeared as a smattering of clouds drifted across the moon, only serving to heighten the sense of unease that enveloped her. The whisper of the wind rose and fell.

And then she caught a rustle of movement, near the trees alongside the bluff. Was her sister up there? No. Not again. The doctors said Brooke would be okay. *I shouldn't have agreed to her going in to work. But how is she back here, without her car? Who is calling for her?*

She heard the woman's voice again, up ahead. Something familiar. "Brooke?"

Feeling a stab of alarm and biting down on her lip, Ellie ran up the road and onto the clifftop reserve. All of a sudden, she heard music somewhere close. An ethereal sound, floating momentarily in the air like that of the disembodied voice, eerie, and then gone. A pipe? She stiffened, turning toward where she thought the sound had come from. The trees swayed, their trunks silhouetted one moment and faded the next as the hard glint of moonlight came and went.

"Hello, is someone there?"

Nothing. She knew for certain now she hadn't imagined the voice. She moved toward the trees, still concerned that something odd was going on with her sister when she caught another flash of movement in her periphery, and then a body slammed full force into her. She began to topple, and she steadied herself, the form of a coated figure in a crooked hat filling her vision. The Piper? He grabbed hold of her, whirled her about, and in one swift action dragged her toward the cliff.

She gasped for breath, straining, pushing back, drawing on energy from deep within, her mind simultaneously spiraling through a tumult of thoughts. How could this be happening? Why was the Piper here? And that voice, calling out... who else was here?

Her arm felt as though it was being pulled from its socket, her body partly pushed, partly dragged by powerful arms. She managed to twist her body, freeing up her left-hand side, survival mode bolstering her like a mule kick. She swung her left arm, her fingernails searching for a face she couldn't see from her position. She didn't find his face but she clawed at the back of his neck. There was an involuntary loosening of his grip and she seized on that. Wrenching her right arm free, she swung both arms, slamming him in the side of the head and he teetered back. For a moment – just a moment – she sensed panic in her attacker, but then within a heartbeat, his fleeting instant of dread had morphed into something else. Sheer rage.

The Piper lunged and he crashed into her. Pain exploded across the bridge of her nose as his elbow connected with her face. As they both toppled, his hands encircled her head, pile-driving her face into the ground. The stony dirt that lined the edge of the clifftop bit into her face as it hit. She felt the pulse of her heart in her throat, hammering away, and for a second her mind went into whiteout, a limbo of fear and pain and shock and that voice, oddly familiar. Calling for Brooke. Who? And then the world boomed back into focus and she rolled, kicking, struggling, pushing herself back up and landing a punch. He reared back, but then he effortlessly kicked out one leg and then the other, collecting her in the head and the side of her body. He lunged again before she could recover, grasping her already toppling form, and dragging her, like a man possessed, he catapulted her over the edge of the cliff.

Ellie thrust out her arms, tried to grab hold of him, of anything, but there was only empty air, and then she was surrounded by nothing but space, the cliff face soaring by as she fell away. Her head turning as she plunged, she glimpsed a shape beneath her, a stunted tree root protruding from the cliff face. Instinctively, she shot her arms out as her body spun but once again her hands closed around empty air, her memories soaring through her mind just as the world around her became a blur of speed, screaming Brooke's name in her head but she never really knew if anything came from her lips.

Chapter Forty-Two

I returned to the café, head lowered, cap pulled down, and made my way to a cubicle and brought up the urban explorer site.

And there it was, Outsider, naming a meeting spot in the back streets of the city.

> *Go there at midnight tonight and wait. When I'm certain you're not the imposter, and I think it's safe, I'll approach.*

I bit down on the side of my lip. *You won't be the only one watching from afar. Two can play at that game.*

The safest place for such a meeting was on the rooftops but Outsider had specified an alley. Which suggested to me that he wasn't an urban climber.

I checked my watch and headed back to my car. I didn't have long to act.

I would be able to drop in at the Bureau field office on the way. I needed to requisition an RFID tag. A razor-thin filament with an adhesive strip, it could be attached to most items and provide a tracking signal. I wasn't certain what I would be facing but I hoped the tag would prove useful.

I'd always found it intriguing how different the FBI offices were, on those rare occasions I'd gone there in the middle of the night. Devoid of the energy of people. The silence, the darkness. As I left with the tag, I searched my memory for all the urban climbing places I used to frequent.

I needed a place near the meeting point but not clearly visible, where I could park, switch into my climbing gear, and then make my way across the city's roofs.

* * *

The first thing was the focus.

It was the only time when all other thoughts were out of my mind. The only time when I *could* switch off.

My only thought, my only focus, had to be the next movement, and then the one after that. One move flowing into the next.

Stretching out beneath was a vast black emptiness. The city nightscape. Streets and walls and balconies and the dark spaces between.

For each new movement, I had seconds to evaluate the risk. Would the structure I was landing on, or the ledge I was stepping onto, hold my weight? Appearances could be deceptive. At night, every structure, every protrusion, could seem larger or longer, tricks of the lights and the shadows.

Panels of glass and steel and slabs of brick, sloped at varying angles, from forty to ninety degrees. I'd trained my fingers to use friction to cling to walls that had limited indents and crevices, but I was out of practice.

Focus.

Exhilaration was always there, adrenaline was always pumping, a fatal drop always only moments away. But the freedom of the sky was like a tonic that only the meshing of body and soul and the elements and the structures of mankind could deliver.

And then there was the silence. The sounds of the world fell away, mired in the streets far below. Up here there was a solace, a beauty. It looked as though the moon and the stars were within reach. It felt as though I could hold the beams of moonlight in the palm of my outstretched hand.

Tonight, though, I was climbing for a very different purpose.

* * *

From a nearby rooftop, well-concealed in shadow, I focused a set of infrared binoculars on the dead-end alleyway below. I watched as another climber – a young man, fair-skinned, red-haired – descended from the next building. He waited in its corner and despite his fair appearance, he had an edge to him, his sinewy body like a coiled spring ready to snap. I scanned the street on the opposite end of the passageway. The street was empty at this hour and then a black SUV drove in and pulled up a couple of blocks back from the alleyway entrance.

A lone figure – tall, in nondescript casual wear and with a hoodie obscuring his features – stepped from the vehicle. He stood still for a moment, and then raised his own binoculars, scanned the far end of the street, and higher to the roof edges. He moved to the alley entrance, and used the binoculars once again, gazing into the far end of the passage.

Seemingly satisfied, he proceeded into the narrow opening. Reaching the far end, he thrust a package into the hands of the climber. It did not seem to me that any words were spoken. The hooded figure immediately turned and retreated the way he'd come.

I wanted to follow him but I had to do something about the photos.

The narrow passage ran behind the next building. The gap between the two buildings was a short one, a distance I had leaped across many times before. But I had to act fast.

I positioned myself, willed myself into parkour mode, and then I sprinted forward and jumped.

As I anticipated, the red-haired climber avoided street level and was taking flight back the way he'd come. I didn't waste a second. I grabbed the climber by the arm as he clambered up over the edge, pushing him aside and ripping his backpack from him as I did. He yelled out in surprise, but I zipped open the bag, removed the envelope, leaped back across to the next rooftop, and was away.

* * *

Back in my car, I turned onto the street where I'd seen Outsider's vehicle. I figured he had five minutes' start on me but I had to at least follow the same direction and hope it was my lucky night. There were few cars on the road at this late hour, although he could have veered off anywhere by now.

Just a few minutes later I saw the SUV ahead, stopped at traffic lights. I slowed down and pulled over. I couldn't allow myself to be sighted or suspicious of following. When he did continue, he drove just under the speed limit, clearly not wanting to attract attention. Now I wished there were other cars on the road to camouflage my pursuit. I pulled out and hung far enough back to keep him within sight but to appear as no more than an inconspicuous set of headlights.

He was moving through the northern end of Beacon Hill, not far from Rainier Valley. I knew this sector to be largely residential with a small but vital business district peppered with cafés, restaurants, and stores.

I saw the SUV turn into an adjoining street. I cruised past so as not to be obviously tailing him and then killed the lights and reversed to the street corner. I glanced down the street and saw Outsider turn into a driveway.

I drove slowly into the street, reactivating my headlights, and past the Craftsman-style two-story home where the SUV now sat in the driveway, and I made a mental note of the car's license plate.

I turned into the next cross street and pulling over, I slipped two photos from the envelope. It was me. The picture made me identifiable to other climbers from the dark blue sweatsuit but thankfully my face was obscured by my hoodie. The vein in my forehead pulsed when I saw the words scribbled down the vertical edge of one of the pictures.

Ilona Farris. FBI.

A telephoto lens had captured me scaling the wall behind my apartment. Whoever this Outsider was, he'd been stalking me.

I doubled back on foot to the Craftsman-style home. It was a tree-lined street and I found a blind spot beside a tree from which I could observe the house. The darkness helped.

I couldn't stay out here all night. Even if I did, the chances were there'd be nothing useful to see. I went further down the street, crossed the road, and moved stealthily to where the SUV was parked. I slipped the RFID tracker from my pocket and attached it to the underside of the car.

I'd had my phone on silent but felt it vibrating as I got back in my vehicle. I clicked it off silent but it had cut out before I answered. I saw there were three missed calls from Brooke Goodman and two missed calls from Will.

I tapped redial for Will.

"Will, what is it?"

"I'm at the Goodmans' home in Port Townsend. I had a call from Brooke, she couldn't reach you."

"What's happened?"

"Ellie Goodman was found at the base of the cliff here. She's dead."

My voice caught in my throat. *Ellie?*

"Neighbors heard a scream," he told me. "They saw a long-coated figure on the street, in the dark. Zach and Zoe are on their way."

"God, no. The Piper." My hand tightened around my phone.

Chapter Forty-Three

My duffel bag was on the back seat. I changed back into my regular clothing and then drove to the Goodman house. I pulled over to the side of the road and alighted from the car, sighting Zach and Zoe ahead of me. I walked up and onto the bluff. A young woman, slender, bespectacled, came forward offering her hand and I took it. "I'm Louise Carter," the woman said. "A colleague of Brooke's. She called me when... when—"

"I'm glad you could be here with her," I said, pressing past, flanked by Zach and Zoe. Brooke was standing a little further back, draped in a blanket, a policewoman comforting her. I approached and embraced Brooke. "So sorry."

Police vehicles and both a rescue truck and a forensic van stood on the bluff, a scurry of activity taking place, night lights illuminating the scene. I was told that Will and the forensic team had driven one of the roads down to the coastal area, from where they could access the base of the cliff.

One of the police officers came toward us, holding up a clear evidence bag that contained a small object. "We found this by the cliff."

I stepped forward, took the bag from him, and held it aloft, squinting. A rounded, black shape, just four by three inches in size.

"A mini 360-degree Bluetooth speaker," Zoe said, moving alongside me and peering into the bag.

I glanced at Brooke, who was looking on. "Is this yours or Ellie's?"

"No."

I donned gloves, removed the device, activated the sound and a voice boomed from the speaker. "Brooke?"

Brooke became agitated, charging forward without warning and snatching the device, her voice rising. "Ellie's voice."

I placed my hand as gently as I could on Brooke's shoulder, deftly taking the device back. "We need that, Brooke."

"*Her voice—*"

"Yes," I said. "I would say that at some point the Piper got close enough to both of you and used a mini recorder to capture her voice speaking your name."

"What? When?"

"You wouldn't have known it was him. Even so, he would have kept himself out of your line of vision so it could have been anywhere, anytime, maybe in a café or a supermarket."

"Stalking us?"

"Yes."

"There are mini recorders, widely available," Zach informed her, "that have in-built sound amplification. The Piper would not have needed to be too close."

"The voice is so loud."

"Those speakers may be tiny," Zoe said, "but they have a projected surround-sound transmission range of around thirty feet."

"He lured Ellie out," Brooke said, sobbing, her chest heaving, "but why… why is it my name being called?"

"Because it was you the Piper wanted to lure," I said.

"Then why kill Ellie?" Brooke shrieked.

"I'm so sorry, Brooke, but I believe it's because…" I hesitated, despairing of having to say the words. "He thought it was you."

Brooke glared at me, aghast. "She'd thrown on my jacket and hood when she went out there."

"And if you'd worn that on one of those occasions you'd been stalked–"

"That was why he thought he was attacking me." Her shoulders slumped, it was as though all the energy was suddenly sucked from her body, and I put my arms around her. "We need to get you inside."

"I don't understand" – Brooke's voice was hoarse – "why Ellie went out there if it was her own voice she was hearing. She must have suspected something was off…"

"Most of us are unaccustomed to hearing our own voice, played back, and this was distant. Ellie wouldn't have recognized it, not immediately."

We moved toward the house.

Zach said, "He wouldn't have just left that speaker here like that."

"He doesn't know it was dropped," I suggested.

Zach frowned. "But he'll figure it out. You think he'll come back for it?"

"He would never take that chance. Not now. But in the meantime, we can check for fingerprints."

"Isn't the Piper most likely to have worn gloves?" he asked.

"Most likely, but we'll know soon enough."

* * *

Later, inside the house, with the clifftop cordoned off as a crime scene and the body raised from the rocks below and taken away, Zoe, Zach, and I sat with Brooke. Brooke's colleague, Louise, provided tea, more for something to distract her friend, but the cups sat untouched on the dining alcove table.

"She was always there for me," Brooke blurted out, "when I was in trouble she was there. Always there." She choked, her eyes wet from crying. Breathing heavily, she resumed, "But when… when she was in trouble and needed me…"

I reached across, my hand resting on Brooke's shoulder, a gesture that seemed useless in a moment like this but a gesture nonetheless. "This isn't something you can blame yourself for. This wasn't something anyone could foresee." We'd had no indication the Piper knew Brooke's home address or had any further interest in her.

Brooke's voice rose and fell as she sobbed. "Why didn't we?"

I winced. *Because the Piper isn't acting like any other criminal we've profiled.* These weren't thoughts I could put into words for Brooke. Not now. Perhaps not ever. All I could do was offer the hope of justice for Ellie. "We'll do everything we can to get this monster," I assured her.

* * *

As we returned to our cars, I stepped alongside Zoe and said, quietly, "I know we're not back at the office but I wonder if you could do me a favor? I've got a car license number and I need the name of the owner."

"I can work remotely with Themis," Zoe said. "Happy to help."

An hour and twenty minutes later I arrived back at my Seattle apartment and was stepping from my car when my phone buzzed. I answered. "How'd you go?"

"I've got a name for you. Or rather, a small business name."

The name didn't mean anything to me.

Faraday Enterprises.

"Can you run some background?"

"Read your mind," Zoe said. "It's set up as a sole trader, owned by a Dr. David Faraday. Youth counselor. He's been running a practice out of his home for the past several years. Consults with various youth and community care service organizations. Runs life lesson sessions at local schools. He's another alumnus of Seattle University."

"Anything else?"

"Very little. Unmarried. His business is small. I can have Themis dig deeper."

"Do that. Where did he go to school? Where did he grow up? That sort of thing."

"What's this about?" Zoe asked.

I couldn't reveal that Faraday knew my urban climbing secret and was attempting to expose me. I hadn't worked out a cover story and was surprised how quickly, on the spot, I invented one. "I'm helping out Seattle Police Department with something."

"That urban climbing stuff?"

I felt a tightness in my chest. Not a conversation I wanted to have. "Yeah, as you know, Seattle PD is clamping down on illegal climbs on buildings. After being called to that rooftop suicide jumper a few weeks back, I've been lending some assistance with that."

"Yes, I'm aware," said Zoe.

"I viewed some CCTV of a particular climber who was always in certain areas on clear nights."

"You were keeping an eye out yourself."

"Yeah. Saw someone in the same gear who fitted the description, walking late at night near my place."

"You followed him?"

"He was parked nearby. I memorized his car's license plate when he drove off. I can't be certain, though, that it's the same person. Just playing a hunch. Leave it with me, and if necessary, I'll run it by Detective Radner."

* * *

Back in my apartment, I shook off my tiredness to sit at my laptop and run a search for any other blog posts or comments attributed to Outsider. There was nothing on any other urban climber sites. I keyed in several keywords to the search bar and then scrolled through the pages of web links that appeared.

I found just two Outsider comments, both from several months ago, and both on an urban explorer site. Like urban climbing, this kind of exploring was mostly an illegal, underground activity, usually because it involved trespassing. Enthusiasts sought out abandoned and derelict man-made structures, in urban and sometimes rural and wilderness areas. Ruins that were often unstable and dangerous. They almost always posted pictures of the fascinating places into which they ventured.

I read Outsider's comments, posted to another user's gallery of long-disused crypts, warehouses, and asylums. Wandering through these places in the dark was not for the faint-hearted. I was reminded of the shaft in the abandoned nuclear plant where I'd once been held captive. Outsider had posted:

> *Explorers are as free as any soul can be, learning so much more than most people will ever know.*

Who was David Faraday and why had he been watching me? Why did he want to expose my secret?

Chapter Forty-Four

Day Six

Early morning and the group reconvened in the UCU briefing room.

I looked over the forensic scene photos of Ellie's body, a lump in my throat. Ellie wearing Brooke's jacket, the hood pulled over her head. The Piper had done his homework but he hadn't known it wasn't Brooke in the house and hadn't expected Ellie to be wearing that outfit. He'd come back to finish the job after Brooke's suicide was averted. Why did he want Brooke Goodman dead?

The mini speaker was on the all-purpose meeting and planning table. "Is there a chance we can track the buyer, maybe from warranty details?" I asked.

Marcia spoke up. "I can send the serial number to the manufacturer."

"Further to yesterday's events," Will said, "the park rangers and local police are concentrating their patrols on the main entry and exit points to the Olympic National Forest, looking out for anything unusual. We've told them there could be movement by the Piper."

"I've been thinking about your question," Zach said to Will, "about how long it would take a child to learn key German phrases and accents."

"And?" Will pressed.

"We're assuming those kids, not being from Hamelin, are most likely from here in the US, and had to learn German. What if these kids already know the German language and it's English that's foreign to them? If they're actually from Germany?"

Will nodded. "Okay, which leads us to how and why are they here."

"Language and cultural exchange vacations," Zach suggested.

"That would make sense," I said.

John stroked his chin. "You're talking about the exchange programs for families or individuals, where each offers hospitality to the other for extended vacations?"

"Yes, a family can live with a like-minded host family for an authentic language and culture homestay," Zach said. "Kind of like a foreign exchange student, except those are limited to young people aged over fifteen. These family homestay programs don't have that restriction."

"But kids in Germany learn English in school as a second or third language," Will pointed out.

"That's true, so it doesn't fully explain why they didn't know English. However, they're young, and some German kids take English as a third language. At that age, they might not have progressed very far with it, if at all."

"It's a hell of a lot more feasible than the lost kids from Hamelin theory." There was no humor in Will's voice.

Zach shrugged. "It was the Piper's behavior *not* fitting the original character's actions that made me alter my focus. Don't forget I also lecture in criminology. Like you guys, I've been looking at where these kids could be from if not from medieval Hamelin."

I saw that the professor couldn't hide the disappointment on his face but his determination to exhaust all options was exactly the input I'd wanted from him.

I looked at Will. I wanted to say, 'I told you so,' but I held my tongue. This wasn't the time for one-upmanship.

Zoe, accessing the net on her phone, was furiously tapping away. "There's a company called Languature Vacations. It has thousands of registered families that can be put in touch with one another for these shared vacations."

"How many German families are here right now?" I asked.

Zoe keyed in the question and scrolled through the resulting data. "There are more than a dozen currently staying in Washington."

"If these kids' families were being hosted here," Marcia weighed in, "then where are the parents?"

"Only one way to find out," Will said. "Marcia, coordinate with that company and contact all those families being hosted."

Marcia headed out as a call from the head of the Poulsbo Resident Agency came through on Will's phone. He flicked it to speaker mode.

"How did you go with Professor Reinholdt?" I heard the Poulsbo woman ask.

"No luck contacting him," Will said. "And further to that, we've established that neither he nor his wife left on their flight overseas, we haven't located their cruise bookings, nor are they at their home."

"As you know, his visit to the agency here preceded my coming on board. I haven't met him but I understand he's been a trusted consultant. Do you think he's met with foul play?"

"Not sure what to think. We're concerned and I've got a contact alert out on him."

"After we spoke last," the Poulsbo chief said, "I went back and had a look at the names on the signature book on the same day as the professor. There's a notation that one of the visitors was there to meet up with the professor, but of course, that's not evident from the signature column."

"Perhaps it's someone who can·help us contact him. What's the name?"

"A youth counselor. Seems he was getting some mentoring from Reinholdt." I felt my throat constrict as she said, "David Faraday."

"Thanks," Will said, ending the call.

"David Faraday." Zoe glanced at me. "That's the name of the possible urban climber you asked for background on?"

Will whirled around to face me. "What? When?"

"Last night. I followed someone I saw by chance on the street." The lie felt bitter on my tongue but I had to stick to my story. "This person's build and gear matched the description I'd seen on Seattle PD's footage."

"Wow," said Zach. "A link between this guy visiting Reinholdt and the police search for an urban climber."

Will fixed me with a hard stare. "Apparently helped by someone who doesn't follow orders."

I stared back, eyebrow raised. "Meaning?"

From the corner of my eye, I saw Zach gesture to his face, mouthing the words '…that eyebrow thing.'

On this occasion, I might have grinned, but I didn't.

"You told me you were completely focused on the Piper case, no helping out on that climber thing."

"It was my own time. I could have been home, feet up, a glass of wine, watching one of those acronym-titled TV crime shows."

"But you chose to unwind by watching CCTV with the Seattle cops."

I shrugged. "Whatever works, Will."

He conceded the point with a nod. "In this instance, it's thrown up the same name as Reinholdt's visitor at Poulsbo. Good work."

My eyebrow rose further. "Thanks."

"What do we know about him?"

Zoe went over to Will's PC and accessed a photo of a house, with the address stenciled across the top of the image. "This is the home and workplace that he rents. He's a youth counselor. He runs a couple of courses a year in the form of group sessions."

"When?"

"Doesn't specify."

I was still, my eyes on the screen. My breath caught in my throat. This wasn't the house I'd followed Outsider to, in Beacon Hill. This was further south, in New Holly. The previous night, Zoe had only accessed a company name and the name of its owner, from the motor registrations. She had no way of knowing that the rental address she'd found for David Faraday differed from the one to which I had secretly followed the man in the hoodie. Was the identity of Outsider someone else, not Faraday, someone driving Faraday's SUV when I'd followed? Either way, it wasn't something I could raise with the team, not without exposing the true manner in which I'd come across the license plate.

"Okay, we need to check him out further and obtain a list of his clients," Will said. "The medical records might be private but we can petition a judge to have them released. First, though, we visit this guy and see if he's prepared to assist."

"I wouldn't pretend to know every counselor and medical practitioner in the city," John said, "but as a psychologist, I'd recognize the name of a Seattle business that's counseling young people."

"And you haven't heard of him?" Will asked.

"No."

Marcia strode back in. "Okay, I've checked out the Bluetooth speaker but there was no warranty taken out, so no buyer details. And word's in from forensics. No fingerprints."

"Nothing at all we can go on?" I asked.

"Not with the serial number, not with a small, low-cost item like this. But the manufacturer has a sophisticated product distribution network and can track the product's batch number. They can pinpoint that batch as being distributed to retailers in and around the Rainier Valley area."

The surprise registered on all our faces. The same area as the New Holly address of David Faraday.

And, known only to me, also close to the area to which I'd followed Outsider. I had to manipulate a way to lead the team to that address as well. "Zoe, can you check if the business, Faraday Enterprises, rents separate premises?"

Zoe nodded.

Despite my tiredness – I had lain awake for a long time in the early hours of the morning, tossing and turning, thoughts spiraling but just out of reach, something about Outsider's blog posts niggling away – my mind was sharper than I would have expected this morning. I recalled Outsider's post on the urban climbing site when queried on what he knew.

> *I make it my business. Believe me, I know more than you could possibly imagine.*

And the months-old post on the urban explorer site.

> *Explorers are as free as any soul can be, learning so much more than most people will ever know.*

I flashed back on my conversations with the Piper. The arrogance. The undertone of menace: 'There is so much you will never know, Special Agent Farris.'

A variation on the same turn of phrase.

A chill coursed through me as though I'd been submerged in a lake of ice. I recalled the Piper's words on the phone: 'I can and I will find you, wherever you are and whenever I want.'

I configured the timings in my mind. I'd suspected someone – the Piper? – of watching me when I'd been in the underground garage, and that was around 5 p.m. Ellie's time of death had been given by the coroner as 7.15 p.m., allowing enough time for the drive of just under two hours from Seattle, starting from I-5 S and taking the Tacoma Narrows Bridge route to Port Townsend, where Ellie had lived.

Outsider's photo handover to StarX had been midnight in Seattle, allowing enough time for him to make it there if he'd been the one coming back from Port Townsend.

The timing was a fit.

Could the Piper, Outsider, and David Faraday be the same person?

My pursuit of a suspected urban climber, on Detective Radner's behalf, now gave me a legitimate opportunity to raise the thought brewing in the back of my mind. "This unexpected link with Faraday has led me to another thought."

They all turned their attention to me.

"I've been thinking about the Piper's knowledge of that abandoned platform and subway tunnels network. I asked myself about the kinds of people who might have that sort of information."

"Urban explorers," Zach suggested. "Another underground subset, similar to urban climbers."

I was pleased Zach had chimed in. Now this line of thinking wasn't coming purely from me. "Exactly. The climbers like the city buildings and monuments. But the urban explorers are a different kind of thrill-seeker, trekking into abandoned, derelict places, often in wilderness areas."

Zoe was on the same wavelength. "The kinds of places the Piper could use."

"He already has," I pointed out. "At King Street Station. And he had to have easily accessible but hidden spots to hold Bethany Gauchi and Timmy Beatty." I reached over to the PC and pulled up a map of the Olympic National Forest. "He had to have a place to hold Dietmar and the others, which brings us back to the forest again. It's a wilderness where he could lead them from one place to another, a place to which he could whisk them away again from right under our noses at SafePlace."

"Zoe," said Will, "can you gather up all the locally known urban explorer maps that are out there on the web?"

"On it."

He turned to me. "Good thinking."

I acknowledged the compliment with a nod.

If only you knew.

They'd all bought into my cover story of how I'd started down this line of inquiry. "Let's just hope we're on the right track."

Will's next directive was to Zoe again. "Can you organize permission from Pan Global Air to check their operating systems? I don't think permission will be a problem, we're looking for any vulnerabilities they may have, so it's to their benefit."

"What am I looking for?" she asked.

"Any illegal code that points to hacking. Any hidden back doors."

"You think their system's compromised?"

"The Piper planted a photo-altering virus at Poulsbo," Will said. "He could just as easily have hacked the airline and cruise company and deleted Reinholdt's name from their records."

"What about Reinholdt not answering his phone?"

"Check his cell service provider as well," I suggested.

Realization dawned in Zoe's eyes. "You think the Piper hoaxed the phone company into changing Reinholdt's number?"

"Not hard to do. And being on a European river cruise, out of regular contact, the professor might not be aware of it as yet."

"Okay, everyone, let's get to it." Will looked at me. "You and I will pay Mr. Faraday a visit over at New Holly."

Chapter Forty-Five

When there was no answer to the doorbell, Will rapped loudly several times on the wide, white wooden door of the two-story townhome.

"No one here," I said.

A middle-aged woman came out of the neighboring house and approached. "Don't see hardly anyone come around to this place."

"Hello," said Will. "Would you happen to know where the owner is?"

"Sorry, no. I don't know where he goes. He's very rarely at the house, drops by every now and then. I've never actually met him."

"I understand Mr. Faraday is a counselor," I said. "We saw information that he runs courses here, in the form of group sessions."

"He may stop by here from time to time and have an office and all," said the neighbor, "but he doesn't run any courses from here. I've never seen people coming by, let alone groups. Are you folk looking to use his services?"

Will played coy. "We'd like to make some inquiries, certainly. Thank you for coming over and taking the time to talk to us."

A call from Zoe came in on my phone. "Checked on Faraday Enterprises. It's registered to the same address in New Holly."

If that was the case, what was the significance of the house in Beacon Hill? Had it been Faraday or someone else who'd photographed me and whom I'd followed there?

"Have you located any online photos of Faraday yet?"

"No. Which is unusual."

"No driver's license ID?"

"Nothing."

Walking silently back to the car, I allowed Will to edge ahead, and I checked the RFID app on my phone. The red dot that represented the SUV was still in the same spot. Was the man in the hoodie still there or did he have another vehicle? I needed a legit reason to go out to that house and in the meantime, I'd have to run a search on the ownership of the house without drawing attention to myself.

As we reached the car, my phone rang again and glancing at the display, I saw that it was Brooke's friend and colleague, Louise Carter. I held up my right forefinger, signaling for Will to wait a moment.

"I'm worried about Brooke, Agent Farris," Louise Carter declared the second I answered. The previous night, it had been agreed for Brooke's safety that she would stay with her work colleague, in a rented city apartment known only to me and Will.

"What's happened?"

"Brooke couldn't sleep. Early this morning she said she wanted to go out walking, needed some 'alone' time, wanted to try and clear her head. I know she's suffering dreadfully, so I respected that. But she hasn't been back all day, she hasn't answered any of my calls. I checked in with the office and with some other friends but no one has heard from her, no one's been able to raise her."

"She could just be shutting the world out," I said, offering a voice of reason even though I doubted it, my fears rising. How could this be happening again? Brooke and Louise were in a safe place. And the FBI had made certain they hadn't been followed when they'd taken the women to the rental.

"I know. Am I overreacting? It's just that... she was zombie-like with despair. I really thought she'd come back and sleep through the day, she was exhausted. She's been through so much. It had just been her and Ellie after their parents died several years back, and she'd suffered depression. After that apparent suicide attempt on the cliff a couple of nights ago, she confided in me about that, she was so confused by it, but *now*, with Ellie…" Her voice faded.

"You're worried something's happened to her."

"Yes."

I pondered the sequence of events. "Dr. Sanders wasn't sure why she acted the way she did the other night, possibly an anxiety attack, brought on by guilt over publishing a story when we asked her not to. He wanted to have a few follow-up sessions with her, to get to the bottom of it. Let me contact Dr. Sanders, see what he thinks about this."

"You think she's having another episode like she did that night?" Louise's panic was evident.

"Let's not rush to conclusions, Louise. Stay by the phone, I'll call back." It was too soon for me to register Brooke Goodman as a missing person.

I tapped in the number for John Sanders as Will looked on.

"Ilona, what is it?"

I told John about the call from Louise. "I'm worried the Piper's got to her, or that she's had another episode like the one the other night." My heart thumped louder when John didn't respond straight away. It wasn't like him to hesitate, I knew that much. "John?"

"We can't rule either out, given all that's happened," he said. "I spoke with Brooke on the phone last night and despite being devastated, nothing gave me the impression she would go off, ignoring calls, creating further panic, but we can't take chances. I'll send a report right now to the Bureau and the Seattle PD to treat Brooke as missing in advance of their deadline, and to consider her a priority."

Ending the call, I stood rigid, my expression grim. "I can't believe this."

Will was watching me intently. "Brooke?"

"Gone. We're putting out an early Missing Persons Alert."

* * *

We had no sooner walked back into the UCU than Will took a call from the ICE director. As he ended the call, Marcia approached.

"You need to see this," she said.

We followed her into the office where the TV was broadcasting a live news feed.

"I've just had ICE on the line informing me of this," Will said. He watched the news report with me and Marcia.

> *In a raid that has taken the quiet Yakima county in Washington by surprise, US Immigration and Customs Enforcement officers have conducted a raid on the Rain Glow fruit orchard. They have arrested the owner, while at the same time rounding up more than a hundred workers believed to be illegal immigrants.*

The reporter, a young man with strong features and a professional manner, swept his hand in a gesture toward the open fields behind him. Officers and workers could be seen.

> *What has set this raid apart from others of this kind is that the orchard's management has, over many years, staged their own 'fake' immigration raids. They have deported their own immigrants while detaining the workers' children for an illegal adoption racket. I'm told simultaneous raids are taking place in Seattle at the offices of both the adoption agency and others discovered to have been knowingly financing the racket, including two high-profile names in Congressman Joe Gauchi and corporate chief Ed Beatty.*

I flashed back on my earlier conversation with Will, that there might be a connection between the Piper and Weatherby's fake immigration raids. But if that was the case, the German heritage didn't fit. And why would the Piper have targeted the Beattys and the Gauchis who were directors of firms that invested in that orchard?

"I hope the woman I spoke to out there," I said, "left there with her son as she said she was going to." I glanced at Will. "Not what an agent is supposed to be hoping for..."

"Either way, the woman won't lose her boy."

"Do you think the Gauchi and Beatty wives knew about their husbands' criminal connections?" Marcia said.

"That will come out in the ongoing investigation," Will said, "but having observed them up to this point, I'd say no. They will have known of their husbands' investments, but not about the criminal adoption scheme. Barbara Gauchi, of course, had secrets of her own." He was referring to the press announcement of her affair.

After the news broadcast ended, and Marcia had returned to her office, Will said, "I need a moment with you."

"What is it?"

He chose his words carefully. "Given the security breaches that have occurred, the assistant director commissioned an urgent triple background check, and an initial twenty-four-hour surveillance."

"On who?" I asked.

"On each of us," Will said.

Chapter Forty-Six

"Why?" I stiffened, registering my surprise.

"As you're aware, the big bosses are watching this new unit and how we function. The Poulsbo, SafePlace, and Brooke Goodman incidents threw everyone for a loop. From the moment the team arrived at Poulsbo, the security breach was activated via the bugs and the PC virus. Before we made this discovery about Faraday, the assistant director had decided on an exhaustive new background check–"

"He suspected one of the team?" I cut across him.

"It was purely due diligence. Rule out any possibility of team members being manipulated or compromised, or that we haven't followed protocol. You would understand that."

"Transparency and accountability."

"Exactly."

"What are they looking at?"

"Our service records. Personal details. Recent cases. You know the drill with these things."

I shrugged. "We can't let any of that distract us from the investigation. And what could they possibly be looking at where you're concerned?"

"I'm on the steering committee that campaigned to have the UCU set up. All of a sudden, right on our home turf, a case perfectly suited to us turns up and we were given a trial run."

"They thought you set these kidnaps up, to help you get this project off the ground? That's crazy."

"No, they didn't think that. They were simply following due process, and as I said, the watch was temporary and only to ensure none of us were being compromised in any way."

I straightened, my eyes serious. "What about the rest of us?"

"This case is all about medieval life and folktales, which means we were most likely to call in an expert in both fields."

"Which we did," I said.

"Who just happens to live and work in Seattle."

"An involvement which helps him promote his book and his theories," I said, seeing where the line of thought was going.

"Yes."

"The internal review needs to eliminate any possibility of suspicion around Zach."

"That's right," said Will. "And the reason I wanted to speak privately with you, is that something came up about John Sanders. A private matter, something he has a right to know, something you might want to point out to him."

"Why would I want to be the one to…?" My voice trailed away as a certain realization dawned on me. "You said the AD had a twenty-four-hour watch on the team's movements. Did they report anything suspicious?"

"No."

I felt a huge sense of relief that they hadn't seen me climbing.

"But they're aware – *you're* aware – that I had drinks with John?"

"Yes."

"And therefore you think I'd be the one to raise a private matter with him?"

"It's just a suggestion, Ilona. You've formed a camaraderie with him."

I didn't hide my annoyance. At the same time, I felt a twinge of horror that the surveillance might have uncovered my urban climbing. I was always ultra-careful that there was no one following or watching when I stole away to one of my launch spots but at some point, someone had watched and photographed me.

"You sure it was the assistant director who wanted me to know this, Will, or is it you?"

He ignored this and pressed on. "You recall the details of the Bureau's background check on John? His parents died in a car crash and he was adopted later at age seven?"

"Yes."

"Growing up in NY, his name was Parnell. John Parnell."

"The surname of his adoptive parents?"

"Yes."

"And his birth name?"

"He used his professional contacts to obtain the adoption records and the details of his birth parents. Their name was Sanders."

"Okay, so he reverted to his real name as an adult."

"Maybe not," said Will.

"What do you mean?"

"The Sanders family died in a car accident on a country vacation."

"Yes. That was in his profile."

"I delved further into that. Just to clarify we had all the details. No loose ends, as we always say."

"And?"

"The Sanders family. A doctor and his wife. Died instantly in a head-on collision. It was over thirty years ago but I accessed the police reports from the county archives."

I felt a sense of unease. "You found something?"

"The accident report had changed the number of fatalities in their car from three to two."

I frowned. "The original report had someone else in the car?"

"Their young child. John."

"But John wasn't in the car. He didn't go on that trip, his profile stated he was with family friends."

"Fair enough." Will spread his hands. "But I also accessed the morgue records. Three bodies signed in. Once again, the records were manually altered later on."

"To show just the doctor and his wife."

"Yes."

"So the first responders could have made an error on their original paperwork."

"That doesn't explain the original morgue records," Will said.

"So you think there was someone else in that car?"

"Yes. Ilona, this smells of a cover-up."

Creases formed around my eyes. "A cover-up of what, exactly?"

"Of a child killed in that accident, reported correctly but later altered, the records filed away and forgotten."

"You think the real John Sanders died with his parents?"

His eyes were solemn. "Yes."

"If that's the case, what happened to the body?"

"Most likely buried secretly in an unmarked grave."

I took a moment, allowing the details to settle. "So the dead child's identity could be stolen and given to a boy in an orphanage. A boy who was then adopted by the Parnells."

"Yes, with the paperwork trail appearing legit."

"Which is one of the ways the adoption agency associated with Rain Glow was operating. The people behind the adoption scam had someone on the inside who could change the morgue records. But John's adoption was through a different agency."

"That's right," Will said. "So we need to check out the adoption agency that John's adoptive parents used. I suspect that the Rain Glow altered records were unintentionally sent to that different agency by the county clerks."

I sank into a chair, taking it in. I felt a wave of sympathy for John. "Do you think John knows? Did he find this out about himself when he looked up details on his birth parents?"

"That, we don't know."

"But the background check confirms he was just seven when he was adopted?"

"Yes."

"Then he must have memories – memories of his childhood with his original family."

"He'd been in the orphanage from a younger age, so probably not."

"And now that we know there was a likely mix-up with his name, we have a moral obligation to pass this on to him."

"You don't think so?"

"Of course, I think so. Just not…" I didn't complete the thought.

"Not an easy subject to bring up."

"You're the unit leader," I said.

"And I'll discuss it with him if you prefer. It was just that you and he seem to have an easy rapport."

"And you know all about that because the bosses have been spying on us, and you've been a party to that. You know what, I didn't come onto this team by choice. I don't approve of being audited in this way, and something else… this doesn't feel like procedure with you, Will, this feels personal. This is you, overstepping the mark."

The anger rose within me as though it had a mind of its own. Even as I fought to suppress it, I wondered whether my anger was really aimed at Will, or whether it was my fear that the FBI had discovered my secret.

"Ilona–"

"When this case is done, so am I. I'll be heading back to my old unit."

"We should talk about this."

"No, we shouldn't." I rose out of my chair and headed for the door, almost colliding with Zoe, who was rushing in.

* * *

"The phone company received a call from Reinholdt," Zoe said to Will, "requesting they change his number due to a personal harassment matter."

Will forced himself to mentally put aside the exchange with Ilona. She was overreacting and he knew from experience it was best to let her sort through that herself. She'd come to see the matter clearly, he was sure. But believing that didn't make it any easier to switch off.

He focused on Zoe. "Except it wasn't Reinholdt who called the phone company," he guessed.

Zoe handed him a slip of paper. "The new number."

"Let's hope international roaming is working and that regardless of the hour the professor picks up."

He tried twice, the phone ringing out the first time. On the second attempt, after it had rung for a while, Bernard Reinholdt came on the line.

"Sorry to disturb you," Will said, and as he spoke he realized Ilona had moved back into the office, listening, "but I need to ask about your consultation with the Poulsbo Resident Agency a few months ago. You had a colleague with you."

"The young lady psychologist I'd been mentoring?"

"Yes, and there was also the signature of a male colleague in the visitor book, whom I believe was meeting you there," Will prompted.

"No one else was with me that day," the professor said.

"David Faraday? A Seattle-based youth counselor."

"Sorry, but I don't know a David Faraday. What is this about, Agent McCord?"

"Following a line of inquiry," Will said. "I also need to tell you that there's been a hoax perpetrated on your phone company and your number has been changed. There's no need for you to be alarmed, but I'll leave it to you to speak with your phone company and change it back. Once again, sorry to have disturbed your vacation, Professor, but thanks for your help."

"It doesn't sound like I've been any help at all," Reinholdt said.

Will's next call was to the Poulsbo Agency chief. This time he asked if their visitor book recorded the time of the visit.

"Yes." The woman checked the records while Will waited and when she came back on the line, she said, "Faraday's visit was at the same time as the others."

"But if he came in after the others and wrote the same time that they had, no one would be checking that?"

"Not necessarily, there wouldn't normally be a reason," the Poulsbo chief said. "Is there a problem, Will?"

"I've been in touch with Professor Reinholdt and he's never heard of David Faraday."

"Your next best bet is to speak with the previous chief here," the woman said, "or perhaps even better, to the front desk secretary on duty that day. She's no longer here, moved across country, but she can be reached at the field office in Massachusetts. In the meantime, I can check our CCTV of the waiting area."

"Do that. But I'm fairly certain you'll find the footage from that day missing."

"Why's that?"

"It seems the virus in the system enabled the Piper to remotely connect," he told her.

"You think he will have deleted that footage?"

"That's exactly what this guy will have done."

Will's next call was to the secretary. He asked her if she recalled the professor's consult.

"Vaguely, yes," the young woman said.

He asked if she remembered the male colleague who'd signed in the same day.

There were a few moments of silence before she spoke. "Yes. It's coming back to me. The man said he'd arranged to meet with Professor Reinholdt in the agency waiting area. They were going to another appointment together."

"But he didn't stay and meet with the professor?" Will guessed.

"No. I remember now. He received a phone call, said it was an urgent matter and he needed to leave. He asked me not to bother the professor about it, that he would send him a text to arrange another time."

"While this man, Faraday, was in the waiting area, was your desk at any time unattended?"

"At busy times I could be in and out of the adjoining copier room."

"Do you remember what Faraday looked like?"

There was a pause. "Not really. Average height and weight, I think, but… it was months ago, and I just can't specifically recall him."

Will thanked her, ended the call, and filled Ilona and Zoe in on the details. "At some point, he's used the distractions there, switched the USB on her desk, and planted the listening devices."

"Clearly," said Zoe, "our so-called Piper hasn't left any stone unturned, or any situation unmanipulated."

"And he's left a very deliberate trail of red herrings along the way," Ilona said.

Marcia strode in. "We've obtained the records held by the Rain Glow adoption agency and Themis has run a search," she said. "The name given to one of the adopted children was David Faraday."

Chapter Forty-Seven

I drove to John's consulting rooms, housed in a community health center in Fremont.

He opened the door and if he was surprised to see me, he didn't show it.

"Sorry if I'm disturbing you," I said.

He flashed his wide, warm, beguiling smile. "You couldn't disturb me if you tried and I don't have any more counseling sessions today." He led me into the room and ushered for me to sit on the sofa. He sat down opposite me. "No further word on Brooke Goodman or the children?"

I shook my head. "Nothing as yet. Police have been advised to be on the lookout for her."

"She was in a safe location so the Piper couldn't have known where to find her."

"I know," I said. "But—"

"They'll find her."

We sat silently for a beat, as I searched for the right approach. I saw in John's expression that he sensed I was there for another reason. "When you started consulting with the Bureau, they ran their usual background checks."

"Of course, but you know that," he said.

"You were raised by your foster parents in NY."

"That's right." He chuckled and made a pretense of looking around the office and up at the ceiling. "I'm not on *This Is Your Life*, am I?"

I grinned, shaking my head. "You were seven when they adopted you?"

"Yeah."

"You decided to revert to your birth name when you were older." It was a statement, not a question.

I saw the look of remembrance in his eyes. His mind flashing back to his childhood. "I was at the orphanage for a couple of years or so, and I barely remembered my birth parents. I suppose reverting to the Sanders name was a way of connecting with them, as an adult. Just a typical young guy trying to find himself."

I bit down gently on my lower lip. I didn't want to upset John by suddenly revealing something that would be a complete shock to him.

Tread gently here.

"When you reverted to your old name," I said, "you looked up the details on your parents?"

"As you do." He grinned.

"And all good. Nothing that didn't make sense?"

He frowned. Puzzled. "Like what?"

I shrugged. "Like anything."

"No," he said. "Ilona, what's this about?"

"The Bureau's been doing its sneaky stuff again. You know. Checking backgrounds."

"They'd already done all that."

"They've been running an exhaustive internal review, because of the security breaches."

His brow furrowed. "Okay. But why these questions?"

"I just wanted to be honest with you so everything's out in the open, about the Bureau… and the checks."

"I appreciate that." His brow furrowed again. "But you asked if anything unusual came up when I was looking into my family. Did the Bureau find something?"

"An anomaly in the paperwork," I explained. "The original accident report listed you as being one of the casualties. You would think it's a clerical error. It was altered soon after." I didn't want to race in with too much information too soon.

John's eyes met mine. "But you think there's more to it?"

"The same changes were made to the morgue records," I said.

"You suspect something… deliberate?"

"Yes."

"Okay. But what?"

"We need to look into it a lot further," I said.

"Something odd about my adoption records?"

"Seems so."

"Oh…" John's demeanor changed. I watched as his shoulders sagged. It was as though he'd been deflated and a look of sorrow passed across his eyes.

I took his hand in mine. "I'm sorry. This must come as a hell of a shock."

"It's okay."

"No, it's really not."

He squeezed my hand. "It brought back feelings of loss... that's all. You think it could be connected with those orchard and adoption agency raids today... and this Faraday?"

"It's a possibility. We've learned that David Faraday was one of the children adopted out by Rain Glow's agency. But regardless, once we've sorted out this anomaly on your birth records, you'll be the first to know what we find."

"Thanks. And as soon as this damn investigation is over–" he took my hands in his, fixed me with that irresistible look of his, and gave me a kiss on the cheek "– there can be more of this if you'd like."

"Like," I said.

Earlier, I'd cursed Will for putting me in the position of coming out to talk to John about this. But right at that moment, I was glad that I had.

Chapter Forty-Eight

Arriving home, I fixed a light meal, and afterward, exhausted, sank back into my sofa, closing my eyes for what I thought was just a moment. I was jolted from sleep when my phone beeped. It was an alert that the RFID tracker was on the move.

I checked my watch. It was late evening; I'd been asleep for a few hours.

What was the man in the hoodie doing at this hour? Was it Faraday on the move or was it someone else in that SUV? Could this man be the Piper?

I threw on my climbing gear and drove in the direction that the tracker was tracing. I knew that the Bureau's surveillance on me and the team had since ended but I kept my eye on the rearview mirror just in case. I didn't notice anything unusual.

On the outskirts of Bremerton, in Kitsap County, there was an empty, long-shuttered aluminum smelter plant, protected by tall barbed-wire fences and dotted with 'No Trespassing' signs. On my screen, the area that signified the plant displayed the tracker's pulsating dot.

As I approached, I googled the plant.

A 190-acre property with half a dozen buildings, it had operated for seventy years. It had been closed twelve years earlier and purchased by a corporation with plans to repurpose and redevelop the site. Due to several changes in management and tight financial periods, that corporation was yet to begin any work there. It remained unused, its derelict buildings in need of demolition.

I didn't know this spot. I drove by, sighting the rusted steel walls of the buildings. Broken heavy-duty equipment littered the grounds, overgrown with weeds. There was a toxic smell in the air. It was a typical, out-of-the-way place for urban explorers, free runners, and climbers, surrounded by a small semi-rural pocket of land.

Was that why Outsider was here? Was he part of an urban explorer gang getting their kicks?

Or was this one of the derelict places, as I now suspected, utilized by the Piper?

I parked my car on a cross street, away from the site.

From the tracker's position, I knew the driver had parked somewhere on the plant, though I couldn't sight the vehicle.

I reined in my sense of foreboding, as I determined whether to sneak in for a closer look. I didn't want to call for backup and have to reveal that it was my climbing secret that led me here. Not unless I could observe what this mystery stalker was doing and whether it exposed him as the Piper. If that was the case, I'd call in the troops.

Despite the fencing and the signs, I knew there would be breaks in the wire through which explorers accessed the plant. I searched for one of those rather than use the main entry road.

I set my phone's ringtone on silent.

I moved along the fence perimeter. It wasn't long before I came upon a break in the wire, partially covered with bush and weed.

I crept through, keeping a vigil on the spaces ahead, and darted over to the first building.

I sighted the vehicle beside the main building. There was a doorway, partly ajar. I gently eased it open further allowing me to peer in, and then step through.

A dark corridor, no sound, and no sign of anything further along. The only faint trace of light was from the moonlight filtering through the doorway.

This would have been the perfect place to hide Bethany Gauchi and Timmy Beatty. If Faraday was the Piper and he'd kidnapped Brooke Goodman, was this where she was being held?

I needed to know for certain before I sounded the alert.

I hoped I could come up with another explanation about how I'd known Faraday – or whoever it was – was out here. Both Will and Detective Radner's suspicions would be further aroused as to what I'd really been up to.

I moved forward, slowly and quietly.

I only needed to see what he was doing. Covertly, from a distance. Then I could retreat, and call for backup if needed.

I inched around the first corner of the winding corridor and I saw a filter of light further along. Was there a side window somewhere there? I pressed on and, as I did, I heard a faint moaning sound and I froze, listening intently, staring hard at the area up ahead.

Someone in pain?

There was a sudden scraping and scurrying overhead, creatures either on the tin roof or in the space between the roof and the ceiling. Thunderous one moment and then gone.

The tone of the groaning sound altered and I recognized that it was the creak of aged timber and metal, mimicking a human in anguish. It faded and the silence that followed seemed just as loud, filling the near-darkness.

And then I felt a harsh breath on the back of my neck, sensed someone close, and I instantly dropped to one knee, spinning around, kicking my leg out, and raising my pistol.

Nothing but empty space.

The waft of air I'd felt had been driven in through unseen gaps.

I steeled myself, leveled my breathing, and crept forward, staying close to the sidewall. As I approached another corner, there was the flicker of a shadow. I took a step back and a figure suddenly appeared from around the edge, a dozen steps ahead of me.

A tall, imposing figure, a flowing coat, an indistinct silhouette in the dim light.

It was as though the Piper had been waiting for me. Surely, that couldn't be the case?

I didn't know if he had a weapon, and I couldn't retreat now that we'd confronted one another. I aimed my revolver, assumed the stance, and called out, "FBI, on your knees and hands in the air."

His long pipe was in his hand. He raised the instrument to his lips, raising his other hand theatrically in the air to signify a performance.

"Lose the pipe," I ordered, "and hands in the air, drop to your knees."

I realized, too late, that it wasn't his musical pipe he'd raised to his lips.

I felt a sting on my neck.

I raised my hand, dabbing at the area of the sting. All of a sudden, I felt faint.

I opened my mouth to repeat the command but this time no sound passed my lips. My throat felt constricted, incredibly dry, and I struggled to swallow.

I'd been drugged.

Instead of fleeing, the Piper walked toward me. His strides seemed unnatural, as though he was walking in... *what?*

Slow motion?

The air around me had taken on an otherworldly glow. The light was muted and flickering as though all the light in the world was reliant on a giant, unseen, wavering candle flame.

This wasn't making sense.

"It's time to go, Ilona." The Piper's voice was a whisper that left just the hint of an echo.

I staggered to the wall and began to slide down it, losing consciousness. My mind flashed on the police officers outside Hilde's cabin. They'd been hit by tranquilizer darts.

I looked up at the Piper as he raised his musical instrument and played. An overwhelming sense of both calm and confusion came over me, ebbing and flowing. Every part of me felt like it was part of the melody being played on that pipe. At one with the music.

My eyes closed as the darkness overcame me.

Chapter Forty-Nine

My eyes opened and I struggled to rise out of a deep sleep. The pull was strong, like a powerful ocean undertow, and my eyelids closed again.

I was conscious of movement. I forced my eyes to open again. I was horizontal, staring up at a dark sky, glittering with stars. A light breeze brushed my face as I was wheeled along. I was on a gurney but no longer in the building.

Try to stay awake.

Think.

I felt myself plunging again, giving in to the sweet seduction of sleep.

* * *

I woke – if you could call it waking. I was in limbo, somewhere between waking and sleeping. I was still on the gurney, I could feel the cold steel through my garments, but I was no longer out in the open. I was in a confined space.

Motion. Whatever I was in, it was moving. I felt bumps and sways.

I felt and heard the crunch of wheels on gravel.

I had to stay awake.

Think.

Think about the case.

Where were the children? Where was Brooke?

Think.

Outsider, Faraday, the Piper. All the same? It seemed he had several addresses, maybe one for each of many different aliases. He had a network of hidden, abandoned places that he discovered via urban explorer sites.

The drowsiness was like a blanket, enveloping me, weighing my body down as though I was tied to rocks.

I gave in again to the sweet relief.

I slept.

Chapter Fifty

Day Seven

Will was always in at an early hour and he wasn't surprised, this morning, when Zach arrived not long after. It was never easy getting rest at this stage of an investigation.

"Couldn't sleep," Zach said.

Will gave a nod of understanding. "Not uncommon around here."

Zoe and Marcia walked in, coffees in hand, and a few minutes later John Sanders joined them.

"No heart-starter?" Marcia said to John, raising her coffee.

John smiled. "Way ahead of you. Already had two."

The three of them pulled up chairs alongside Zach. Will did the opposite, standing up and moving about, restless.

"Where's Ilona?" Marcia asked.

Will glanced at his watch. "Not like her to run late for our briefing." He pulled out his phone and called her number.

It went to voicemail, and he left a message. "Ilona, are you far away? We're starting the meeting and then I'm heading over to Faraday's with a warrant."

Will ended the call and phone still in hand, wasted no time addressing the team.

"To bring you all up to date, the adoption agency associated with the Rain Glow Orchard falsified morgue records and stole the names of deceased children. Those names were used by the adoption racket, but to complicate matters, the odd record slipped through the cracks, mistakenly sent out by unsuspecting bureaucrats to other agencies." Will exchanged a glance with John but had no intention of talking about John's personal details in front of the others. "We also know that David Faraday was one of the names in the Rain Glow records."

"Joe Gauchi and Ed Beatty are both directors of investment firms that have a financial stake in the Rain Glow Orchard," Marcia said to the group, "and ICE has established they were involved in the adoption racket. So apart from the ransom, there's another reason for the Piper kidnapping their children. He knew we'd explore the fathers' backgrounds, ultimately leading us to the orchard and the adoption firm. We just don't know *why* the Piper wanted to lead us there or how that ties in with the missing German children."

"But it does seem to fit with this self-styled vigilantism of the Piper's," Zach said.

Will outlined the roles everyone would be taking for the rest of the day. "And John, the moment we have any news on any of the children, you'll be alerted."

"I'll be ready 24-7," John said.

* * *

Will arranged for several local police officers to meet with himself and Marcia at David Faraday's home in New Holly.

The first thing Will noticed was how bare the premises were. The first-floor rooms had only basic sets of furniture, a kitchen that hadn't been used recently, and a barely stocked fridge.

The second-story rooms were empty, except for a study and the main bedroom. The queen-size bed hadn't been slept in. The study had several filing cabinets and a desk and chair.

"There are no photos on the walls or the mantelpiece," Will observed as he sorted the group into teams of two for the search.

He and Marcia were rifling through the cabinets when she called out, "Look at this." She displayed several credit cards and business cards, with three different names, one of which was David Faraday. The other two names meant nothing to them. No photo IDs.

"He's been operating under different aliases," Will said, "and this house is not much more than a front for his counseling business."

"There's a list of assignments here." Marcia held up a sheet of paper. "He ran occasional classes at some of the local schools."

"Which schools?"

Marcia was speed-reading through the schedule. "Two of them are the schools which the Gauchi and Beatty kids attended."

* * *

From Faraday's house, Will phoned Zoe with the discoveries they'd made.

By the time he and Marcia returned to the UCU, Zoe had called the school that the Beatty boy attended. "I spoke with the teacher who was in the classroom on the day of Faraday's visit. She remembered the interactions he had with the students."

"And one of them was Timmy Beatty?" Will guessed.

"Yes."

"When Timothy saw Faraday in the park, behind those trees, it was a face he knew."

"So Faraday could motion for the boy to come to him and the boy wouldn't have been afraid," Zoe said. "But how did he lure Bethany Gauchi away?"

Will rubbed his chin, wishing he had the answer. "Where are we with the urban explorer sites?" he asked her.

"Themis has pulled down maps and GPS coordinates and Zach and I have been going through them."

"Still no sign of Ilona?" Marcia asked.

"No."

Will slipped his phone from his pocket and made another call to her.

"Voicemail again," he said, pocketing the phone.

Marcia's stare was intense. "This isn't like Ilona."

"I'm sending some agents over to her place." Will didn't voice his deeper concern, that there was something else going on, something to do with how she'd been led to the David Faraday identity in the first place.

Where was she now, at the most crucial point of the investigation?

Chapter Fifty-One

Will, Marcia, and Zoe entered the office where Zach was poring over multiple screens of abandoned sites maps. "There's a heap of these throughout the National Park and Forest," he said without removing his gaze from the screens. "Like this: the ruins of a Second World War military watchpoint. And there's abandoned ranger points and the wreckage of a bridge from half a century ago."

"Those are too far from the perimeter, and too far up for reasonable access," Zoe pointed out.

"Agreed. One thing in our favor is that these explorers love to take photos and post them online with details of their exploits. So I've started speed-browsing a range of sites the explorer community frequents." Zach diverted his gaze from the screens and turned to Will. "Did you contact Ilona?"

"Agents have been to her apartment," he said. "No sign of her or her car."

Zach rose slowly from his chair, deep in thought. "Will, the Piper knows her number, has phoned her, taunting her, if he's found out where she lives…"

"I've got a BOLO out on her, Zach. We'll find her."
Will's phone rang. As he listened, he motioned to Marcia,
saying, "Write this down."

Grabbing a pen and pad, Marcia scribbled as Will read
out a suburb and street name and GPS coordinates.

"What's this?" Zoe asked.

"A police patrol found Ilona's car out there."

Zach had already pulled up an urban explorer map that
matched the coordinates. "Bremerton. There's an
abandoned aluminum smelting plant there."

* * *

In a matter of seconds, a quiet, deserted, semi-rural
strip of Bremerton was transformed into a hive of activity.

An FBI Tactical Aviation MD530 chopper flew
overhead, its loudspeaker issuing an order for anyone in
the smelting plant to walk out of the buildings with their
arms held high.

Armored FBI vehicles took up strategic points around
the fenced perimeter.

A SWAT team broke through the wire and spreading
out in duos, they entered the first line of buildings at the
main entrance.

Grouped at the fence, the UCU team waited.

Zach, Marcia, and Zoe all felt their anticipation rise as
Will took a call from the SWAT team commander.

The voice of the commander crackled over the line.
"No sign of Agent Farris or the Piper but we have found
something strange."

"What is it?" Will asked.

There was a pause, a blast of static, and then the
commander came back on the line. "Several rooms with
makeshift beds and new padlocks on the doors. Looks like
it's been used recently to lock people in," he said.

Chapter Fifty-Two

Before

The boy reached the top of the steep slope. The man in the long coat that they'd all been following was joined here by several other men. All in long-coated suits.

The boy looked back one last time. There was the cluster of cabins where they'd all lived, their little village at the bottom of the hill, on the clear grounds at the rear of the Rain Glow Orchard.

Now he and the others were herded by the group of men and they walked further, over the cusp of the hill to where he saw a fleet of minivans.

On the side of one of the vans, the boy saw a name. One of the words caused him to gasp. Orphanage.

And then he was clambering into the back of it.

He remembered the men coming to the village earlier in the day, and talking with their parents. He remembered the children were told to wait outside, to remain quiet, and they'd all been given something to drink.

After that, he'd felt strange, as though he wasn't in control of his body. The other children had not been acting like themselves.

There was a part of him that knew they'd all been affected by the drink they'd been given. And that his memory was fading in and out.

He would not forget his parents.

He would not forget these men, or that orchard where his parents had worked, or the name of the orphanage on the side of the van.

One day, when he was older, when he was stronger, he would come for these bad men and he would turn their own evil ways against them.

PART THREE

Chapter Fifty-Three

I opened my eyes.

My arms were raised above my head and I couldn't move them.

I looked down at my body. I was in a seated position in an abseiling harness, my arms bound to a metal rod that ran along the upper part of the structure.

I was hanging just above ground level. I glanced about, my view taking in rock formations and wooded hills. In the distance, I saw the blue haze of the mountains.

I could see that I was in an elevated region of the Olympic National Forest.

I swallowed hard. Once again, I was coming up out of a drugged state.

Flashes of memory. Being led out of the vehicle. I'd stumbled groggily for a short period, half out of it, pushing through thick brush on a steep, stony trail, climbing higher and higher. It was a landscape of rotting logs, ferns, and mosses. The Piper had been ahead of me, pulling me along.

I vaguely remembered being in a room at the abandoned plant the night before. It was as though my head was breaking the surface of a deep ocean, my lungs filling with air.

I remembered the drowsiness. The loss of self-control.

I called out. "Are you there?"

As my close-up vision came into sharper focus, I saw the cable. It ran from the harness to a rusted iron winching machine. Behind that, a gear wheel extended out from one of the old iron bunkers that were grown through with shoots and shards of vegetation.

What was this place?

I remembered waking in the moving vehicle. I recalled the bumping, rolling upward tilt. It must have been a different vehicle, built for rough terrain, taking the unsealed trails from a lower trailhead and switchbacking up the steep hillsides. I remembered hearing the sloshes where the Piper had crossed streams.

I knew that the elevation gain in parts of the forest was considerable, anywhere up to four thousand feet and in some spots higher.

He had turned this abandoned, isolated bunker and its tools and machinery to his own use. Just as, I realized now, he had done with the cluster of cabins I could see further down the hill. This was an old logging town, long since abandoned and grown over with tentacles of weed and fern. He'd refashioned it like a medieval village. It hadn't taken much, cutting away some of the vegetation, and dumping bales of straw over the old timber roofs.

And then I saw him approaching from the cabins, coming out of the shadows.

* * *

He stood at a distance, watching. In addition to the wide-brimmed straw hat, largely obscuring his face, he wore a mask. And then he spoke, his voice harsh and guttural behind the mask, and I detected the trace of a German accent.

"The children of the privileged, their parents paying through the nose for an expensive camping trip." He gestured back at the cabins.

I glanced at the cabins. "Except they were living in your hidden medieval town." But why, I wondered, did the children believe they were from the Middle Ages? I hardened my voice. "I'm a federal agent. You need to untie me."

"I'm afraid you've got too close to the truth."

"My team will be on their way."

"Your team has no idea you're here, or that you're even in trouble. Because you couldn't risk them knowing about your little climbing escapades."

He had to be the one who'd been watching me. I thought of the parking lot at the mall and the sense someone was lurking there.

"What have you done with the children?" I demanded.

"You figured they were on a language exchange vacation," he said, "so you should have guessed that having served their purpose, helping me create the Piper persona, they were of no further use to me. It wasn't difficult to have those privileged children signed up for a three-week camping trip, run by a youth counselor as a health and well-being experience."

"Which is why no one was missing them. What have you done? Where are they?"

The team's theory had been right, but that didn't give me any consolation here and now. How did the Piper know Zach and I had theorized the kids were part of a language and culture exchange vacation?

"You've got a listening device at the Seattle office as well?"

"Listening device?" His voice affected amusement. "I suppose you could call it that."

What did he mean?

I wanted to scream at him.

"What do you want?" I said through clenched teeth.

"Maybe I'll boast about a few things, get them off my chest. Things I can't share with anyone else because I'm a lone wolf."

"That was the reason for your phone calls to me? To gloat?"

"One of the reasons."

"And it's safe to tell me more, now?"

"Safe? Yes."

"Because I won't be around to tell anyone else."

There was a cold finality in his silence.

* * *

I strained for a glimpse of his eyes but they remained in shadow from the wide brim of the hat.

"Despite all my false trails, you started to get too much right. Impressive."

"You were listening via the bugs."

He laughed. "In the event you found them, they were always there as another red herring."

"But they led to you, *David*," I said, mocking his rhetoric, using Faraday's name to see if it brought a response, but he didn't react.

"Is that what you think?"

I scoffed. "You still expect me to believe you're a supernatural being and that's how you could hear and see us?"

"Nothing supernatural about it." Now his voice had a quiet chill. "But back to how well you *were* doing. I'd watched your climbs and your visits to the internet café and it wasn't hard to see the connection. I knew that an attempt to expose your secret would distract you and help disrupt the investigation. Another piece of gameplay."

"You wanted me to see that post."

"Yes, and I expected you'd be watching the meeting point. I knew your priority would be to try and get those photos from the climber instead of following me. But, resourceful as ever, it seems you managed to do both. What I didn't anticipate was that you'd find a way to track me to the Bremerton plant. But after all that, it's worked in my favor. I had sensors all around that abandoned place so I'd never be caught by someone coming onto the property."

I was sickened by his tone of superiority.

"Always prepared. As I was when I studied the routines of the park rangers. I played a hunch the ranger's reporter sister would post the story. That gave me, in Brooke Goodman, a susceptible person to manipulate."

I knew that the worst thing you could call a psychopath was a 'psychopath.' It would only infuriate him further. What you could do, if you were skilled enough and handled it properly, was to play to his ego. "So you've done it. You've run rings around the FBI, and you've panicked the public with fear of the unknown."

"It's early days but the seed is planted: the fear that your children could be kidnapped by a shadowy figure, maybe supernatural, maybe not. What parent wants to take the chance that the authorities can deal with it and save their child? *No* parent. Instead, they'll follow my orders."

There was an eerie stillness to him and then his manner became more expansive.

"The perfect child kidnap operation, targeting those parents who deserve to be destroyed financially."

"While you listened in to everything that was going on with the investigation."

"You still think the bugs were how I knew everything that was going on?"

Even in the distance, there was something disquietingly familiar about him.

"Who knew the most about the medieval era? Who had the most to gain by making it all appear real?"

I glared at him. Another red herring? "Are you trying to set up one of the team members?"

"And who got the chance to lead their own special unit?"

I stared hard.

"No answer?" he goaded.

"You're wasting your breath if you're suggesting that anyone on the team had anything to do with you." Even as I spoke, I wondered if John, Zach, or Marcia had known

David Faraday, by a different name, without ever realizing it. Had Faraday tricked one of them in some manner, learning what had been transpiring within the UCU? I allowed my anger to boil over. "None of them would ever knowingly be a part of something like this."

The Piper moved in close, his body just inches from mine, his head angled so that his hat's wide, droopy brim shielded his upper face. "Wouldn't they?"

He knew I couldn't move my arms. He was enjoying the power. Taunting me.

"Perhaps that's the one thing that should remain a mystery, the one thing you will never know."

But there's one thing you're not expecting.

I craned my neck and tilted my head, wrapping my mouth around the extended brim of his hat and biting down. I jerked my head, lifting and ripping the hat from his head before he could react. I spat it out, and it fell away as my eyes reverted to the exposed part of his face.

Chapter Fifty-Four

I stared at him.

Despite my fury, my frustration, and my sense of hopelessness, a great sadness erupted from deep within. I felt a tear welling up in my left eye.

He smirked, shaking off his surprise and then removing the mask over his mouth.

"John?"

How could this be? How could John Sanders be standing there, with the peaked hat and the long, flowing coat with colored trims?

"I debated whether to reveal myself but it seems you've made that decision for both of us. Impressive.

Beeindruckend, meine Liebe." He dropped the pretense of the accent and the deep, throaty tone.

I felt my energy draining from pure shock. It was as though I'd been knocked around like a punching bag and now I'd been deflated. Everything I'd ever felt, everything I'd ever believed, nothing more than a lie, the very inner core of my confidence in my own judgment, shredded.

I continued to stare, silent, my mind racing. The face and the voice might have now belonged to the man I knew as John Sanders but I was looking at a stranger who could also speak German. How many things were there that I didn't know about this imposter? It was as though I was seeing him for the first time. My mind drew on the discovery that as an orphan he'd been given the identity of a deceased child. I realized that the man before me had been one of the South American immigrant children stolen away from Rain Glow, decades before, his identity changed and then changed again when he'd been adopted out and raised by an American family.

In that instant, John Sanders's jet-black hair, dark eyes, and smoldering looks fitted this hidden heritage.

I swallowed hard, breathed, and struggled to find my voice. "You were one of the Rain Glow children."

"I deleted my name from the Rain Glow agency's records and inserted it into another adoption group. One of my early computer hacks. Insurance so that my name would not appear when the authorities began investigating Rain Glow. I replaced it with the fake Faraday name. The FBI's search for him is another wild goose chase."

"And you created a whole host of aliases."

"With hidden rear exits at my homes and my counseling rooms," he declared. "Ensures I'm never observed when I move about and switch from one identity to another."

When it came to John's background and his progress into the twisted mind I now saw, there, ultimately, only one word worth uttering. "Why?"

My eyes never left him and his features seemed to morph right in front of me. This wasn't the gentle, charming, compassionate persona I'd known. This was a man with a hard and haunted expression, a tortured glare in his eyes. An exposed soul.

"We hit it off better than I could have hoped," he said in a self-possessed manner. "Not part of my initial plan. Just something that happened. And I would've preferred this moment hadn't come or had come much later."

He spoke without emotion. Even his voice now sounded to me like the voice of a different man. He strode to the edge of my vision, gazing out at the mountains.

"There's a maverick side to you, something I can appreciate. I've spent a lot of time up here, planning all of this, as well as letting off steam. Hiking and climbing the rock face. So I can understand your urban climbing addiction. The least I can do is let you die doing the thing you love."

I remembered the moment I shared with John on the beach. He remarked on the sedate nature of his counseling work, and how he'd liked to get away to blow off steam. Jogging and biking.

There'd been a lot more to it than that.

He paced back. "It's not an urban landscape but it's the ultimate climb. Depending on the difficulty, and the temperatures, you may be gone in a few hours or you may last a day or so."

"What about Brooke? What have you done with her?"

"She's the very least of your concerns."

"Was she drugged like me? How?"

As my mind began to absorb the shock of what I'd learned out here, I refocused. My agent training was slowly kicking back into play. I had to forget about my relationship with John. I had to snap back into survival mode. The man before me wasn't just an imposter and a child kidnapper. He was a murderer.

"I phoned her, posing as David Faraday, after her Dietmar article. Told her that I could give her an interview, with my expert opinion on what might be troubling the boy. She didn't remember afterward, of course."

"How could she not remember?" Even as I said it, the only other possibility dawned on me. If not drugged, then how could a mind be manipulated like that?

"There's a certain karma to all of this." He spoke with cold indifference. "Meeting with her for an interview about Dietmar, I was easily able to place her under hypnosis, implant the suggestion that she would do whatever asked by the voice she heard after listening to the Piper's tune, and have her forget both about me and that interview taking place."

I exhaled a breath in frustration. "Hypnosis. And your post-hypnotic suggestions always used music as the trigger."

"When she heard the tune over the phone, she followed my instructions and sent the post about Berthold and Anna, and then walked out to the cliff's edge where I expected she'd slip and fall."

"For what reason?"

"Eliminating loose ends, as the erased memory would resurface. Unfortunately, her meddling sister got in the way."

"So you went back to finish the job. But you got it wrong, pushed her sister instead."

John didn't respond. He glared at me.

"And when you realized your mistake, you went after Brooke again."

He quickly seemed to shrug this off. "None of that matters now."

I couldn't let this master of deception have all the control. "Zoe's gathering data on explorer sites in the forest. The team will find this spot."

He sat down on the stump of a log, gesturing once more to the cabins, an air of calm about him. "I'd searched a raft of derelict sites, not the mainstream ones, but chatter from underground blogs on the dark web. Your team may zero in on this place eventually, but it won't be any time soon."

* * *

He allowed himself a moment of reflection. The woods were quiet, as though the forest creatures were watching in silent dread. There was just the rustle of the leaves from a brisk breeze that carried the scent of cedar and damp moss.

"These run-down huts were perfect. From here, I was able to prep the children, lead them through the forest and into the cave, scorch their clothes, and then, of course, spirit them back here from the Retreat."

"Prep them? Is that what you call your inhuman process?"

There was a faraway look in his eyes. "Hypnotherapy is a science by which people can access their repressed childhood traumas. But it can be just as effective for brainwashing and implanting false memories."

I had heard of this. "False memory syndrome."

His gaze wandered and then settled on me. "The children were conditioned to believe that they had followed the Piper from another time and place. I had to be very careful, however, not to leave them under your care for too long. The hypnotic state wears off after a day, possibly two, and I could only reactivate it once by having the children hear the tune."

"Which you knew we'd have them whistle or hum for us."

He rose to his feet again. "And, of course, you did."

"Tell me how these false memories work." If I kept him talking, I had longer to think of a way to escape. I sensed he could easily be drawn into a broader explanation of his grand illusion.

And I was right. His voice lifted, his eyes once again flittering over the majestic landscape that dwarfed us. Striking, scattered rock formations rose above the treetops.

"The first step is to create an atmosphere of trust, getting the subject to talk about their past while they're hypnotized. Have them flesh out the details. And once they're steeped in true memories, that's when I introduce a *false* memory, interspersed with the real."

I detected a warped sense of pride in his words.

"I don't expect you've come across the term 'imagination inflation'? It's about repeatedly asking the subject to try and remember something that never happened. They already have trust in you that the event is real. After attempting to remember many times, their mind is tricked into recalling it as a real event and that effect is magnified under hypnosis."

I was reminded of the first call I'd received from the Piper. 'I can make people see and hear what I want them to see and hear.'

Pictures formed in my mind as I listened to him recount the methods he'd employed with the children.

* * *

From time to time, the Piper allowed the children to play outside in his makeshift medieval village, immersing them in the environment. But mostly they sat in the cabin, lured into a hypnotic state, where he repeated the same session, over and over, immersing them in the dialect, and the day-to-day life of a child in the Middle Ages. He implanted false memories of medieval parents.

"We've looked at pictures of Hamelin. Now, imagine the town in your mind. Visualize the cobbled street, the straw-thatched roofs of the stone houses. Try to remember the long journey you took from there, through the woods and the caves. Do you remember?"

After a while, they began to nod. Later, they answered his questions themselves, drawing on these 'memories,' filling in the gaps.

"Try to remember the Ratcatcher and how he played the pipe and how you followed him. Think back on your fear of what he might do to you and your parents."

The children shuddered.

"Do you remember?"

* * *

"Everyone thinks their memories are the truth of what happened in the past."

John had become immersed in his passion for the subject.

"But even without false memory implants, our own memories of everything are a perception, Ilona. The result of details being forgotten and our minds naturally creating new details to fill in the spaces, something first explored in experiments at the University of Washington years ago."

"You hacked the children's memories," I said. "Made them temporarily forget their real lives."

"Prompted each step of the way by a tune. I'm no great musician but I cobbled together a melody from haunting folk songs, just the one short piece, practiced over and over. That was my post-hypnotic trigger."

I challenged him. "But Hilde was found with ripped clothes, something was different, something didn't work."

"Sometimes the hypnosis meets with resistance. I was forced to restrain her but then, that played into the narrative, anyway."

"Along with her wearing a medallion you'd had manufactured."

"Forged by a talented craftsman for one of my aliases."

"All of this in just a short period," I stated, baiting him to keep talking.

He nodded. "The first two weeks devoted to the prepping, the final week starting from when you found Dietmar."

I changed tack. "I get it. You were very young when your parents were deported by fake authorities and you were placed in an illegal orphanage. Then you were told your parents had died in a car crash. They brainwashed you and later you were adopted out. But you remembered the Rain Glow name. When you were older you looked into it and figured out the truth. You wanted revenge but there are other ways to have led the FBI to organizations like Rain Glow, John. Why kidnap and ransom children?"

I shivered at the bitterness in his response.

"You make it sound simple but it's anything but. Your so-called authorities fail time after time. Apparently, my parents tried to find me but have both since died. My adoptive parents were abusive alcoholics who died bankrupts. They'd lived off the rental income from a small apartment block my adoptive father inherited from his parents. But he never spent a cent on that place and when the tenants complained the building was infested with rats he just laughed. And kept drinking. Eventually he was closed down by the health authorities. But I can thank him for the rats. That image reminded me of the folktale." His mouth formed into a hard line. "I excelled at languages, which got me to college on a scholarship. I learned French, Spanish, German, but I majored in psychology. I saw a way, not just of exacting revenge, but of creating a financial empire so that I would never be at the mercy of the corrupt." He spread his hands as a gesture of triumph. "I knew of Bernard Reinholdt's retirement plans and positioned myself to take on his assignments, giving me an 'in' to the FBI. I was certain the Bureau would be called on but just in case, I also had my devices planted with other law enforcement parties."

He started to move around, and my heart beat faster. Was he ready to act?

I had to keep him talking, keep him caught up in the swell of his own brilliance.

It was as if he'd read my mind, when he said, "Don't think I haven't noticed your ploy to keep me talking. But I'll be long gone before your precious team comes charging in." He became still, sizing up the next step of his plan.

Hold his attention.

"You brought me here in the early hours, but where were you after that? Did you go back to Seattle to put in an appearance at the morning brief?"

He answered with a knowing smirk and then stretched his neck and loosened his shoulders in preparation for the next step. "And now it really is time to put an end to this."

Chapter Fifty-Five

"Do you really need to have me strung up like some piece of meat?" I wasn't certain there was any point in appealing to whatever humanity might have been locked away in there. Probably no point but I had to try every angle. If there was any part of him that had genuinely felt a connection with me, could I draw that out? "You never felt anything for me?"

He ignored me, averting his gaze and examining the equipment. "You're strung up because that's how the harness is structured. And as I said the one thing I do respect is that maverick side to you. That's what I'm allowing you to be in your final moments."

How could I keep him talking?

"You don't have to do this, John. You don't have to keep trying to get revenge endlessly."

"That's where you're wrong. And I'll do whatever it takes to bring down the real criminals who masquerade as pillars of society."

"You think you've won but the FBI will hunt you down." I was counting on raising his anger with an argument he'd be compelled to address. Another delaying tactic.

A dark grin spread across his face. "They will never find me and they will never stop me." He turned and walked back to an old wooden table, grabbing an item from its surface.

My gaze took in the table. It ran the full length of the large, single cabin that stood further back.

He turned back again and strode toward me.

What now? Had I angered him too much?

As he loomed in front of me, I saw the wide, sharp blade of a hunting knife in his hand.

* * *

The knife rose in front of me and then John dug it into the rope that was wound around my right wrist. Several hard slashing cuts later, the remaining strands of rope splintered and fell away, freeing my hand.

"You will have the dignity of dying as you attempt to climb out of this." He placed the knife in my free hand and he stepped briskly away. "It will take you a long time, in that harness and using just one hand, to use the knife to release your other arm. By then, you will either be at the bottom of this fissure or close enough to it."

"You call this a fighting chance?"

"I call it an honorable way to die. And you won't be the first or the last urban climber to fall."

Think.

As a young girl, I had partly climbed out of an impossible-to-climb hole.

I survived once. Could I do it again?

I knew this situation bore no resemblance to that earlier one.

At that time there had been a savior, someone who found that tunnel and was there at the top to help.

This time there was no one coming to save me.

* * *

The device was in the shape of an A-frame, the sides of its base weighted down at the cliff's edge by heavy iron stabilizers. It was leveraged so that it could raise the harness at an angle and swing it out over the cliff edge.

In the center of the A, cables fed through a pulley wheel and then ran to where it was bound around a boulder further back. Sitting behind the boulder was the gear wheel.

"It's more than a thousand-foot drop," he said. "I've rigged the pulley with industrial winch cable, more than enough to lower you to the base, or close enough to it, and there's no other way out but to climb."

"You're a regular MacGyver."

"A one-man band has to be a jack-of-all-trades. It's why I also mastered the essential art of cyber-hacking over the years."

"You engineered all this to drop me down this crevasse?"

"No." His demeanor was reflective again. "A long-since abandoned logging company left this equipment here. The winch was used for shifting logs further down by the river. It didn't take me long to rig it up for this."

"I was a kidnap victim *too*, John–"

He sneered. "You were a child of privilege that I doubt was ever in real danger. I suspect your abduction was part of a plan with a very different agenda."

"What are you talking about–?"

"How long were you incarcerated," he cut across me viciously, "one or two days? There are so many others who suffered something worse and suffered it for years. But Little Miss Privilege was treated like a heroine, and then, of course, had to grow up and become an agent to prove how good she was."

"That's what you think of me?"

It would be very easy for John to push down on the lever, activating the gear wheel.

"Perhaps you were always meant to die at the bottom of either a shaft or a ravine. And the holier-than-thou Mr. Will McCord can grieve for the rest of his life for bringing you in on this case."

"You don't want to do this," I said, my voice calm. I wouldn't let him see panic. "You know that if you cause an agent's death, you're bringing the combined weight of the government forces down on you."

He didn't respond. He maintained eye contact as he moved alongside the lever.

"There will be sub-zero temperatures down there overnight," I said. My feet cleared the edge and the harness began to lower me down the cliff face. Above my head, the clifftop rose as my body descended.

As the cable stretched and groaned and pockets of wind whistled through the narrow chasm, the harness bounced and I bobbed up and down, my back and sides hitting the cliff wall.

I looked down. The walls were sheer in some places, with clumps of weed and crevices and cracks in others. Mostly all I could see stretching down below was an abyss of total darkness.

I averted my eyes. *Do-not-look-down.*

I tried to look up, tilting my head but I could only see the rock face and a sliver of disappearing sky.

I felt the cold air seeping into the exposed areas of flesh – my face and my hands. It felt as though the sheer expanse of wall on either side of me was infinite, and closing in. I felt terrifying loneliness, a feeling I knew from my time in that hole, so long ago.

Insignificant, like an insect lost in a universe of nothingness.

Chapter Fifty-Six

Will tried calling Ilona again. Her silence chilled him to the bone. He checked his office PC for messages, and then after speaking briefly with the assistant director, he headed to the main command room. Given Zach's contribution to the team and the fact a deep background check on him came up crystal clear, Will had approved a suggestion from Zoe that she introduce Zach to their AI software. It would enable him to play a greater part in their search for the explorer sites.

He entered the spacious room where Zoe and Zach sat before the console, trawling through reams of data.

"Themis's primary purpose is to collect crime reports daily and apply unique algorithms, comparing them to cold cases," Zoe was explaining to the professor as they worked. "As a result, *she* predicts cases with the highest probability of remaining unsolved."

"Which is what led this team to the lost boy," Zach said.

"Yes. And as you're seeing right now, we can also use Themis as a highly targeted search engine."

"So, what have we found?" Will asked.

Zoe swiveled in her chair. "I've run a program to resurrect deleted blog posts from a raft of explorer sites."

"We think the Piper hacked those sites," Zach said, "and deleted certain data."

Zoe's fingers flew across her keyboard. "The system has zeroed in on this."

Themis's Greek-accented tones filled their ears. "There was a timber logging operation in this region of the National Forest." An accompanying image appeared on the large screen. "It was closed over fifty years ago. High up on a slope were the lodgings and equipment sheds of the workers. The remaining cabins are rotted through and overgrown. Urban explorers discovered the ruins a few years ago, and posted photos to one of the sites."

"The site was hacked and the posts erased?"

"Yeah," said Zach.

"And it's not the only one," Zoe added. "But this one fitted the search parameter of something abandoned, unknown, and within a half-day access to the entry points."

* * *

Will reviewed the secretive urban explorer sites and agreed that the logging village was at the top of the list. At the same time, he knew that for every location they traveled to that was the wrong one, precious time was lost.

Time in which Ilona could disappear forever.

Zoe walked across to the printer to retrieve photos she'd printed out.

Marcia entered the area. "I've been in touch with each of the state universities. Faraday undertook advanced courses at one of them, in both cyber technology and–" she took a breath "–hypnotherapy."

"Hypnotherapy," Zach repeated. "Before each of the German children disappeared, John had them hum the tune they'd heard the Piper play. It could have been used as a post-hypnotic suggestion."

Marcia drew a breath. "If David Faraday had a personal interaction with Bethany at her school, he could've applied that same technique. A trigger to lure her away."

Zoe placed the photos she'd printed across the console desk. "These are the German exchange vacationers currently being hosted by Washington families. Anyone you recognize?" She hadn't been at Poulsbo or Port Ludlow herself, so she hadn't seen the children.

Will, Marcia, and Zach grouped around the desk and looked over the pictures. Almost immediately Marcia gasped, as Will pointed out four of the photos. "These are the four we knew as Dietmar, Berthold, Anna, and Hilde."

Zoe checked the photos selected against the data on the screen. "They were on a youth camp run by one of the David Faraday aliases. All four are now back with their host families."

"Without remembering the experience they've been through?" Marcia wrung her hands in frustration.

"Hypnosis," said Zach. "Most likely, they've been conditioned to remember only that they were on a camping trip."

Marcia shifted her spectacles. "Hypnosis? That could have had them believe they were from the thirteenth century?"

"They never said they were from the thirteenth century," Zach reminded everyone. "Only that their home was Hamelin. They could describe their houses, and that they'd been led away by a man playing a pipe. Hypnotically immersed so deeply in false memories that those faked recollections became their reality, either until the hypnosis wore off, or he released them from it, which he's done when he's returned them to their parents."

Chapter Fifty-Seven

The Piper's ears pricked at the sound of a motor roaring in overdrive, and the screech of wheels across dirt and stone.

His head whipped around and his eyes widened in disbelief. It was his all-terrain SUV, pushing up the slope through the thick undergrowth, rolling onto this flat stretch of land beside the crevasse. It picked up speed as it stormed toward him, coming from the side so it wouldn't crash over the edge.

How was this possible? This was a pocket of the forest that wasn't used by campers and hikers. He'd made certain of that when he'd first started spending time up here. And each time he came here he scoured the area to make sure there was no one around.

He squinted at the vehicle but the sun glinting off the tinted front windows meant he couldn't see who was driving. He wouldn't have left his keys in the ignition if he'd thought there was any chance of…

Who the hell is in that vehicle?

Realizing the driver wasn't going to stop he leaped to the side, crashing to the ground as the vehicle thundered past. It sideswiped the long table, splintering it and sending it toppling.

Even as the Piper pushed himself to his feet, the vehicle's wheels spun, reversing at top speed, and then swung in his direction and charged forward. He jumped to the side again. Before he'd regained his equilibrium the vehicle reversed, turning in his direction and then flying full throttle toward him. He leaped out of its way again. This time the SUV smashed into the large cabin, the bullbar crushing the front timber wall.

The Piper couldn't keep this up and this attacker wasn't going to stop. His vehicle had been turned into a deadly weapon against him.

He ran into the thick undergrowth and headed up the slope. The driver would have too much difficulty trying to negotiate the vehicle through this part of the terrain. It would need to wind its way around the hills and then along a higher section of the ridge.

When he was certain the coast was clear, he'd double back and surprise his would-be assailant.

Survival mode kicked in. He was fuming but he wasn't going to let this unexpected development stop him.

As he ran higher, he glanced back. The woods were thick but there was just one point, and one brief moment, when he saw through a break in the canopy. It afforded a view of the ridge's edge from which he'd fled. He caught a glimpse of a figure that had alighted from the vehicle and had raced to the winch's lever, stopping the harness's descent.

* * *

The harness jolted to a stop. I had lost all sense of time. I wasn't sure how long I'd been in descent. I raised my eyes up and then down.

Why had it stopped?

There was no time to ponder that. I needed to cut my other hand free while the harness was still and while I was not bouncing and banging against the cliff.

I tilted my face upwards again, scanning the steep rock face. I was looking for narrow ledges and rocky overhangs. Heavy shadow fell across the chasm, making visibility of the higher areas difficult, but I could see at least a couple of craggy outcrops. And there were enough crevasses, cracks, and fissures in the cliff face to act as handholds and footholds.

If I could free this hand then I could try and climb this.

I slashed away viciously at the rope. A couple of times the blade slipped and gashed my arm but I wasn't going to let that stop me.

My breath was ragged, my heart thumping, anxiety coursing through me.

If the winch started up again before I could cut through this… What was going on up there?

My muscles ached, my bruised back and sides sent bolts of pain, but sheer adrenaline and determination fueled me. I swung the knife again and again at the thick coil of rope.

Again and again.

The rope thinned and began to splinter. Angling the blade's tip, I picked and sawed at the remaining strands and then the final pieces disintegrated, and my left hand was free.

I looked up at the towering wall above me.

Did I have the strength to do this?

A climb like this required tremendous agility, one-hundred-percent focus, and every last ounce of strength.

No choice.

I stepped out of the harness, swung the cable holding the harness, and then using the swinging motion, leaped across to the cliff wall and clung to it.

Many of the cracks in a rock face form distinct lines and I knew to follow these. Some of the cracks were barely wide or deep enough to fit my fingertips, others enabled a stronger handhold.

I climbed.

I might have been able to climb the harness cable but I expected the harness to resume its descent at any moment. Regardless, the cable was further out from the cliff face.

Even where there were only the mildest of indents between cracks, I jammed my body as hard and close as possible between those cracks. The cracks were just wide enough that I could extend my arms to each of them. Using the friction this created I wriggled, squeezed, balanced, and swung in an upward motion.

I couldn't arch my neck safely to look up higher, and I knew not to look down. Sweat glistened on my forehead and my hair was damp. Every nerve and tendon groaned. I didn't have the feeling I was making much progress.

"Keep going. Concentrate on the wall, on the next fissure, the next outcrop of rock."

There was a voice in my ear.

The same voice I'd heard all those years before when I was in that box at the bottom of that deep hole.

Mom?

"You can do this, my darling. You have the strength, and I'm right here with you."

I climbed, no sense of time, and I was aware that the winch hadn't moved.

I reached a thick wedge of rock, giving me a more secure ledge onto which I could fit most of my body.

From here I was able to strain my neck and look up.

The clifftop wasn't that much further.

Or was it?

The distance was hard to distinguish.

And then I heard a voice calling. Too far away to recognize it.

A face was peering over the edge of the cliff far above.

Was it John?

I resumed climbing.

The minutes passed. One handhold after another, my body making use of every fissure and crevasse, no matter the depth or the size, all could be used to assist my ascent.

I was closer now and on another thick overhang of rock. I looked up again.

I could hear the voice, louder now. But it wasn't John.

I saw the head, bobbing at the edge, peering down. Close enough now, I squinted, the sun in my eyes, and I saw the face floating there, gazing down at me. At first, I thought I must have been hallucinating.

Chapter Fifty-Eight

I reached the clifftop, panting for breath, and I scrambled over the ridge onto solid ground, helped by the hands of the person who'd saved me. I lay there gulping in air, looking at the face of Brooke Goodman. "How…?" was all I could manage.

Brooke thrust a flask of water at me. "Glad I hung on to this. Drink."

I drank from the flask, my eyes taking in the SUV, the smashed table, and the crushed wall of the old equipment cabin.

"How did you get here?" I asked, after a minute.

"I started to remember snatches of that phone call," Brooke said. "After what that psycho must have done to me, somehow placing me in a trance, and after he killed Ellie, I wanted to be there when he was caught. Just to watch. I figured that was as close as I could get to revenge. And I'd be front row to report the story."

"But you knew the FBI wouldn't let you tag along." My strength was returning. Looking into Brooke's eyes, I saw that the young woman had channeled her despair into anger, into a vigilante-like determination to see justice done, that it must have started before her sister's death and had ramped up to the nth degree over the past day and a half.

"Maybe it's a crazy way of thinking, but I thought if I watch you, follow you without being detected, then I'd be close enough when you moved on him."

I thought back to the parking lot at the mall. I'd sensed someone stalking me. I'd chased someone down the exit stairwell only to find they'd disappeared into the dark streets. But it hadn't been John.

Brooke.

Yesterday we'd reported the woman missing, but she'd simply cut off all contact, single-mindedly pursuing this obsession of secretly being on hand for the pursuit of the Piper. "But surely you couldn't be watching me 24-7?"

"I watched your apartment or the FBI building when you were there, until late." She shrugged. "Haven't had much sleep. I followed when your car drove off late last night. It wasn't easy staying far enough back, especially when you hit the rural area. I lost sight of you but after a while, I reached the smelting plant. It was a dead end. I drove around, spotted your car."

"And you waited?" I was incredulous.

"Yeah. After a while, I saw you on a gurney being loaded into the back of an SUV with an enclosed canopy. I followed, making certain I was way back with lights turned off." She threw a glance over her shoulder, making certain there was no sign of the Piper. "My phone battery was almost dead, so stupid of me, and I couldn't get a signal. And then I realized we'd entered the National Forest on a rough trail going up a mountainside. I stayed on it a long time but it wasn't safe driving without lights so eventually, I got out and hiked." She flashed a self-deprecating grin. "I was organized enough to have a flashlight with me and I could see the tracks."

"It must have taken hours."

"Lost count. Three or four. I thought about turning back at least fifty times, but at the same time I couldn't just leave you to the mercy of this monster, not without at least trying to keep going."

"I'm lucky you did."

"As it turns out, I was closer than I could've hoped. When I first reached these ruins, I didn't know what they were. And then I heard the SUV coming up the same trail from behind. I couldn't figure out how the hell that was possible."

"The Piper left me here and must've driven out by another trail that was better for the descent. That's why you didn't see him on your way in." I took a deep breath and tucked my hair behind my ears. "He went to the morning FBI briefing, as Sanders, to keep up appearances. Same as he must've done when he took the children from SafePlace."

"Sanders, the psychologist, is the Piper?"

"Yes. But, Brooke, he hypnotized you during a pre-arranged interview, implanted post-hypnotic suggestions, and erased himself and the interview from your memory."

Clearly stunned, the young reporter took a moment, catching her breath. "So, he came back from the UCU briefing with this insane idea of dropping you down to the bottom of that crevasse?" Her eyes were wide, filled with horror. She gestured to the SUV. "He left the key in the ignition…"

"I have to go after him."

"What about your team?"

"We can't get a phone signal here," I said. "I need you to take the Piper's vehicle and get down to the ranger's office and raise the alarm."

Brooke shook her head. "Ilona, you should come back with me."

"He would be long gone by the time we could get help."

"But you can't tackle this psycho on your own."

"I don't intend to. But he's on foot. He can only travel so fast. At the very least, I might be able to pick up the trail and know where he goes."

"Ilona, I don't like—"

"I need you to go, Brooke. I need you to get down to Quilcene and call the FBI."

* * *

The stony path John had taken rose through rock formations interspersed with diverse vegetation. As I ran higher, I saw the trail was traversing a mountainous ridge from which wooded gullies and hills sloped away.

I was drawing on all of my rough-terrain training. I sidestepped the uneven stretches of ground, the small boulders, and the sword-shaped ferns.

He had a long head start on me, but I was racing at breakneck speed, oblivious to the cuts and scratches from rocks and branches.

After a while, I heard the sound of movement further along.

I was closing on him.

I rounded an edge, past the overhanging canopy of the forest to an open stretch along the ridge.

John was within sight now, and he had come to a stop beside an opening in the earth. A deep crack in the rock of the mountainside. Slabs and layers of stone lined this side of the crevasse with a wall of solid rock across the divide. That opposing rock wall rose far above us, one of several pillars in the mountainside.

John turned to face me. I slowed my speed as I approached, assessing the scene.

Why had he stopped here when the widening ridge ran off into swathes of forest and furrows between the boulders? Multiple ways to try and lose me.

He threw a glance behind himself at the fissure. "You've had an extraordinary piece of good fortune," he said, turning toward me again, "and you might be able to outrun me. You'd certainly be able to outfight me. But as formidable as you are, Ilona, there's one thing I can beat you at. You don't know this mountain like I do and you can't outclimb me up here on these cliffs."

He slipped the long coat off. He took a few steps forward toward me, then spun around, ran, and launched himself across the divide. There was a ledge across the gap, a little lower down, and as his feet touched that narrow strip, his hands and fingers gripped the uneven wall, a human spider.

I ran to the edge and looked down. This wide crack was nowhere near as broad as the crevasse I'd just climbed out of, but it was deep and rocky and deadly enough.

I could see that the top of the rocky tower he was climbing opened onto a narrow plateau. From there I guessed it sloped down into thousands of acres of hills and forest.

He knows how to disappear in a landscape like that, I thought.

I threw another glance across at him as he began to scale the cliff.

I gauged the distance. Fourteen to fifteen feet. I could manage that crossing.

I had to keep him within sight.

I took several steps back. It was important to get up just enough speed to cover the gap without crashing too heavily into the rock face, and then bouncing and falling.

I sprinted forward and leaped.

* * *

John was several feet above and despite the danger, he was climbing fast.

He reached the top, pushing himself up and into position to clamber over.

There was a sudden blur of movement.

I saw the seven-foot wingspan of a golden eagle appear as the great bird darted out from behind the cliff's edge. I knew that in wilderness areas these birds sometimes nested on sunny, rocky crags where the elevation gave them a 360-degree view of the world around them.

Threatened by a human climber pushing himself toward its plateau, the eagle had reacted, and immediately behind it, a second bird flew out, wings flapping, its massive body just inches from John.

Startled, he lost his grip and reeled backward. He fell, sliding down the rock face, scrambling to get hold of a crack or an outcrop. He grabbed hold of one with his left hand, his body swinging out from the rock like a barn door as he attempted to regain his equilibrium. As he fought to establish balance, his right hand reached toward another handhold.

In that split second the first of the birds soared downward, sweeping by him, its centrifugal force destabilizing him further.

Frozen to the spot, clinging to the rock face, I watched helplessly.

John's left hand lost its grip, his whole body careering too far backward and he plunged, a guttural cry escaping his lips.

In the blink of an eye his body plummeted past me. It took only a few seconds for the cry to fade completely, and with the eagles soaring away, what was left was only stillness and silence with barely a whisper of wind.

I thought about the theories put forward over the centuries about what had happened to the Hamelin children. One of those theories, I recalled Zach telling me, was that they had been taken to Transylvania. There were towering rock cliffs and soaring golden eagles in that account. The irony was not lost on me. If the legend was real and John Sanders had really been that legendary Piper, then it was as though the lost children had exacted their revenge, up here on this mountain in the realm of those eagles.

I didn't move. My body was pressed against the rock, arms spread, my fingertips digging into a line of cracks. I slowed my breathing, giving myself a chance to absorb the sudden turn of events.

Silence. Peace.

It was as though neither the golden eagles nor the man, whom I could only think of now as the Piper, had been there. It was as though time stood still and nothing at all had ever happened on this lonely, elevated point where I clung to the rock face, a lone human, at one with the elements.

Chapter Fifty-Nine

Aftermath

Will looked up from his computer screen when I appeared in his doorway. After Zach and Zoe had identified the abandoned cabins, Will and a SWAT team arrived at the old logging village where they found me and Brooke. I had spent a day in hospital, mainly for observation and treatment for the gashes on my arm. My story was that the Piper had kidnapped me from the parking station beneath my apartment building, and holding a knife to the back of my head, forced me to drive my car to the abandoned Bremerton plant. Brooke had followed the car that night and verified the story but she didn't know that the Piper wasn't in the car. Back in the field office, I'd had a debrief with the team and spent the afternoon writing up reports.

"This is an internal video," Will said, ushering me closer, "of Dietmar, Berthold, Anna, and Hilde in a group session with Bureau psychologists."

I moved closer, looking at the screen.

"Eventually," he said, "each of the kids will need to be told about what really happened during their so-called youth camp. They will need to know that should any of the erased memories from that time resurface, the memories are real and that counseling will always be available to them."

"The parents?" I asked.

"They've already been told. They believed the kids were on a trip to another part of the state. They are being given ongoing counsel on how to deal with the kidnapping, both for themselves and their children."

I watched part of the discussion between the psychologists and the four young people whom I'd known by names that weren't their own. "They're all okay?"

"They're fine." Will turned to me. "Are you?"

"Yes." I stepped back, my eyes still on the live feed coming via the screen. "If it hadn't been for Themis's prediction, those kids would have returned home without us ever knowing and the kidnaps would have continued."

He nodded. "The bosses have given the green light to a full trial of the unit."

I didn't look at him. I'd turned to the window and was gazing out on the city nightscape. A constellation of lights peppered the sides of the buildings. "That's good news, Will. You'll do great."

"We'll do great."

"I won't be joining the team."

"You *are* this new team," Will said. "We worked well together, we always did. I told you we could make it work."

"For this one, yes. But not going forward."

"Why? Because of our past? We cleared all that up."

I turned back to face him. "Did we?"

He didn't answer and I knew that was because we both knew there was something still there. I answered my own question for him. "Timing's all wrong, Will. It always will be."

"Why?" was all he could manage.

"For one thing, a few nights ago I almost had sex with a psychopath, thinking he was a nice guy."

"We were all fooled, Ilona. Look, it's late, we're both exhausted. If there's bad timing then that was probably me bringing this up now, tonight. Let's speak in the morning."

In my mind, I was once again having a simultaneous dialogue with my inner critic. *What are you doing? You've been through hell. This is not the time to be making rash decisions.*

"It's for the best," I responded to my other self. *You're transferring the anger you feel at John onto Will.*

Is that what I was doing? I closed down the inner dialogue. "I won't be here in the morning," I said to Will.

"Where will you be?"

"Taking some personal time and then back to my old job."

"Ilona, the transfer's underway."

"Reverse it."

"Ilona–"

I cut him off as I turned away and headed for the door. "Good luck with the new team, Will."

* * *

I strode out of the building without a backward glance. I would say my goodbyes to Zoe, Zach, and Marcia another time. Right now I needed a couple of days of sleeping in, lounging around the apartment, shutting the world out.

I thought of the Seattle cityscape, its buildings, its monuments, its bridges. The freedom and excitement of soaring and leaping and becoming one with those elements. That was what I really needed. Nothing too strenuous. And certainly nothing out in the wilds.

Here in the city.

An exhilarating climb to indulge myself, shake off everything that had happened.

No sleep-in tomorrow. That would have to wait. I had other plans.

Chapter Sixty

There was a corner of an office block's roof, shadowed by a retaining wall, near the stairwell exit door. I pulled myself up and over the ledge and onto the roof. I moved quickly to the shadowed corner and stripped off the hoodie, sweatpants, and slipped out of the sneakers. I placed the items into the duffel bag I had hidden there.

Transformed now into a young woman in a tank-top, sawn-off jeans, and sandals, I picked up the bag and entered the stairwell. I walked calmly down the twenty-four floors of the exit stairway and out onto the street.

It was a twenty-minute walk to my inner-city apartment.

I was on the front steps of my building, digging for my key when a black sedan pulled up on the street alongside me.

I turned, frozen to the spot, recognizing the government-issued vehicle.

Two men in dark suits, men I didn't know but could instantly tell were federal agents, alighted from the car.

The taller and older of the two men had striking, hawk-like features and graying, swept-back hair. I knew the face. An assistant director at the FBI.

How had they discovered I was the climber?

Was it from the surveillance they'd run on the team? Or had Detective Radner been onto me all along and tipped them off?

Panic surged through me. My life, my career, and my reputation. In tatters. Why had I pushed the envelope so far, allowing this to happen?

They strode toward me, clearly primed to launch into action at the slightest sign of trouble, or of my attempting to flee.

They must have been watching me, waiting for the chance to catch me in the act.

"Special Agent Farris." The older man flashed his badge. "I'm the assistant director of the Criminal Investigative Division, Washington DC."

"Yes, sir?" I marshaled all my stamina to stop myself from shaking. I didn't want to show any sign of weakness in this, my lowest moment, arrested by the very same law enforcement agency I loved.

"I understand," said the assistant director, "that you declined the offer to join the newly formed Unsolvable Crimes Unit?"

"That's right."

"I am here in person to make a special request," the AD said, "I wonder if I could persuade you to reconsider? We would like you to come on board with a wide brief as to the cases you accept, as second-in-charge of the unit."

I drew a slow breath, calming my nerves. I held my mouth in a firm line, not wanting to betray my thoughts of just a few moments ago. Did I really want to walk away from the UCU and this offer of a promotion? It was exactly the kind of team with the type of opportunities I craved as an agent. And Will had been right, we did work brilliantly as a team.

I didn't need to think twice. My eyes met those of the assistant director. "You have a deal," I said.

THE END

If you enjoyed this book, please let others know by leaving a quick review on Amazon. Also, if you spot anything untoward in the paperback, get in touch. We strive for the best quality and appreciate reader feedback.

editor@thebookfolks.com

www.thebookfolks.com

More fiction by Iain Henn

DEAD SET ON MURDER

Eighteen years after disappearing without a trace, Jennifer's husband's body turns up, yards from her home. Apparently without aging one bit. She knows something is seriously amiss. Fortunately homicide detective Neil Lachlan shares her concerns. But when the case overlaps with a manhunt for a serial killer, it will put Jennifer's life on the line.

FREE with Kindle Unlimited and available in paperback!

THE GREATEST BETRAYAL

Liz Carter is the proud owner of a successful advertising business when she begins a whirlwind romance with handsome airline pilot Callan McKenzie. Yet after his estranged ex contacts him, he disappears without a trace. Liz resolves to move on with her life, but a chain of events has been set in motion that threatens all she holds dear.

FREE with Kindle Unlimited and available in paperback!

Other titles of interest

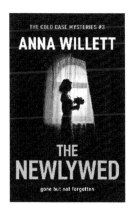

THE NEWLYWED
by Anna Willett

When newlywed Jane Wilson disappeared many years ago, her husband immediately fell under suspicion. But all the police had was his testimony and no evidence. Examining the cold case, Detective Pope has a hunch that Jane was witness to a serious crime. Something dragged her back to Seabreak and made sure she would never leave. And whatever that was, may well be alive and ready to act again.

FREE with Kindle Unlimited and available in paperback!

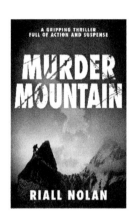

MURDER MOUNTAIN
by Riall Nolan

Wanted by the FBI and hiding out on a remote island in the Pacific, Peter Blake has an unwelcome visit. He's been rumbled by a man who "trades in information" and the price for not being handed over to the authorities is to use his mountaineering experience to lead a team on a dangerous mission to recover a fallen satellite. If he fails, it will cost him his life.

FREE with Kindle Unlimited and available in paperback!

YOUR COLD EYES
by Denver Murphy

A serial killer is targeting women. He is dressing them up and discarding their bodies. Detectives become convinced that it is something about the way the victims look that is making them be selected. They need to find out just what that is, and why, to hunt down the killer.

FREE with Kindle Unlimited and available in paperback!

Printed in Great Britain
by Amazon